THE NEVSKY PROSPEKT AFFAIR

DENISE BEDDOWS

SPELLBOUND BOOKS

CHAPTER ONE

London's Oxford Street was buzzing with shoppers at four o'clock that cold November afternoon. Signs proliferated exhorting shoppers to take advantage of the many bargains and reductions to be had on that so-called 'Black Friday'. Forty-two-year-old Walt Edelman emerged from the perfume emporium clutching his wife's gift which was wrapped in pink tissue paper and tucked into a small, glossy designer carrier. He knew she loved anything jasmine-scented so he guessed she would like the fragrance he had chosen. He could not have imagined, however, that he would never actually get to give it to her.

As he stepped out of the overheated shop, a haze of rose geranium, lavender and sandalwood scents followed him, dissipating the instant it hit the traffic fume-laden air. Not wanting to lose his grip on the precious perfume bottle, he tucked the little bag inside the larger bag of toys from Hamley's Toy Emporium. Pleased with his purchases, he glanced at his watch and decided he had time for a pint of warm British beer and maybe a bite to eat before he had to collect his suitcase from the hotel and head off to Heathrow.

He remembered there was a nice pub just behind Oxford underground station, so he headed around the corner into Argyll Street. Inside the pub, light from the bar's chandelier reflected off the numerous wall mirrors, creating a bright and welcoming atmosphere. He liked British pubs. They seemed to be more welcoming than some of the bars in his native Washington, which were often just sterile places where people – men, mostly – went to get drunk. He headed for the bar and ordered a pint of one of the cask beers. Glancing at one of the menus, he saw they offered pre-theatre dinners, so he ordered the beer battered haddock and chips as well. He quite liked British chips, which were a little more substantial than the French fries he usually had at home. Settling himself down at a vacant table, he took a long draught of his beer.

As a devotee since his teens of ice-cold Budweiser, he had found it strange, at first, that the Brits liked their beer served at room temperature, but nowadays, having made so many business trips to London, he got it. It was all to do with the flavour. A Bud could not be served at room temperature. It was meant to be drunk ice-cold, so that the chilled bubbles knocked the dust from the back of your throat. He'd once let a Bud get warm and had tasted it, just by way of experiment. It had tasted like wet straw. The beers the Brits enjoyed, however, were more flavoursome and were meant to be savoured rather than gulped down ice-cold. Nowadays he enjoyed trying out different British cask beers whenever he visited. When his meal came, he was pleased to see it was a generous portion. As good as it was, however, he was looking forward to tomorrow night's home-cooked dinner with his wife and kids back in Washington.

As he sipped his beer and ate his food, he observed the pub's clientele. Most seemed to be shoppers, laden with bags, and there were couples who were, he presumed, having supper before heading into the nearby London Palladium Theatre. Most were chatting away excitedly. There were also two burly men who had come into the bar just after him but who looked more like workers, calling in to enjoy a couple of beers on their way home whilst sitting out the evening rush hour. One of the two men went to the bar and returned minutes later with two bottled lagers. Both had sombre faces and they wore similar padded black polyester jackets. Edelman noticed that, unlike the rest of the bar's customers, the men barely spoke to one another. He guessed they must be weary after a day's toil. He noticed them watching him and he wondered if they were regretting having chosen the bottled beers when they could have been enjoying a more traditional draught beer such as he had ordered. He smiled and raised his glass to them, but they looked away.

By the time there was only a ring of foam remaining at the bottom of his pint glass and a few chips left on his plate, he felt pleasantly replete and ready to continue his journey. He carefully consigned the bar receipt to his wallet so he could add it to his expenses claim back in Washington. As he stepped out of the pub, clutching his shopping bags and his briefcase, he noticed the crowds had become even denser. It was dark already, and there was a light dusting of frost on the winter pavements. His breath turned to vapour in the cold evening air, as he joined the long shuffling queue which inched its way towards the tube station entrance. He now thought perhaps he should have given the pub a miss and set off before the rush hour had commenced, but, what the heck, it was too late now. In any case, he only needed to get to his hotel with enough time to collect his luggage before taking a taxi to Heathrow airport. Gradually, the queue descended the steps and passed through the ticket gates, before fanning out in different directions towards the Bakerloo, Central and Victoria lines.

Squeezing onto a packed Victoria line train and squeezing out again to change at Green Park onto the Piccadilly line, he had to strap-hang all the way to Hammersmith. The train was uncomfortably crowded and he had something of a struggle to manoeuvre himself and his bags towards the doors in order to alight at Hammersmith Broadway. The crush on the platform, too, was unrelenting, at least until he reached the steps leading up to the exits. More people seemed to be entering the station than were leaving it, and, to his annoyance, they weren't all observing the 'keep left' rule. Travellers rushing to try to catch the train which he had just quit were galloping down the steps on both sides of the central handrail. Several of them knocked into him in their haste.

Edelman clung tightly onto his shopping bags and tried to keep up the pace set by the commuters around him. Inexplicably, however, the black-jacketed individual immediately in front of him stopped dead and Edelman involuntarily collided with the man's back. At the same moment, he felt someone behind him simultaneously yank hard on the shoulder strap of his laptop case which was slung over his right shoulder. This threw him off balance and spun him around and, to his alarm, he began to topple back down the steps. Suddenly, his senses were strangely heightened and the world seemed to drift into slow motion as he fell. If he had hoped the passenger behind him would break his fall, he was to be disappointed. He felt another violent tug on the shoulder strap. This did not feel accidental. He suspected he was being targeted by a mugger. Encumbered by his shopping bags, however, he was unable to throw out a hand to grab the central handrail to check his descent. He could not see who had pulled him down. The last thing he saw, indeed, the last thing he would ever see, was the shiny steel handrail as it came rushing up to smash heavily into his forehead.

People gasped as they saw him fall. There were even more gasps as blood began to spurt from his ruptured frontal artery. The black-jacketed man behind him pushed past the casualty, crushing the perfume bottle and the toys beneath his feet, as he bent down and snatched Edelman's laptop case from where it had fallen. None of the commuters paid the thief any heed, distracted as they were by the injured and bleeding man on the steps. Black jacket man and his identically dressed companion kept walking briskly up the steps towards the station exit.

A couple of passengers rushed to help the casualty. Others, exiting the platform and in too much of a hurry to get involved, ducked under the central rail and made their way up the 'down' steps, forcing the descending passengers to funnel sharply to one side. Several impatient and unsympathetic commuters tutted at the inconvenient hold-up.

A young man, who gave the impression he knew what he was doing, knelt and tried to stem the arterial bleeding from Edelman's forehead using his woollen scarf, whilst another passenger checked her mobile phone for a signal to summon an ambulance. She baulked at the strong scent of jasmine which oddly surrounded the casualty. Station staff were notified of the incident and they came rushing. They quickly cordoned off that side of the steps and marshalled passengers into two orderly single columns on the other side of the central rail. By the time the ambulance staff made it through the rush hour traffic to Hammersmith Broadway station, however, Walt Edelman was deceased.

On the Monday morning, Adrian Curtis, Director of the Security Service's Counter-espionage section, welcomed Corey Hart into his office at Thames House. As Senior Case Officer with America's National Security Agency, Hart was one of Adrian's regular contacts at the US embassy and he enjoyed a good rapport with Adrian and his section officers.

'So, Corey, what's this incident you mentioned on the phone? A fatality on the underground, I think you said?'

'Yeah. A US citizen. Walt Edelman. A Washington-based roving diplomat. He'd been attending a meeting of the SCG in London on Friday and was heading back to his hotel when he fell down a flight of steps at Hammersmith Broadway tube station. He was due to fly back to Washington Friday night.'

'SCG, that's the ... Security Co-operation Group, right?'

'Yeah. It's a fifty-five-state international organisation that looks at security in European countries, and, when I say security, I mean everything from economic and cyber security and cross-border crime and trafficking, to acts of aggression and military conflict. It's the largest international organisation of its kind.'

'And, if I may ask, what was Edelman's role in the organisation?'

'Well, he was one of our US delegates who regularly attended SCG meetings in London and Vienna, but he was also involved with the SMG, that's the SCG's Special Monitoring Group in the Ukraine.'

'And, given the Ukraine link, you suspect his death may not have been an accident?'

'Well, so far, there's nothing to suggest that, although you and I know that killing people by pushing them down stairs, under trains or outa high windows are methods of assassination favoured by the Russians.'

'True,' Adrian agreed, 'and there've certainly been many such deaths of late in Russia. We've had a few here in London, too.'

'Our consular staff were advised of the incident and they believe his attaché case is missing. Edelman had it with him when he left the meeting, and the staff at his hotel confirmed he hadn't been back to check out, and the case isn't in his room.'

'Do you know what was in his case?'

'Not for sure. We don't know if he had a laptop with him. He woulda had a copy of the agenda and his briefing notes for the meeting, but we don't know what else. Our people collected his personal luggage from the hotel but he had no paperwork in his room. He'd made some purchases in town after he left the meeting, some gifts for his family, and they were laying by the body.'

'Was it robbery, perhaps?'

'Well, his billfold was still in his pocket. From the timings on some receipts that were in it, we know he'd visited some London stores and had eaten a pub meal before he set off to return to Hammersmith where his hotel was at.'

'Have the police checked CCTV at the station?'

'No. They've decided it was an accident, so they're not keen to devote resources to checking it out.'

'And I suppose his briefcase could have been snatched by an opportunist thief. It does happen, you know. Someone faints on the underground and a pickpocket moves in, pretending to help them.'

'Yeah, I guess. But Edelman was a fairly athletic guy and light on his feet. Despite that, it looks like he hit his head with some force when he fell. Looks like he fell hard and fast – too fast to put out a hand to save himself. He was on the left-hand side of the stairway, so he'd have been going up the steps when he fell back down and somehow twisted around to his right, hitting his face on the central handrail.'

'Ouch,' Adrian winced.

'That's not an impossible move, but it's kinda unusual, especially in a tightly-packed crowd. My impression is that his injuries were greater than if he'd just tripped and fallen. Maybe someone pushed him real hard from in front, or maybe pulled him violently from behind – or both.'

'Actually, there's a common ploy used by pickpockets on the London underground. If you're their mark, one pickpocket gets in front of you, the other one behind you, and everyone's rushing along, then the one in front stops suddenly. So, when you collide into the back of him, it feels natural that the one behind you bumps into the back of you, too. You expect to feel the contact. What you don't realise is that the fellah behind has taken advantage of that contact to pick your pocket.'

'Yeah, I guess they do that trick on the Washington Metro, too. But Edelman didn't have his pocket picked. He still had his money. It seems more likely to me that he was knocked or pulled back down the steps so that his attaché case could be snatched. Maybe the thief didn't intend to kill him. On the other hand, though, maybe he did.'

'Well, if, as you say, he had a role to play in monitoring developments in Ukraine, then, like you, I wouldn't rule out either foul play or Russian involvement. Do you think he could've been carrying anything sensitive in his case?'

'It's possible. There were ... certain sensitivities involved in his work in Ukraine. The people he was in contact with out there, those special monitors, they were tasked with reporting to the SCG on activity in the Russian-occupied areas. Of course, the Russians wouldn't have considered those guys as mere *rapporteurs*. They'd consider them to be spies. I guess they'd have liked to know who the monitors were and where exactly they were at.'

'Is it likely Edelman would've been carrying that sort of information?' Adrian frowned.

'We don't know for sure. The thief wouldn't know that either. His case might have been taken just in case he was carrying sensitive information. Or maybe just the fact that Edelman was the guy in charge of them coulda made him a target for assassination.'

'I read that the SCG states all pulled out their own nationals when the Russians began their big invasion of Ukraine,' Adrian said, 'but they left behind the monitoring staff. They were locally engaged Ukrainian nationals, weren't they?'

'Yeah. Our intel suggests a lot of them are still there, trapped in Russian-occupied regions.'

'Why wouldn't they evacuate the monitors, though?'

'I don't know, Adrian. It sucks, though. All I know is that, in February of twenty twenty-two, the SCG abruptly terminated the contracts of their Ukrainian staff. Seems those men and women were left to fend for themselves. No salary. No visas issued to travel to a safer country. *Nada*. Maybe it was thought they'd just move away into safer areas within Ukraine. But it's not easy to re-locate when you have no money coming in. And then the Ukrainian authorities put a halt to all men of military age leaving the country. I guess the local employees had no choice but to stay put.'

'That seems rather harsh. Do we know if those chaps are safe?'

'Dunno. I'm told Edelman made an impassioned plea on their behalf at the SCG meeting last week. I'm not getting much information from the SCG, though. See, that's the problem with these big international groups. There's no single individual able to take big decisions. They're consensus-led. Every action has to be decided by mutual agreement of all the participating states. The invasion was sudden and I guess they were thrown. It was a knee-jerk reaction to just get their own people out.'

'I agree it was sudden, but not unexpected, certainly not by the intelligence agencies. Anyway, Corey, I agree with you. Edelman's death definitely needs looking into. I'll get the CCTV footage at the station retrieved right away.'

'Thanks, Adrian,' Hart breathed a sigh of relief. 'That's much appreciated. We won't worry too much if it really does look like a genuine accident. But, if it looks like murder, then we'll have real cause for concern.'

Adrian felt his American counterpart looked deeply concerned already. He wondered whether there was something Hart wasn't telling him. He escorted his visitor down to reception, reunited him with his mobile phone from the security lockers and saw him safely off the premises. Hart's driver and car were awaiting him outside. Once on board, Hart closed the soundproof glass separating him from the driver, took out his mobile phone and punched in some numbers. He had to try three times before he managed to get connected, though it was just to an answerphone service.

'Hi, it's Corey,' he said. 'Listen, Honey, I'm worried I didn't hear from you. It looks like you may have been compromised. You need to get outa there asap. Call me when you get this and get yourself to a safe place. I need to know you're okay.'

CHAPTER TWO

The Moscow pavements were icy and treacherous as fifty-year-old Verona Brooks made her way along the *Smolenskaya* Embankment. She was glad of the fur-lined, crêpe-soled, ankle boots her sister had lent her. A chill wind whipped up the surface of the Moscow River and all the passers-by seemed to be swathed in scarves and fur-lined hats. Verona decided one of her first purchases, once she got settled into her new posting, would be one of those fur hats, as her knitted woollen cloche hat offered little defence against the biting wind.

Naturally, the Russian weather came as quite a shock, especially as her two previous postings had been Kuala Lumpur and Delhi – the one providing tropical, humid heat and the other an intense dry heat. The Moscow climate would take some getting used to, she thought. A little way further along the embankment she arrived at the British Embassy.

As she approached the Embassy complex, she was surprised to see a bronze monument on the pavement outside. It comprised statues which were unmistakably of Sherlock Holmes and Dr Watson, the latter being seated on a bench. She guessed this would be a great spot to take a selfie, when spring came and it might be warm enough to sit out of doors. Even more surprising, however, was the street sign at the corner. Instead of announcing the street name as *Smolenskaya Naberezhnaya*, on which street the UK Embassy occupied the huge plot at number ten, the name of the street now read, in English, 'Luhansk People's Republic Square'.

This threw her for a moment, but she recalled from the war news bulletins that Luhansk was in Russian-occupied Ukraine, so she guessed this was some kind of propaganda stunt on the part of the Russians. Presenting her posting letter to the Russian guard outside the gate, she waited, shivering, whilst he phoned her details through to the security office within.

'Berrooks, Berrooks,' she heard the Russian shout down the phone.

After what seemed like an eternity, but was probably less than five minutes, a smiling Embassy security officer appeared.

'Miss Brooks? You're the DHM's new PA, aren't you? We were expecting you yesterday. You must be frozen. Come on in.'

Once her teeth had stopped chattering, Verona began to explain about the complex routing she had been obliged to take, owing to the Russian invasion of Ukraine, and the consequent cancellation of direct flights in and out of Russia. That's why she hadn't arrived until late the previous night, and the embassy driver had collected her on arrival and dropped her at her accommodation a few blocks away. However, the SO didn't seem interested in hearing about that. He ushered her into the reception area and into a small side room where she was seated before a camera and asked to remove her hat. She blinked at the unexpectedly blinding flash, so the SO had her pose for a second head and shoulders shot, this time with her eyes open.

'Right. Just complete this chitty with your personal details, will you. I'll have your embassy swipe pass ready by lunchtime and I'll get a couple of your photos sent round to MID. That's the Ministry of Foreign Affairs. They'll issue your diplomatic ID card – eventually,' the SO informed her, and he picked up the phone and dialled an internal number.

There seemed to be no-one answering, so he tried a couple more extensions.

'Ah, Lauren. Are you able to come down and escort the DHM's new PA up to his office? Ta.'

Moments later, a young, dark-haired woman appeared and offered Verona her hand.

'Hi. I'm Lauren Bird. I'm PA to the First Sec Trade. Follow me and I'll take you to the DHM. Have you met him already?'

Verona said she hadn't met Peter Cross previously. Her posting had come at fairly short notice, she explained, and she'd barely had time to shop for warm clothes and arrange despatch of her heavy baggage before she was required to be in post.

'Yes, well, your predecessor, Alice Bartram, she had to bring forward her departure date as she needed medical treatment,' Lauren explained. 'She had to have an operation.'

Lauren lowered her voice, 'a hysterectomy. She was at that age ... well, you'll know more about that than I. Anyway, she left in a bit of a hurry as she'd got a date for her op. Hopefully, though, she'll have left you written instructions about stuff.'

Verona was disappointed that she wouldn't have a proper handover from her predecessor. She didn't imagine the outgoing PA would have had much time to commit to paper all the important 'stuff', not if she'd been in need of medical treatment. Lauren led Verona into the suite of offices occupied by the Deputy Head of Mission and pointed out the desk in the outer office which Verona was to occupy, before knocking on the door of the inner office. Peter Cross stood up as they entered. Verona guessed him to be of a similar age to herself. He had dark, thinning hair, a somewhat expanded waistline and a fairly bland countenance.

'This is the new Alice,' Lauren announced and she turned to Verona with a baffled expression. 'Sorry, I didn't catch your name.'

'Verona Brooks,' Verona informed her.

'Okay, well, Verona, I'll leave you to the DHM's tender mercies and I'll pop back at lunchtime to collect you and show you where the cafeteria is. See you later.'

'Ah, yes,' Cross said. He made no move to shake her hand but withdrew a file from the open safe behind him.

He seemed slightly flustered at her arrival, and yet Verona knew he would have been expecting her. Perhaps he didn't feel at ease welcoming a new PA, she thought. He handed her the file and a bunch of keys.

'These are the keys to your desk drawers and Alice has left you these full instructions *viz a vis* office procedures, and so on. You'll have had a copy of the post report before you left England, I suppose?'

Verona confirmed that she had, although she expressed her disappointment that she hadn't been allocated an apartment within the embassy complex, especially as the post report had suggested *all* staff were so accommodated.

'Yes, that's unfortunate,' he said. 'Problem is that we're a bit over complement at the moment. You may know the

Russians expelled fifty of our staff after we accused them of poisoning the Skripals in Salisbury.'

'Yes, I heard.'

'That meant we were able to accommodate the entire staff of the Canadian Embassy. Their former building was pretty much falling down around their ears, and their new one's taking forever to build, owing to corruption in Moscow's public works department. Since the Canadians joined us, we've also had a few more of our chaps sent out here, you know, *viz a vis* the situation in Ukraine. They need to be accommodated here in the main complex so they can move quickly if necessary, and they work in shifts. So, our embassy's full to overflowing again. Anyway, I understand they've allocated you the transit flat on *Nevsky Prospekt*. Hope it's a nice one.'

'Well, it's a bit small and dingy, to be honest ...' Verona began.

'Good, good,' Cross interrupted. 'Now, you should find all the information you need in the folder – instructions about signing our office keys into the SO's keep before you leave the building, local circulars, etcetera. Have a read of that and then get yourself logged-on and check the e-mails for our section. Oh, and the tea station for this floor is in the corridor just outside our office suite.'

Considering herself dismissed, Verona retreated to the outer office, sat at her desk and unlocked the drawers. Amidst all the usual stationery items, her predecessor had thoughtfully left a jar of instant coffee, some coffee whitener and a tube of artificial sweeteners. Verona decided to make herself a coffee first. She located the tea station out in the corridor and noted also the location of the nearby ladies' room. She decided her first task would be to re-organise her work station. It was always the first thing she did on arriving in a new office. Moving to a new post in a new country every three years or so was something of an upheaval, and it wasn't exactly fun being the 'new girl' for the first few weeks, but it was a situation she was used to. It helped if one could introduce an element of familiarity into the working environment, she felt. Her desk here would be organised exactly as all her previous desks had been.

Her first priority was to ensure everything in her desk drawers was arranged in a certain logical order, as she felt that was conducive to efficiency. She didn't think she was pernickety or obsessive or anything like that, but she liked to be able to lay her hands on what she needed without too much hunting around. Pens, notepads and her stapler, for example, needed to be in the top right-hand drawer and easily to hand if she needed to jot down phone messages. The coffee and a coffee mug should be in the top left-hand drawer. Once her heavy baggage would arrive, she would substitute her favourite china cup and saucer for her predecessor's abandoned 'Keep Calm and Carry On' mug. She noticed there was only a small supply of printer paper in the larger desk drawers, so she would make it a priority to check Alice's instructions on obtaining stationery supplies.

The rest of her first morning in post was taken up with answering e-mails, reading all the local instructions and perusing the floor plan of the embassy which Alice Bartram had thoughtfully left for her. It was a little disappointing that there was no-one available to take her around on a familiarisation tour, as she had always done with her own successors in previous posts. However, with the help of the plan, she determined she would take herself on a walking tour of the building after lunch and introduce herself to some other members of the diplomatic staff.

The morning passed fairly quickly and soon Lauren appeared to take her to lunch. As they lined up at the counter in the embassy's cafeteria, Verona selected a sandwich for herself. Lauren chose some of the cooked items.

'I usually opt for a hot lunch,' Lauren explained. 'Saves me having to cook in the evening. Food in the local supermarkets isn't very exciting anyway. We've a little commissary here with some imported English goods, but it's not a huge selection. Personally, I can live without Marmite.'

The cafeteria was quite busy but Lauren steered Verona to a table where three other young women sat.

'Girls, this is the new Alice Bartram,' she announced again.

'Verona Brooks,' Verona added.

She found it mildly irritating to be introduced as her predecessor's replacement rather than as a person in her own right. Then again, it happened with new arrivals in most posts and, to be fair, it was the easiest way of letting people know what a new person's grade was and in which section they were to be based. She wondered, though, whether Lauren's use of the term 'girls' to greet the others was intended to emphasise the newcomer's middle-age. Lauren duly introduced the others.

'This is Daisy Rogers, she's the Ambassador's PA. Tiffany Munro, she's the Defence Attaché's PA. And Caroline Howard, PA Political Section.'

The girls were already clutching their knives and forks and tucking into their lunches, so there was no formal handshaking.

'So, welcome to Moscow, Verona,' Caroline smiled warmly. 'Where were you previously?'

'Delhi,' Verona informed her, 'and before that Kuala Lumpur. Karachi before that, too.'

'Ah, you'll find Moscow very different, then,' Caroline remarked. 'Which floor is your flat on?'

'Oh, I'm not in the embassy complex. There wasn't a flat available. They've put me in a fourth-floor apartment in one of those big old buildings a few blocks away on *Nevsky Prospekt*.'

'Oh, poor you,' Tiffany said.

'Well, at least it's within walking distance,' Caroline consoled her. 'And those boots will be good when the snow comes. Although it usually gets at least a foot deep here. You might want to pick up some knee boots as well.'

Verona was acutely conscious that she had forgotten to bring her indoor shoes to change into. There'd been so much to think about on her first day, and, having arrived in the city quite late the previous evening, she hadn't slept a great deal on the lumpy mattress in her over-heated flat, and so wasn't thinking clearly. She had hoped no-one would notice her boots.

'I do actually have other footwear, but things were a bit rushed this morning and it didn't occur to me to bring my indoor shoes with me. You'll get to see my ankles tomorrow, though, I promise,' she joked.

'Have you got transport?' Lauren asked.

'Yes, I've bought Alice's car. She's left the keys in my desk, but I haven't seen it yet. I believe it's parked here in one of the embassy parking bays.'

'That old banger?' Tiffany smirked. 'May as well leave it there. You won't need it for getting to the embassy. When the weather hits minus twenty it takes so long to get a car started that it'll be quicker to walk.'

'But it'll be very useful in the spring, for getting out of the city, I mean,' Lauren added, reacting to the look of dismay on Verona's face.

'So, what's your apartment like?' Caroline asked. 'Is there anything you need? Do say, as I'm sure we can lend you whatever you might be short of. There's an embassy float, too, you know, mugs and plates and kettles.'

'Oh, thanks, Caroline. It's a bit dingy, but it seems to be fully equipped already with stuff from the float – all mismatched of course. The flat's a bit overheated, though. I guess I need to find the thermostat and turn it down a bit.'

'You'll be lucky,' Tiffany shook her head. 'Those pre-war apartment blocks don't have thermostats. They're all heated with scalding hot water pumped around from a big old boiler in the basement.'

'Have you found any bugs yet?' Caroline asked.

'What, like cockroaches, you mean?'

'No, listening devices,' Caroline said.

'They'll have done a security sweep before they marched her in,' Lauren added. 'But it won't hurt to do a bit of a sweep yourself from time to time, Verona. Check out the lamps, unscrew the telephone handset, that sort of thing.'

'Look, Verona, we're all going out this evening to a nightclub. Would you like to join us?' Daisy asked. 'It must be a bit lonely just sitting in your flat.'

'That's very kind of you, but a nightclub wouldn't be my cup of tea. After all, you wouldn't take your maiden aunt to a disco, would you?' Verona joked.

'Ooh, get Miss Prissy, here. A disco!' Tiffany snorted.

'Don't they use the term 'disco' nowadays, then?' Verona blushed with embarrassment, but quickly covered her embarrassment with a quip. 'That's what they were called when *I* was alive.'

Verona's first impressions were that that dark-haired Lauren, fair-haired Caroline and party girl blonde Daisy were nice enough, but clearly Tiffany was the catty one. There was one like her in every post, of course. There was always that one individual who got to feel good about herself by denigrating others. Tiffany would be the embassy's gossip, too, Verona suspected. Well, she'd met Tiffany's type before, and forewarned was forearmed.

'So, Tiffany, where were *you* posted prior to Moscow?' Verona asked.

'This is my first posting,' Tiffany said.

It was Verona's turn to smirk.

'Oh, poor you. Who did you upset that they gave you Moscow first time out? I was lucky. My first posting was New York. The winter weather there was pretty severe, too, but the social life was great. And the shopping.'

'Speaking of the social life,' Lauren chipped in, 'we have a Wednesday film club every week here in the embassy. We get some of the latest films and recordings of UK television programmes sent out via the diplomatic bag. Plus, we have a few boxed sets we can watch whenever the bag's delayed.'

'It's been delayed a lot lately, since they stopped the direct flights from London,' Caroline added. 'Do come on Wednesday. It starts at seven o'clock, and some of us have the canteen special beforehand. This Wednesday it's chicken curry. That might make you feel like you're back in India, even if the weather doesn't.'

CHAPTER THREE

At Thames House, thirty-five-year-old Operational Intelligence Officer Harry Edwards was running through the CCTV footage from Hammersmith underground station which, unfortunately, did not cover the set of steps where Walt Edelman had suffered his fatal fall. Using the digital passport photograph Corey Hart had e-mailed across for comparison, Harry had spotted Edelman exiting the train amidst the crowds of rush-hour commuters, and he could just glimpse a strap on the American's shoulder, which he guessed was attached to either a laptop case or briefcase, but, as Edelman left the platform and began to ascend the steps, he was soon out of view of the cameras.

Harry played the footage numerous times more, this time observing, not just Edelman, but those passengers around him, in particular, those following immediately behind him. He concentrated on any males who looked strong enough to have pushed or pulled a fit forty-two-year-old with sufficient strength to cause his head to collide with fatal force against the stair handrail.

Predictably, there were quite a lot of potential candidates amongst the evening commuters. Next, he surveyed the footage from the cameras by the station exits, searching for sight of those same strong-looking males. Not all of the likely candidates he identified actually left the station. Hammersmith being an interchange, some had transferred to different trains, which meant he could eliminate some of the passengers. Harry played both sets of footage a dozen times, each time focusing on different potential killers, until his eyes were beginning to feel the strain.

Suddenly, Jo Laska was by his desk holding two cups of coffee. The tall, attractive blonde placed one of the cups by his keyboard.

'You haven't stirred for ages, Harry,' she smiled. 'Thought you might need a strong one.'

'Thanks, Jo. Where's Kirpal when we need him? I'd forgotten how tedious this can be. I'm not cut out to be a desk jockey.'

'We're all missing young Mister Kohli,' Jo agreed, 'but he seems to be enjoying life in the frozen north. I imagine his work at the new Cyber Warfare Centre is a bit more exciting than what you're doing. What exactly are you doing, by the way?'

'Looking into the Black Friday murder.'

'The *what*?'

'That's what the boss is calling it. Adrian has a great sense of the dramatic. A visiting American diplomat fell down the steps at Hammersmith Broadway tube station last Friday, hit his head and died. The police say it was an accident, but it could be murder. Here, have you got a moment to have a look at this?'

'Sure,' she said, pulling up a chair and taking a sip of her own coffee. 'What are we looking at?'

Harry ran the footage of Edelman disembarking from the train and he pointed at the screen.

'Check out these two individuals, the ones in the black quilted jackets,' he urged. 'Watch them carefully and tell me what you notice about them.'

'Casual dressers,' Jo surmised. 'Don't look like businessmen. Or manual workers. More like tourists. A bit glum-faced. They're not communicating with each other.'

'Yes, and they're not carrying anything. No luggage or briefcases. No newspapers or paperback books.'

'Maybe they just had a short journey, so they didn't have time to read anything,' Jo suggested.

'I caught them on footage embarking at Oxford Circus, where Edelman also embarked. Same tube train Edelman caught. That's a twenty-minute ride, maybe long enough to make it worthwhile at least picking up a free copy of the *Metro*?'

'Maybe they aren't interested in what's going on in London. Or maybe English isn't their first language. Can you zoom in on their faces?'

Harry brought up images of the faces of each of the two men in turn. One had a broad face with slightly hooded eyes. The other had dark hair and eyes and a neatly trimmed short beard. Harry pressed the print key on his keyboard to produce an image of their faces. Then he brought up another piece of film footage.

'Now take a look at this. This shows them passing through the station exit onto Hammersmith Broadway.'

Jo leaned further forward to watch the footage.

'Can you re-play that bit. Stop, just freeze it there. What's that slightly lighter stripe on the shoulder of that one's jacket? I didn't notice that stripe in the earlier footage – when he was up on the platform, or at Oxford Circus. Did you? What do you think it is?' Jo asked.

'I think it's the shoulder strap of a briefcase or laptop case. Edelman was carrying a laptop case with a shoulder strap like that at Oxford Circus, but it wasn't found with his body. I think these men took his case. Have another look at their faces, Jo. What do you make of them?'

'Definitely Slavic. Could be Russian. Is there anywhere else they might have appeared on CCTV?'

Harry picked up a photocopy of the deceased man's receipts which Corey Hart had provided.

'It's possible. Fancy a trip up to town, to Oxford Circus?' he asked.

Forty minutes later, Harry and Jo entered the Argyll Arms and approached the bar. Glancing around, Harry was pleased to see security cameras in the bar and dining areas.

'What can I get you?' the barman asked.

Harry produced his warrant card, 'We're interested in some individuals who were in here on Friday night. Would you still have the CCTV footage from that night?'

'I've no idea. I'll ask the manager though.'

The barman turned to the back of the bar, picked up the phone and dialled an internal extension. Minutes later, the manager, a fair-haired woman in her fifties, joined them.

'Hi, I'm Tanya Taylor, duty manager. How can I help?' she asked, as Harry and Jo again produced their warrants.

'How long do you keep your CCTV footage?' Harry asked.

'Thirty days,' she advised. 'What date are you interested in?'

'Last Friday. Early evening,' Harry said, showing her the receipt. 'Around about the time shown on this receipt.'

'Yes, we'll have that. Follow me,' she said

She led them along the corridor to a small back office which Harry suspected might once have been a broom cupboard, and the three squeezed inside. The manager selected a DVD from amongst several others kept in a wall-mounted rack. She checked the date which was written on the DVD and she placed it in the DVD player.

'I take it this is for the purposes of a criminal investigation?' she asked, 'only we're always being lectured about the legislation on surveillance.'

'Yes, it is.' Jo reassured her. 'Your cameras will certainly have captured images of a possible murder victim, and we believe it's even possible his killers are on here, too.'

'Oh?' the manager was intrigued, and she held the fast forward option until she reached the time indicated on the receipt.

They all watched and saw a male customer standing at the bar with his back to the camera, whilst the barman stood at the till registering the customer's order. The customer picked up his pint glass from the bar, turned and looked around for a table. As he did so, Harry pointed to the screen.

'Yes, that's the victim. Can you run it forward more slowly this time?'

The manageress obliged and she stopped the DVD each time another customer appeared at the bar, until, eventually, two men in dark, padded jackets, approached the bar. One caught the barman's attention and took out his wallet, whilst the other, resting one arm casually on the bar top, turned around and glanced across in the direction in which Edelman had walked off with his drink. Harry and Jo could clearly see his neatly clipped beard, as he walked off, out of shot, in the same direction as Edelman, leaving the other man to pay for and pick up two bottles of beer.

'That's them, isn't it? Jo said, excitedly.

'Yes, that's them. May we take the DVD?' he asked of the manager.

'Of course.'

Outside in Argyll Place once again, they headed for the underground.

'Where to, now?' Jo asked. 'Back to the office?'

'I'm thinking of following the next part of the journey Edelman took. Fancy coming with me to Hammersmith?'

'Yes, why not?

Around twenty-five minutes later, they disembarked at Hammersmith Broadway and made their way from the platform up to the ticket hall, via the same set of steps Edelman had taken. Thankfully, there was nothing to mark the spot where Edelman had died; no blood trail or any indication that someone had bled out and breathed his last on those steps. Once outside on the street, they stood and glanced around them.

'Edelman was staying at the Novotel,' Harry said. 'It's only a five-minute walk away, but, of course, he didn't make it back there after his meeting.'

'So, are there any enquiries we can make at the hotel?' Jo asked.

'None that won't already have been made by US consular

officers,' Harry said, thoughtfully, 'but whoever made those enquiries wouldn't have known about our two po-faced men in black jackets.'

Harry spotted a taxi rank some thirty metres away and so they headed across towards the line of taxis which was awaiting the imminent arrival of rush hour commuters. Approaching the first taxi in the rank, Harry took out his warrant card and the printout he had made of the close-up images of Edelman's fellow passengers.

'Where to, Squire?' the taxi driver asked as he opened his side window.

'Evening, Mate. I wonder if you were here on Friday evening, and whether you might have seen these two men?'

'Fraid not,' the driver said, without even glancing at the images. 'I don't normally work evenings. I'm only here now cause my cab was in for service this morning. Can't afford to lose half a day in this game. You might ask the other cabbies, though. Most of 'em do work evenings.'

Harry thanked the man and proceeded to make his way along the line of taxis, asking each driver in turn, but with no success. It had been a long shot but one he had he thought worth taking. He and Jo were about to give it up as a bad job when a fifth taxi pulled up at the rank. Once again, Harry produced the image. The driver took a long look at it.

'Was they two foreign gents?' the driver asked.

'Very probably,' Harry replied. 'Why, d'you think you might have picked them up?'

'Possibly. I had these two fares what spoke some sort of foreign language to each other. Early evenin', it was. No luggage, 'cept for one of 'em had a brief case. No tip, neither. Miserable buggers.'

'Can you recall where you dropped them?' Harry asked, excited now.

'Yeah. Kensington Palace Gardens.'

'Do you remember which number?' Jo asked.

'Nah. It's closed to traffic these days. Had to drop 'em at the end of the road,'

'Many thanks indeed, Mate,' Harry grinned, as he and Jo headed off, back in the direction of the tube station.

'You know what's at Kensington Palace Gardens, don't you?' he asked.

'Of course,' Jo grinned back. 'The Russian Embassy. So, what's next?'

'Back to the office. I'll send these images off to UK Visas and ask them to do a quick check with recent visa issues to Russians. Those two might have been sent over here especially to do the job. I'll also check with ports' police to see whether they appear on airports' CCTV. With any luck, we might find out who they are before they fly back to Moscow.'

'You'll be lucky,' Jo shook her head. 'I imagine they'll be long gone by now.'

CHAPTER FOUR

VERONA RETURNED TO HER APARTMENT BLOCK IN *NEVSKY PROSPEKT* on Thursday evening and climbed the stairs wearily. It was only half past six, but it was already quite dark and very cold. As soon as she entered her apartment, however, the heat hit her. Kicking off her boots and divesting herself of her heavy coat and woolly hat, she crossed to the large lounge window and flung it open. The stifling hot air was immediately drawn out. Unfortunately, the traffic noise from the street was simultaneously drawn in.

She sighed deeply. This was only the fourth day of her latest posting but already she hated the tiny one-bedroomed flat. Maybe it would be better when her heavy baggage arrived, she thought, though she had no idea when that would be or even if it had been despatched. She walked around the small lounge, checking the lamps, and then repeated the same little ritual in the bedroom. Then she lifted the telephone handset and listened for any unexplained clicks which might indicate she was being bugged. There was nothing. She guessed the Russians must consider her as dull as her embassy colleagues obviously did. Clearly, she was neither interesting enough nor important enough to be spied upon.

Sitting down on the rather lumpy sofa, she reflected that, in her thirty years with the Diplomatic Service, she had never asked to cut short a posting. Then again, in all of those thirty years she had never felt this unhappy. None of her postings thus far had been so unpleasant that it had made her want to quit. It was generally considered amongst Foreign Office staff that the worst posting possible was Ulaanbaatar. The Mongolian capital reputedly was the coldest and dullest capital city in the world, and so it was considered a punishment posting. However, she couldn't imagine Mongolia would be much colder and drabber than her current situation.

New York had been wonderful, despite the fear most of its residents had of street crime. Pakistan, had been a very different experience, yet despite the restrictions of living in a Muslim country, she had made many friends in Karachi's diplomatic community, chiefly through the amateur dramatics scene. Kuala Lumpur had been a vibrant city, and she had come to love Malaysian food. In her recollections, however, India had provided the best experiences of all, from the snowy peaks of Kashmir, seen from the deck of the ornately carved wooden houseboat on which she had holidayed, to the marble palaces of Rajasthan, one of which nowadays was a grand hotel in which she had stayed. Her European postings, although less exotic, had been close enough to home that she could fly back to London for the odd week, or even just for a weekend, whenever she had wished. Each of her former postings had offered delights along with the drawbacks, yet, so far, Moscow was cold, unfriendly and depressing.

She knew it would be wrong to admit defeat so early on by

asking to be short-toured, but she couldn't help feeling sorry for herself. She couldn't decide whether to give Moscow a bit longer before she spoke to whoever in the mission was charged with staff welfare, or whether she should request a transfer sooner rather than later. She suspected her heavy baggage had not yet been despatched, given the war in Ukraine, so maybe her request might be received more favourably now than later. She felt they ought to accommodate her wishes, especially as she had given the Foreign and Commonwealth Office her unstinting service for the best part of three decades now.

She began to wonder why her predecessor, Alice Bartram, had cut short her own tour. Surely, it would be normal to return to post after her medical treatment? Her operation and recuperation would probably have taken at least a couple of months, maybe three at most, but they could have brought in a temporary floater to cover her post until her return. She wouldn't have needed a long-term replacement. Verona guessed Alice hadn't been happy here either. Presumably, her surgery had been a convenient means of escape. But at least Alice had been accommodated within the embassy complex. As Tiffany had delighted in telling Verona, Alice's apartment had been quite a nice one. Well, of course it had.

Verona's self-pity was suddenly interrupted by a gentle knock at the door. She was quite surprised. She couldn't imagine who would be calling, since she didn't know a soul in the city, apart from the DHM and the other PAs, and she couldn't imagine any of them would wish to visit her. They had everything they needed within the embassy complex. She didn't think they'd either need or want to venture down to *Nevsky Prospekt*. She opened the door slowly and looked out.

The dark-haired, middle-aged woman who stood before

her door was clutching something covered with a cotton napkin.

'Hello, British Lady,' the woman smiled and tapped her chest with her free hand. 'Olga Petrenko. I livink downstairs. Apartment one. Welcome to you.'

She removed the napkin and presented a plate with a freshly baked cake upon it.

'*Medovik*,' she announced. 'Russian honey cake. I maked it for you.'

'Oh, how very kind. Do come in, Olga,' Verona ushered her neighbour into the flat.

Olga spotted the small dining table in front of the lounge window and she crossed the room and, with a slight flourish, placed the cake in the centre of the table.

'Olga, I was just about to make coffee. Will you have a coffee with me?' Verona enquired.

'Oh, yes. Thank you,' Olga smiled broadly and Verona caught a glimpse of a partial gold filling on one of her neighbour's front teeth. Somehow, the gold made her smile appear even warmer and friendlier.

The rather ancient electric coffee machine in Verona's kitchen was persuaded to produce two cups of strong coffee which she brought into the lounge on a tray with milk and sugar. Olga had seated herself on the lumpy sofa and was gazing down at a copy of *Country Living* magazine on the coffee table. Verona had picked it up at Heathrow Airport and, since it was the sole item she had which might lend the flat something remotely resembling a decorative touch, she had positioned it on the rather scratched coffee table. Olga declined the offer of milk, but shovelled a generous amount of sugar into her cup and gave it a robust stir. Verona suddenly recalled something she had read in the post report about Russians being offended if offered 'naked' tea or coffee – that meant a beverage which was not accompanied by cake or biscuits.

'Shall I cut us some of your cake, your *Medov* ...?' Verona asked.

'*Medovik*. Oh, not for me, thank you. It is for you. I maked two. One is for my family and this one is for you.'

'Thank you so much. I've never had *Medovik*. I shall enjoy it.'

'You are welcome to it,' Olga replied, in her quaint and heavily accented English, and her gaze took in the lounge before again coming to rest on the magazine.

'I say, Olga, would you like this English magazine? I brought it from England and I've read it several times already, cover to cover.'

Olga seemed delighted.

'Oh, yes please. My son will read it, too. Aleksandr. He studyink English. My English very bad. My husband, Vitaly, he have no English. But Aleksandr very good in English.'

'Well, Olga, your English is a million times better than my Russian. I only had a couple of lessons before I arrived. I had to come out in a hurry, you see, to replace a lady who needed medical treatment.'

'And what is your name?' Olga asked.

'Oh, forgive me. I forgot to say. I'm Verona. Verona Brooks.'

'Verona. Pretty name for pretty British lady.'

'Oh, thank you, Olga.'

Verona noticed her visitor glancing at the open lounge windows. She realised this must look odd, having her windows wide open in the middle of November.

'I had to open the windows,' she explained. 'This flat. The heating. It gets too hot. Unbearably hot.'

Fanning her face with her hand, she puffed to emphasise the point.

'Ah, yes. Heating pipes is too much hot,' Olga nodded. 'You need ... uh ...'

Olga made a winding gesture with her hand as if opening an imaginary tin of sardines, but her English did not run to explaining what it was that Verona needed. Draining her coffee cup, Olga stood up. Verona rose also and handed her the magazine. Olga clutched it to her bosom, as if it were something quite precious.

'Thank you for this. Aleksandr and I will enjoy. And if you ... any problem ... anything needing ... please come ask me. Apartment one. Downstairs.'

'Oh, I will. Thank you so much. So lovely to meet you. *Da svidania.*'

And, almost as suddenly as she had appeared, Olga was gone. Verona was quite touched at her neighbour's generosity. She hadn't expected Russian people to be at all friendly, especially given the UK's support for Ukraine in the present conflict. In fact, she'd been warned to expect some hostility, especially here in the capital. That warning had increased her apprehension at living away from the embassy enclave. Suddenly, however, Moscow didn't seem quite as bad as it had ten minutes ago. She made herself another coffee and cut a slice of Olga's cake. It was very good. As she helped herself to a second slice, she decided that, maybe she would give Moscow another chance. Yes, maybe she would.

. . .

The following day, Friday, Verona walked home from the embassy via the little supermarket on the corner where she bought a few food items for the weekend. The accommodation officer who had checked out the apartment prior to her arrival and had left the float items had also left her some coffee and tea bags in the cupboard and some milk in the oversized refrigerator, but these had now run out. It had been a bit of a challenge working out what everything on the supermarket shelves was, since she couldn't read the Cyrillic script. Her brief introduction to the Russian language had only comprised a few essential spoken phrases. She now bought more coffee and milk and some cheeses and fresh fruit, as well as something she guessed was a kind of breakfast cereal. At least, the illustration on the packet looked like a sack of porridge oats being admired by a cute mouse who was dangling from a stalk of wheat. It made her smile.

Having put her milk, cheese and fruit in the fridge, she left the dry goods on the kitchen worktop. She hadn't yet decided how she would arrange the little kitchen nor where she would store everything. Normally, the first thing she would do on arriving in a new billet was to re-arrange her kitchen, just as she arranged her office desk. It was a sort of ritual and it gave her some satisfaction and made a strange place feel a little more homely. She supposed her reluctance to sort out cupboards here was because she hadn't actually wanted to stay. Once again, she flung open the lounge windows to reduce the temperature. She congratulated herself on having at least made it to the end of her first working week, and she had survived it – more or less.

She decided to run herself a hot bath and have a relaxing soak. Whilst the bath filled, she went into the stuffy bedroom, threw off all her clothes and put on her dressing gown. It was a Malaysian batik cotton gown and, whilst not ideal for the Moscow climate, it was ideal to wear in her overheated flat. She had just turned off the hot tap and diluted the scalding bathwater with more water from the cold tap, when there was a knock at the door. Fastening her dressing gown, she went to answer the door. She half expected to see Olga from downstairs, since she didn't know anyone else who might visit. To her surprise, however, there was a young man standing there. She clutched at the neck of her dressing gown in an unconscious gesture of modesty. She was slightly alarmed at the sight of the large wrench in the young man's hand.

'Miss Brooks?' he said. 'I'm Aleksandr Petrenko. From downstairs. You already met my mother, I believe.'

'Oh, yes. You're Olga's boy. She mentioned you.'

Aleksandr grinned and raised the wrench in a non-threatening way.

'She said you have problems with the heating. She asked me to come and fix the radiators for you.'

'Oh, would you? I didn't know how to turn them down. It's so stuffy and hot in here. Please, come in. Do forgive my not being dressed. I was just about to take a bath.'

'Then I'll be quick,' he said, and he went around each of her radiators in turn and made some adjustments to the valves using the wrench.

'Is it okay to go into your bedroom?' he asked.

'Just let me check,' she blushed, as she dashed in and grabbed her discarded undergarments from the bedside rug and stuffed them under her pillow.

Aleksandr adjusted the bedroom radiator and then did the

same in the kitchen. His task completed, he looked around the small, shabby kitchen.

'Do you have a problem with rodents?' he asked.

'No, I haven't seen any. Why do you ask?'

He pointed to the packet of cereal on the worktop.

'You bought rat poison,' he informed her.

'Oh, is that what it is? Clearly, I've bought it by mistake,' she blushed again, acutely embarrassed.

She was so relieved her radiators had been adjusted. As Aleksandr explained, the ancient valves could only be adjusted with a heavy-duty wrench. She was relieved to hear gurgling noises from the radiators, suggesting the apartment would shortly be cooling down. She was even more relieved that the young man had spotted the rat poison. She might well have eaten some of that for breakfast. She felt rather foolish, but extremely grateful.

'Thank you so much, Aleksandr. You're a life-saver – literally. Let me pay you for your trouble'

'Please, call me Aleks, and no payment required. We are neighbours, after all. And I am pleased to get the chance to practice my English with a real English person.'

'Well, your English is excellent. I have virtually no Russian, I'm afraid.'

'In that case, if you need anything translating, just come downstairs and ask me. I will always be glad of an opportunity to speak English with you.'

'I will. Well, Aleksandr, it has been lovely meeting you. And thank you for pointing out that I'd bought rat poison. Can't believe I did that. What a *faux pas*!'

'Er, a *fowpah*?'

'Oh, that's French. *Faux pas.* Literally a false step. A mistake.'

'Ah, so now I have learned some French, also. A *fowpah.* Well, thank you Miss Brooks, and goodnight to you.'

'Good night, Aleks.'

She closed the apartment door behind him, then went and climbed into her pleasantly warm bath in her now pleasantly cool bathroom. As she lay back in the warmth, she thought things were looking up ever so slightly. Maybe her apartment would seem a little more tolerable, and maybe Moscow would be a little more bearable now that she had met Olga and her very personable son.

CHAPTER FIVE

At Thames House, all was quiet in the Counter-espionage section until an excited Harry Edwards called out.

'They're still here, Jo.'

'Who?'

'The two Russians. Come and have a look.'

Jo left her desk and crossed over to where Harry was again trawling through images on his computer.

'SO18 sent me these CCTV images from Heathrow. These are all the passengers who passed through the departure gate for that Friday evening's Moscow flight. The odd thing is, there's no sign of our po-faced friends at the boarding gate, and yet they do appear on the security cameras at the check-in desk for that flight.'

'That *is* odd. So, you're saying they actually turned up at the airport and checked in, but they didn't go through security and embark. What about their luggage? Did it have to be offloaded?'

'No, they didn't check-in any luggage. And it seems they no longer had Edelman's laptop case.'

'So, do we think they returned to their embassy?'

'Probably not. Heathrow's external cameras show them being dropped off earlier at the terminal by the driver of a vehicle with Russian Embassy plates, and then they checked in, but then they're seen on the external cameras again, leaving the departures building twenty minutes later and hailing a taxi.'

'That's very strange. Can we trace the taxi and find out where they went?'

'The taxi's index number isn't very distinct, as it was fairly dark, but I've asked SO18 to get me any footage from nearer the taxi ranks. Might be able to narrow it down by a process of elimination and by checking the timings the various taxis left the rank.'

'And have UK Visas confirmed who the two Russians are?' Jo asked.

'Yes. They've sent me their VAFs.'

'VAFs?'

'Visa application forms. The biometrics check out with the CCTV images. At least, we now know the identities the men used. SO18 found their booking and check-in details on APIS – that's the advanced passenger information system. They were the only two passengers who checked in for that flight but didn't turn up at the gate. They didn't pass through passport control either. I see from their passport detail on the VAFs that they're Russian military intelligence.'

'How do you know that?' Jo asked, intrigued. 'It surely doesn't give that as their occupation in their passports, does it?'

'No, but Russian passport serial numbers include the number of the passport office which issued them. Passports issued to GRU officers are always issued by the same passport office. It's one which is used almost exclusively for their intelligence staff. Their official procedures are so predictable.'

'Wait a minute, are you telling me that we can tell from their passports which of the Russian applicants for UK visas are spies, yet we issue them with visas anyway?'

'Yes, but it's more helpful to be able to identify which ones are GRU agents and to issue visas to them than to deny them. If we were to refuse them visas, and we're legally obliged to give reasons for the refusals, the Russians would change their passport-issuing procedures and we'd lose that advantage. So long as we can identify them as GRU, we can keep track of them.'

'Oh, I see. Well, that makes sense, but, clearly, we didn't keep track of this pair, since it looks like they bumped off an American official.'

'Yeah, well, no system's perfect. It's only as good as the people operating it – that's assuming you've got *enough* people to operate it. Russian state-sponsored crime and terrorism needs all the surveillance we can throw at it, and our surveillance capabilities aren't limitless. Plus, it's not the only source of threat the UK faces at the moment. There are other hostiles besides the Russians that we need to keep eyeballs on. It's just unfortunate that these two slipped in without us being notified.'

'If this is a terrorism-related incident, shouldn't our Counter-terrorism people be involved?' Jo reasoned.

'Yes, but we don't yet know that's what it is. The police have persuaded themselves Edelman's death was an accident. And we can't say for certain that these two Russian goons were responsible. It's not as clear cut as it would be if he'd been shot or poisoned, or if they'd been caught in the act on CCTV. It could be pure coincidence that they were near the scene when a US official tripped and sustained a fatal head injury.'

'A US official who happens to be engaged on security issues connected with Russia's invasion of Ukraine, you mean? And he suffers a fatal injury within yards of two Russian spies. Do you *really* think that's a coincidence?'

'No, Jo, of course I don't. As our former detective colleague continually reminds us, there's no such thing as coincidence.'

'And, there's the issue of Edelman's missing attaché case. Whoever took it didn't take his wallet, so I imagine it's no random robbery. Plus, there's the shoulder strap that wasn't on the Russian's shoulder before Edelman died, but then, moments after he had fallen, it was.'

'Yes, and I didn't identify any other nearby passenger who'd suddenly acquired an attaché case,' Harry agreed.

'And the Russians had been in the same bar as Edelman just prior to boarding the same train as him. And on the same tube trains.'

'That's right. I have absolutely no doubt they targeted Edelman, then killed him and took his case, but it wouldn't stand up in a court of law as it's all circumstantial. It's intelligence but it's not evidence. I'll print out the details for the boss and see if he wants to involve C-T.'

Moments later, their colleague, Dave Lloyd, appeared, carrying a mug in one hand and a china cup and saucer in the other. The fifty-year-old former detective deposited the cup of Earl Grey tea on the desk of his wife, Carole Murray, the section's senior analyst, and, clutching his own mug of coffee, he came across to see what Harry and Jo were up to.

'Ah, speak of the devil,' Harry grinned. 'We were just talking about you.'

'Oh? All good things, I hope.'

'Well,' Jo said, 'we were wondering what you'd make of this scenario. Two Russians follow a US government official into a bar ...'

'Is this a joke?' Dave asked.

'No,' Jo continued, 'far from it. He's a US official who's receiving intel from western assets based in Russian-occupied Ukraine. Then, the two Russians travel on the same train as him to Hammersmith.'

'Yeah, sounds dodgy enough so far,' Dave said.

'And, at Hammersmith,' Jo explained, 'they all ascend the same set of steps from the platform. But the American somehow stumbles and launches himself head first into a handrail with sufficient force to kill him. Meanwhile, the Russians step over his dying body and exit the station, and the American's attaché case disappears. One of the Russians seems to have something slung over his shoulder as he leaves – something he didn't have earlier. Coincidence or assassination?'

'There's no ...' Dave began.

'... such thing as coincidence,' Jo and Harry chorused.

'We knew you'd say that,' Jo laughed.

'So, have we got a handle on the two assassins?' Dave grinned, as he pulled up a chair and sipped at his coffee.

'They took a taxi to Kensington Palace Gardens,' Harry said.

'Where the Russian Embassy is,' Dave interjected, 'another non-coincidence.'

'And then they checked in for a flight back to Moscow last night.' Harry continued.

'Mission accomplished, then,' Dave nodded.

'Yes, but they didn't catch that flight,' Jo added. 'They doubled back for some reason. They're still here, which is odd.'

'You're right, that is odd.' Dave agreed. 'GRU assassins always take off for home right after they've killed.'

'Yeah. So, tell me, Dave,' Harry asked. 'Have you heard from your Russian contact recently?'

'You mean *Kray*?' Dave put down his coffee. 'Not for a while, not since his former colleague from his days at the Russian Embassy was killed. Understandably, it knocked him sideways a bit. He says his friends are all dying off. Or, as he puts it, they're melting away like snow off a roof in spring.'

'Do you think it would be worth your while catching up with him. He might still have some contacts left at the embassy. He might have an idea what's going on.'

'Yeah. I'll give him a call and see if he'll meet with me. He's a wise old owl and I like to keep in touch with him. Actually, I quite like the old boy. He may be ex-KGB and a trained killer, but he's quite likeable, really.'

Harry could see, via the glass partition which separated their office from that of the head of their Counter-espionage section, that Adrian Curtis was alone and seated at his desk. Tapping on Adrian's door, Harry entered.

'Morning, Boss. May I update you on the Edelman enquiry?'

'Sure, Harry,' Adrian waved him to take a seat and Harry slipped the CCTV image printouts on his desk.

'The CCTV doesn't actually cover the spot where he fell, but I've identified these two characters who were clearly following him. They were drinking in the same bar where he had supper, then they took the same underground trains as him all the way to Hammersmith Broadway. When they pass through the station exit after Edelman fell, one of them is wearing a strap, maybe the strap of a laptop case, over his shoulder. Yet he isn't seen wearing it or carrying it in the earlier CCTV images. Looks like he stole Edelman's laptop.'

'Do we know who the two men were?' Adrian asked.

'Yes. They're GRU. The names they're using are Igor Ignatiev and Zoltan Cherny. They took a taxi from Hammersmith Broadway and were dropped off near the Russian Embassy. They're also seen later that night, on security footage at Heathrow where they checked in for a flight to Moscow.'

'They've gone, then,' Adrian said.

'No. Oddly enough, they doubled back and didn't catch the flight. They're still in the UK somewhere.'

'Good work. So, it looks like the Americans were right. It was an assassination. 'The Black Friday Murder' – has a certain ring to it, don't you think? It's odd that they didn't flee the UK, though. Presumably, their flights were booked by their embassy and they would have been escorted to Heathrow by an embassy driver. Looks like, for some reason, they wanted their embassy to think they were leaving, when they weren't.'

'Should we alert C-T?'

'Let me run this past the DG first,' Adrian said, as he stood up. 'She may want to inform the Americans personally. Sometimes, a return favour might be needed. She might want to use this info to barter.'

Adrian always welcomed the opportunity to discuss cases with Helena Fairbrother. They had always done so in the days when they were both operational officers and enjoyed a close working relationship. Of course, back then, they'd been rather more than colleagues. Even though their intense physical relationship had petered out following Helena's steady elevation up the ranks to the Security Service's top post as Director General, he still enjoyed her company and, he felt, she enjoyed his. Helena was putting on her coat as Adrian entered her office.

'Are you about to leave?' he asked, 'only there have been developments regarding the death of the US diplomat at Hammersmith.'

'I've been summoned to the Cabinet Office for a JIC meeting, but do fill me in before I go,' she urged and, still with her coat on, she sat back down at her desk.

Adrian recounted the results of Harry's enquiries.

'Do you want me to pursue this or should I hand it over to C-T?' he asked. 'And do you want to let Corey Hart know yourself, or should I give him a call?'

'A Russian assassination of a US official on UK soil?' Helena mused, as she ran her fingers thoughtfully through her short and neatly styled brown hair.

Adrian suddenly remembered what it felt like to run *his* hands through her hair. He quickly dismissed the memory.

'This is a serious development, Adrian,' she continued. 'I'll need to let the JIC know about this right away. Let's keep this quiet otherwise, though, just until we get the JIC's view. I'll let Corey know as and when I get the go ahead to do so. The PM must be informed first, as a matter of form, and I'll need to let Bob know, too,' she reasoned.

Adrian guessed that, by 'Bob', she meant Sir Robert Vanbrugge, Director General of MI6. It seemed to Adrian that, nowadays, unlike in the past, there was good rapport between the heads of the two principal intelligence agencies, though he sometimes wondered whether there was actually a little more to the relationship between the two DGs. The two were certainly on first name terms lately, and they had attended several meetings together down at the Secret Intelligence Service's Moncton Fort, meetings which had necessitated overnight stays at the fort. Helena was single, of course, but Vanbrugge was married. Then again, so was Adrian, and, although he was Helena's former lover, he knew that her private life, and whom she might or might not be seeing, was none of his business these days. All the same, he couldn't help being curious.

That afternoon, Dave Lloyd was already seated in the lakeside café in Battersea Park nursing a coffee when his contact arrived. Nikolai Volkov, or agent *Kray*, as he was officially registered at Thames House, was still a bear of a man and mentally sharp, despite being in his mid-seventies. His expression brightened on seeing his handler. Dave stood up to receive the expected bear hug from a man who had once been a Russian intelligence officer and trained killer, but who now lived a quieter life in this affluent part of London.

'David. How are you, My Friend?' Nikolai beamed.

'I'm as well as you look, Nikolai.'

'And how is your lovely wife, Carole?'

'She's fine, too, thanks. She sends you her best wishes. So, lemon tea as usual?'

'Yes, please, David,' Nikolai sat down again.

'I think they still do that lemon drizzle cake. Can I tempt you?'

'You can indeed.'

Dave went to the counter and returned with a pot of tea and two slices of cake.

'How's your son and his family? Still in France?' Dave enquired.

'Yes. I went over to visit them last month. Konstantin keeps trying to persuade me to go and live with them there. It would be nice to see more of my grandchildren, but London has been my home for several decades now. My wife is buried here. I have several old comrades buried here, now, too. I'm too old to pull up my roots, never mind to start learning French.'

'Do they visit you?'

'No. Never. Konstantin no longer does the Kremlin's bidding, and he's of less use to Putin whilst he's living in France. He hopes that, so long as he stays there, they'll leave him alone. He can run his UK businesses from there.'

'And how's your delightful little granddaughter, Katya?'

'Not so little now, David. She's already fluent in French. She was always the bright one in the family. A little star. I can't forget how you rescued our little star and me when we were abducted. Things could have ended so differently. I will always be indebted to you.'

'And what about you, Nikolai? Is Putin leaving you alone? No more thugs sent to try and eliminate you?'

'No. Putin has much greater worries these days than an outspoken KGB retiree. I may be a thorn in his side, but he has many thorns in his eyes. Things are going very badly for him in his war in Ukraine.'

'And, given the situation in Ukraine, do you find it difficult being a Russian in London right now?'

'No. It's fine. When first I came to live in Battersea and I got to know my neighbours, I told them I was Ukrainian. They still think I'm a retired building contractor from Kyiv. I don't see much of my neighbours but, since Putin took the insane decision to invade Ukraine, whenever I do bump into them, they're all wearing blue and yellow ribbons in their lapels. That means I have to wear one, too.'

'Is that a problem for you?'

'Not at all. You knew my late wife was Ukrainian, didn't you? No, it's just that, whenever I see the neighbours, they express their sympathy and support for Zelensky and the Ukrainian people. I try to look deserving of their sympathy, but I feel shame. I am ashamed at what Putin is doing over there. So many lives lost, both Ukrainian and Russian. It's a terrible situation.'

'Actually, the Ukraine situation is one of the reasons I asked to meet you. There's been an incident in London and I wondered if, with your connections, you might have heard anything about it.'

'What sort of incident?'

Dave explained about the American government official and his unfortunate 'accident' at Hammersmith underground station, and how the two men who had been following him then headed towards the Russian Embassy before checking in for a Moscow flight which they failed to catch. Volkov asked him for more details of the incident. He sipped at his tea, thoughtfully for a while before he spoke again.

'It doesn't sound to me as though they intended to kill him,' he opined.

'It doesn't?'

'No. Pushing or dragging a man down a staircase isn't a sure-fire way of killing him. No self-respecting GRU assassins would use that method. We certainly wouldn't have in my KGB days. No point in doing something so clumsy when they could have pushed him under a train and made it look like an accident or suicide.'

'Fair point,' Dave conceded.

'A good assassin uses the best weapon he has to hand, and, in an underground station, a train is the best weapon. You say he was walking *up* the stairs when he fell back *down* again, yet he didn't land on his back but on his face?'

'Yes, he fell face first, with some considerable force, against the metal handrail. It burst an artery in his forehead and he bled out.'

'And you say they took his briefcase? Did it have a shoulder strap? Was he carrying it on his shoulder when he fell?'

'Yes. He's captured on CCTV embarking from a train with the case over his shoulder and he was also carrying shopping bags. He probably didn't have a free hand to hold the handrail, but there's no CCTV coverage of the actual incident.'

'So, a sudden and violent pulling of the briefcase strap on his shoulder would have spun him around and that may be why he'd have been facing down the stairs when he fell. Perhaps he was also pushed from above at the same time. That suggests to me that they were after the briefcase. That briefcase, and not the American, was the primary target.'

'Yes, that makes sense.'

'Do you know what was in the briefcase?'

'Well, the Americans aren't trusting us with that information, but given what the victim's area of responsibility was, it's possible it had something to do with western interests in the Ukraine.'

'Was there a laptop in the case?'

'Again, the Americans aren't saying, but all US officials carry laptops, don't they?'

'Then whatever information was on that laptop will be in Moscow by now. Let's hope it was fully encrypted.'

Volkov took a bite of his cake and savoured the sweet, citrus flavour. He grinned at his handler.

'What is it they say, David? When life gives you lemons, make lemon drizzle cake.'

'Yes, it's my favourite, too. Cake is an antidote to most of life's cares. We don't eat cake often at home, though. Carole is always on at me to keep my weight down. So, do you get any crumbs from Moscow these days? Heard anything which might interest my firm?'

Nikolai savoured his cake and rinsed it down with a sip of his tea whilst he considered Dave's question. He put down his cup and glanced over his shoulder to ensure they were still alone in the restaurant.

'Well, your people might be interested to know that there is much dissatisfaction within the military intelligence service at the moment.'

'Do you know why?' Dave asked, as he used his napkins to dab away some lemon-flavoured crumbs from his lips.

'You will know that, following Putin's half-baked notion to invade Ukraine, most western countries began expelling Russia's diplomats, especially those diplomats who were Russia's declared and undeclared intelligence officers. Hundreds of them have been sent home – from USA, Canada, virtually all European countries, plus Australia and New Zealand. You can imagine how many that would entail.'

'More than six hundred is the figure I've heard,' Dave added.

'Well, those who are civilian intelligence officers, you know, Foreign Ministry employees, they've been found government posts at home in Russia. Their wives, too, have been given priority for jobs in government offices or with local authorities. They've also been allocated decent state housing, and their children have been given places in good schools. But the story is very different for the GRU employees – the expelled military intelligence officers.'

'Different? In what way?'

'They've been housed in military barracks and their families placed in sub-standard housing. Their wives are not being offered employment. Their overseas allowances have been stopped and they are struggling to find state school places for their children.'

'Why aren't they being looked after the same as the Foreign Ministry staff, then?'

'I'm not sure, David. Some say it is because Putin is disgusted with the military's performance in Ukraine. Others say it is payback because it was the military strategists' intelligence which had persuaded him Ukraine would be a pushover, and that the west would have neither the will nor the finances to arm Ukraine. He blames the military for his unwise decision to invade Ukraine, and for his continued lack of victory.'

'Didn't he recently sack a bunch of army generals?'

'He did. Also, GRU behaved badly in the Crimea. Shooting down a civilian airliner was a very bad move. Putin was forced to deny that's what they had done, despite the remains of one of their *Buk* missiles being seen in the wreckage. It brought discredit upon Russia. And the military's war crimes in Ukraine's Bucha and other occupied areas have also shamed the Kremlin. And so they should.'

'I'm guessing it's not good to have so many disaffected military intel officers kicking their heels back in Russia. What do you think will happen?'

'Your guess is as good as mine, David. But maybe the west should be prepared for some defections. And defectors have stories to tell.'

CHAPTER SIX

THERE WERE SEVENTEEN SOULS CRAMMED INTO THE BASEMENT OF THE apartment block in the Ukrainian port city of Kherson. They comprised six women, eight children of various ages and three men. Mr Stasiuk, a man in his early fifties, was the building superintendent. His wife, Darhya, was a portly woman with a heart condition and bandaged legs. Over the past couple of years, the block's residents hadn't seen much of Darhya, since she was frequently unwell and had spent much of the time in her apartment. However, since the Russians had taken over the city, this little band of neighbours had taken refuge in the basement and were now thrown into each other's company for most of each day and night.

Marina Ivanova had often made time to call on the Stasiuks, to chat to Darhya, and she had often collected groceries for the couple whenever she went shopping for herself. The Stasiuk's son, Roman, had recently come back from the frontline severely wounded. In addition to having lost the lower part of his left leg, he bore the mental scars of one who had fought the invasion of his homeland in the face of months of unrelenting bombardment. His wounds had at least brought him a reprieve from the Russian shells.

The Stasiuks had been pleased to have their son home again and alive, albeit not fully intact. To Marina, Roman seemed much older now than his twenty years. She had known him since he was a small boy. Back when she was fifteen and he was five, she would occasionally babysit for the Stasiuks, and little Roman had sweetly declared he would marry Marina one day. She had no idea what horrors young Roman had seen, but his experiences had clearly traumatised him.

Thirty-year-old Marina had not married. A modern languages graduate and career-woman now, she was glad she had no partner and no children to worry about. Marriage and motherhood had not held the same appeal for her as it clearly had for some of the other women who sheltered in the basement with their fretful infants and fearful teenagers. Though she had occasional relationships, she shied away from commitment. She told herself that all the best ones were married anyway. In any case, dating married men made it easier for her to walk away when the relationship lost its excitement. Her most recent lover, Andrey, had been the kind of man she could perhaps have spent the rest of her life with. He was a good man and she had fallen in love with him. That had been a mistake, however, as he had left her to go and fight the Russians, and she had not seen him again – at least not until she'd had to identify his tortured and mutilated body. His remains had been found in an infants' school commandeered as a Russian military headquarters.

Marina had seen her own mother worn down by housework and childbearing and by struggling to keep their household going on the meagre pay Marina's father earned – when he was actually working, that is. For most of his adult life, Bodhan Ivanov had been a drunk. Marina had no idea where her father was these days – dead, probably. She knew where her mother was, however, for she visited her grave regularly. The local cemetery was one of the few places the Russians had not destroyed or pillaged.

Mr Stasiuk was hammering at something. Marina went to see what he was up to. She found him at the top of the stairs, nailing a metal sign onto the heavy entrance door to the basement.

'Look,' he said, and he indicated the metal sign plate with the large red lightning symbol emblazoned upon it. 'It's the sign from the plant room door. It says *'No Entry to Unauthorised Persons. High Voltage.'* Those bastards will think twice about trying to get into our basement now.'

'Good job. Well done,' Marina congratulated him, although she wasn't so sure the Russians would be so easily fooled. 'You will let *me* in, though, won't you? When I come back tonight, I mean?'

'Of course, so long as you give our special knock.'

Mr Stasiuk had worked out a secret signal for Marina and the others. On her return from her nightly forage for food and supplies, Marina was to tap out the rhythm of the opening bars of the Ukrainian national anthem. Then she would be re-admitted to the subterranean sanctuary. Of course, it wasn't just food which Marina was venturing out to acquire. Food was becoming scarcer, especially since the Russians had looted every store and supermarket within a mile or more of their block. Increasingly, she had to make her way around the kitchens of bombed out apartment buildings. She risked being buried, should the ruins collapse, but there were still some tinned goods and bottled preserves to be found in the larders of deserted homes. Fresh provisions, however, were becoming harder and harder to source, especially as winter slowly turned the fields to iron and the fruit trees to skeletons.

Marina's main mission, though, was to make her way to the upper floors and rooftops of the buildings which still stood. From there, she could observe the comings and goings of the Russian troops. She could take a note of their artillery positions and movements and could even photograph their equipment. From certain vantage points, she could take the odd photograph, provided she ensured that the flash from her camera phone did not give away her presence. The intelligence she gleaned could then be phoned through to her contacts. Her immediate supervisor would ensure the information was passed in swift time to local military commanders and to central command in Kyiv. Unlike peacetime gatherers of intelligence, she could witness the immediacy and usefulness of her observations, since the submission of her reports on the enemy's positions would usually be followed fairly promptly by military action in the neighbourhood.

There had been especially fierce fighting in the city in recent weeks, and her superiors had told her that the Ukrainian's resistance in the city was beginning to bite. The Russians were on the back foot and, any day now, they would begin to retreat. It would not be long now, she felt, before the enemy would quit Kherson, and perhaps not long after, other zones of occupation would be cleared and the invaders would be beaten back to the Russian border. From her vantage point this particular evening, Marina could see there were still many Russian troops swarming around the city streets. There were numerous vehicles around with their distinctive white painted letter 'Z' on the side.

Mr Stasiuk kept a random selection of paint tins in his caretaker's store cupboards, and, a few weeks ago, since the battery on her phone had died, Marina had taken a tin of white paint and a brush out with her on her night reconnaissance mission. She had used the paint to complete the rest of the letters around the letter 'z' to make up the word 'NAZI' on as many of the parked Russian vehicles as she could. Some might have thought it a foolish and futile gesture, childish even, but it gave her a deal of personal satisfaction. Whilst the Russians were engaged in removing her artistic endeavours with paint stripper, they weren't killing or torturing her fellow citizens. It was a very small victory in a very big war. The Russian propagandists might describe the purpose of their invasion of Ukraine as 'de-Nazification', but the Ukrainian people, and indeed most of the world, knew who the real Nazis were.

It certainly did appear, as she headed out on this cloudless, moonlit night, darting from corner to corner, and from one ruined apartment block to the next, that the Russians were gradually moving out. There were still pockets of their men roaming the streets, beating or shooting any unwary civilian who should be caught out after curfew. Some of the Russians were on organised patrols, but others were looting, not that there was a great deal left to be looted. The locals, too, had been reduced to stealing food, since all the usual infrastructures had collapsed. Tonight, the pickings were very slim, but Marina gathered what she could. Kherson was a ghost town. The banks were closed. Normal trade and services had ceased. Most citizens, like Marina, were out of work.

Marina told herself it no longer mattered so much that her

job with the SCG's Special Monitoring Group had been terminated after the foreign nationals had left. Sure, she was disappointed she hadn't received either salary or severance pay since the SCG's withdrawal, but then money was no longer the standard currency in Kherson. It couldn't buy food or essential supplies, since the shops and warehouses were emptied and closed up. Many had not just been looted, but also burned out by the vengeful Russians. Scavenging and stealing were the only ways of surviving amidst the ruins. She had taken care to consume only canned or bottled foods which appeared unopened. Lately, however, she had been feeling sick. Darhya warned her to be careful eating foodstuffs the Russians had left behind, in case they had poisoned these. She also warned Marina to make sure she wasn't ingesting asbestos or other hazardous materials whilst rummaging around in the ruins. But Marina knew her sickness wasn't due to either of those things.

She dodged the patrols and made her way back through the darkened streets. There was the sound of shelling coming from the outskirts of the city, and she occasionally took shelter in the ruins to let the heavily armed patrols pass. It had been a couple of days since there had been any electricity in her building. Several times, she had slipped into deserted buildings to try to find a working electrical socket for her phone charger, but there was no electricity to be had anywhere now. She suspected that one of the many loud explosions she had heard earlier that week would have taken out the city's electrical generating capability.

She wasn't sure she would now be able to pass on her latest observations. Maybe they wouldn't be needed. Perhaps the liberation of Kherson wasn't too far away now. She prayed that was the case, as she approached her own apartment block. She hung back in the shadows for a while as she spotted one Russian military truck taking off away from the building whilst another one was still parked outside.

Moments later soldiers came out of the building carrying white goods. She realised they were taking the last of the washing machines from the apartment block's laundry. *'What is it with the Russians and washing machines?'* she wondered. So often had she witnessed military trucks heading out of the city, laden with stolen washing machines and refrigerators. She had even heard, via the BBC radio news, that some Moscow official in overall charge of the country's military recruitment centres had been sacked for agreeing to give one of those centres an undeservedly good report in return for a bribe. The bribe he demanded was not a financial one, however, but a very expensive American washing machine.

She had seen reports suggesting that the Russian domestic goods industry – like most other areas of Russian production – was beset with problems caused by incompetence and corruption. It wasn't only their washing machines which were poorly put together, but their munitions, tanks and trucks, were often faulty, too. Of course, Marina had contributed to the breakdown of a number of Russian trucks. Whilst sugar had still been available, she had poured some into the petrol tanks of any Russian vehicles she had come across. There was no sugar left now, but sand seemed to do the trick just as well.

She waited until the second truck had pulled away before heading back into her building. She regretted that she was returning with very little food for her fellow residents, since she had been unable to find much in any of the ruins. She told herself she would have to travel further tomorrow night. As she approached the door to the basement, however, she saw that it was ajar. She could see bullet holes in the door. It was clear that, despite Mr Stasiuk's warning sign, the Russians had forced their way in. With some trepidation, she crept silently down the cellar steps, fearing she would find the occupants dead. In the dim glow of candlelight, she saw Mr and Mrs Stasiuk seated on the floor. Mercifully, they were still alive. In her lap, however, Irina Stasiuk cradled the body of her son, Roman. His eyes were closed and there was a bullet hole in his forehead. It was fairly obvious that he had been executed.

'Where are the others?' she asked, afraid that she already knew the answer.

'They broke in and demanded access to girls,' Mr Stasiuk said. We had hidden them behind the packing cases when we heard the bastards arrive. But they found them. They took all the women and girls, even Mrs Pavluk's nine-year-old twin granddaughters. They took Mrs Pavluk, too. They left my Irina and told her she should bury our son.'

Marina looked around the dimly lit cellar. The Russian rapists were no respecters of age. They would brutally assault the women and the teenagers, also the little girls and their grandmother, too.

'Old Mr Pavluk put up a fight to save his granddaughters,' Stasiuk continued. 'So did my Roman, but the bastards shot them both.'

Marina now spotted the body of the grandfather lying motionless against the back wall of the cellar. She stepped across to him, bent down and felt for a pulse. There was none. These were people she had known since childhood. These were her neighbours, her friends. She could remember the births of all their children. She had celebrated with their families. She looked up at the caretaker's bloodied face. It seemed Stasiuk, too, had put up a struggle.

'Marina,' Stasiuk, said gravely. 'You must go. You must get out of here right now.'

'Why? You think they'll come back?'

'They will. They also demanded to know where you were. They asked for you by name. They had your name written down on a paper. I said you'd been killed by a sniper last week. But I don't think they believed me. You must go.'

Marina was shocked. So, they knew who she was and what she was. She extended her hand and shook Mr Stasiuk's. She handed him the two jars of pickles, which were all the food she had been able to find that evening, and she quickly gathered up the holdall containing the few clothes she had brought down with her into the basement. She headed towards the steps again. Turning to take a last look at the shocked and grieving Irina Stasiuk, who still clutched the body of her boy to her, Marina didn't know what to say. Irina looked up at her, bewildered and traumatised.

'Mrs Stasiuk, I'm devastated for your loss,' Marina said. 'I couldn't have loved your Roman more if he'd been my own son.'

'They took the washing machines,' a shocked Irina said indignantly. 'They took all the fucking washing machines!'

CHAPTER SEVEN

THE MEMBERS OF THE JOINT INTELLIGENCE COMMITTEE HAD assembled in the Cabinet Office that afternoon and were awaiting the arrival of the Prime Minister. Ivan Thompson liked to keep people waiting, whether it was members of his actual Cabinet who met every Monday morning to discuss the events, meetings and issues to be tackled in the week ahead or specialist committees such as the JIC. Helena thought he was especially tardy when attending the JIC meetings and she felt this was because he wasn't entirely comfortable discussing intelligence issues. The Directors General of MI5 and MI6 often took a contrary line to that which Thompson espoused, and he was positively scared of the Cabinet Secretary, Sir Henry Mortimer. Helena guessed that, for Ivan Thompson, if there was one thing more dismal and depressing than a cold, rainy winter's day, it was the prospect of his being challenged by Sir Henry and the JIC.

'Well, Helena,' Sir Robert Vanbrugge asked his MI5 counterpart. 'Are we going to make the PM's day today, or break it?'

'I rather think the latter, Bob,' Helena grinned. 'There's an issue of Russian interference I have to raise. He won't like it.'

'Oh, good,' the MI6 Chief rubbed his hands together.

Soon, the green baize-lined door, which linked the Cabinet Offices in Whitehall to Downing Street's Number Ten, was flung open and the PM stomped in. Leaving it to someone else to close the door, and taking his seat at the conference table, Thompson unzipped his customary black leather conference folder and slammed it down on the table. Noticing the fact that all the other JIC members had already helped themselves to coffee, he rose again and crossed to the side table to pour a cup for himself. As he pumped at the large vacuum flask, however, only three or four drops of coffee emerged. He shook the flask but it was empty. He spotted the biscuit plate which customarily accompanied the conference coffee and which, on his instruction, usually bore his favourite custard creams, but it now bore just a white paper lace doily and a few tiny biscuit crumbs. He grimaced. This was not a good start to his working day. He re-took his seat at the conference table.

Helena glanced across the table at the document which was uppermost in the prime ministerial folder. Although, from her perspective, it was upside down, she spotted the distinctive crest of the Security Service. She enjoyed the proud symbolism embodied within that crest, with its circlet made up of five-leaf cinquefoils – the five signifying the organisation's origins as military intelligence's 'Section Five' – the five-petalled red roses, reminiscent of the personal seal of Walsingham, Queen Elizabeth the first's spymaster, and the parliamentary portcullises, signifying the organisation's remit to protect democracy. The strange, mythical beast within the symbolic circle was a fantastical and literal 'sea lion', whose lion's head represented the army, whilst its wings stood for the air force and its fish's tail for the navy.

Guessing that this was probably the latest Security Service report she had sent the Prime Minister, Helena also noticed another larger brown circle on the page. It was quite obviously a coffee stain, presumably a ring left by Thompson's breakfast cup. She felt this was typical of the PM's careless disdain for the official intelligence reports he regularly received. At least, she thought, he hadn't left the classified report lying on the breakfast table. She wondered, however, whether he had actually read it, or had he simply used it as a convenient coaster?

'Right. Good morning, everyone,' Thompson said, briskly, as he turned over the printed agenda his secretary had prepared for him and prepared to scribble notes on the back of it. 'Let's try and kick off with some good news, shall we? So, Jonah, anything to report on the government efficiencies front?'

Helena glanced at Vanbrugge and raised her eyes to heaven. Surely, this wasn't a topic for the Joint Intelligence Committee? Their remit was to discuss issues of terrorism or serious organised crime, anything which represented a threat to the realm. Jonah Rhys-Maddox, Minister for Brexit Opportunities and Government Efficiency, shook his head, glumly. His long, bland countenance seemed even longer and blander than usual.

'My efforts to get senior civil servants to return to their desks has met with a disappointing level of opposition,' he lamented. 'This really will not do. Covid is dead and gone, now. There's absolutely no excuse for working from home. We need to introduce some disciplinary measures to force them back. *You* need to sort them out, Henry.'

Sir Henry Mortimer, Cabinet Secretary and head of the Civil Service, smiled benignly at Rhys-Maddox.

'Well, I have to tell you, Jonah, that, since they've adopted the working from home strategy, productivity has actually increased, and by quite a margin.'

'I find that very hard to believe,' Rhys-Maddox said.

'The figures will confirm it,' the Cabinet Secretary assured him. 'Most London-based civil servants normally spend at least two hours each day commuting to and from London, and they take an hour out for lunch. Commuting, even if one manages to get a seat on the train, really takes it out of one. With homeworking, however, they arise, fresh as daisies, to start work first thing each morning, kiss the wife and kids goodbye as they push them out the door, then they sit at their own desks, or even kitchen tables, bashing out reports, developing projects and so on, using their secure, networked laptops, until the work is done. They can have coffee whenever they want and they don't break for lunch. They eat lunch as they work.'

'Yes, but, dammit, when we see them during online meetings, some of them are wearing tee shirts, and even pyjamas. They don't even put on a collar and tie for a zoom meeting with their ministers. That's just not acceptable,' Rhys-Maddox complained.

'It's true,' Sir Henry agreed, 'that some of them work in their pyjamas and slippers, but they're not wasting time on showering and dressing up. They are ploughing on with their work and responsibilities in a degree of comfort. Wearing a suit and tie is no guarantee of the quality of a person's work, is it? And a comfortable civil servant is a happy civil servant. And a happy civil servant is an effective civil servant. And, of course, whilst working at home, they're using their own heating. We've been able to turn down the thermostats in Whitehall and even close down some offices. It's actually saving us money having work done at home.'

'Saving us money?' the Prime Minister queried, impressed at this suggestion. 'How much d'you think we're saving with this working from home business, then?'

'Oh, hard to quantify, exactly,' Sir Henry said, 'but I would expect a reduction in Whitehall's winter running costs of at least a third, maybe more.'

'And how much would a third of those running costs work out at, would you think, Henry?'

'Oh, perhaps three or four million,' the Cabinet Secretary replied. 'And it's also solved some of the problems we've had around the necessity for desk-sharing. So many civil servants were having to desk-share, that we had to stagger their working hours. That has meant paying them shift disturbance allowance. In some cases, we've had to fork out for taxis to take employees home outside public transport hours. Of course, Covid and lockdown and the working from home policy has saved those payments.'

'Good God!' the Prime Minister spluttered. 'But why were they having to hot-desk and work in shifts?'

'Because you set up new departments which required large numbers of additional staff, but we didn't have enough civil service buildings in which to accommodate them.'

'Which new departments?' the PM asked.

'Well, for instance, there was Jonah's new Ministry for Brexit Opportunities and Government Efficiency.'

Sir Henry was aware of Jonah Rhys-Maddox glaring at him, but he continued:

'And, following Brexit, huge numbers of the civil servants employed in the European Commission had to be brought home and re-absorbed into home departments. We had to do that or we'd have had to cough up a small fortune in redundancy payments.'

'Ah, yes, I'd forgotten about them,' Thompson nodded.

'So, you see, Prime Minister, having so many staff working from home is creating significant financial savings. You might say they're consuming their own smoke.'

'Consuming their own smoke, eh?' Thompson smiled. 'Yes, I like that phrase.'

There was a short silence as the Prime Minister scribbled down the phrase on the back of his agenda sheet. Meanwhile Rhys-Maddox silently fumed. The MI6 chief, Sir Robert Vanbrugge, raised a custard cream from his saucer and brandished it somewhat theatrically before taking a small nibble and replacing it on his saucer. Helena took advantage of the silence to interject.

'Prime Minister, I need to raise a rather serious issue – an intelligence-related issue – if I may.'

'Does it concern home working by your staff?' Rhys-Maddox asked.

'No. My staff do not work from home. No, it concerns murder.'

Knowing that she now had the attention of everyone in the room, Helena continued, in defiance of the PM's neatly typed agenda.

'An American diplomat suffered fatal injuries at Hammersmith Broadway tube station recently. Although the police believed it was due to an accidental fall, my officers have reviewed nearby CCTV footage, and have interviewed individuals in connection with the incident, and we are satisfied this was an assassination carried out by two Russians who then stole the official's laptop and papers and delivered them to the Russian Embassy.'

There was yet another momentary silence as the committee members took all this in. It was MI6 chief who next spoke.

'Do we know if the laptop had anything sensitive on it?'

'The Americans can't be sure, Bob, but the official did have access to the personal details and locations of western assets in occupied Ukraine. Indeed, he was in the UK to attend a meeting of the Security Co-operation Group to discuss the safety and welfare of those very same assets. So, it is possible he was carrying their details on his laptop, although these might have been encrypted. However, we don't know what papers he may also have had with him.'

'Who was he?' Sir Robert asked. 'Was he someone we knew at the embassy here?'

'No, Bob. He was a Washington-based roving diplomat. Walter Edelman.'

'Can we be sure it was the Russians who had him killed?' the Prime Minister asked.

'Oh, yes,' Helena assured him. 'We've confirmed the identities the two Russians were using. We have good reason to believe they were GRU – military intelligence.'

'And I suppose they've fled the country already?' the PM asked, hopefully.

'No,' Helena said. 'Strangely enough, they're still here. We've circulated their details and the photos from their visa applications so, if they try to embark from any UK port, or if they're otherwise apprehended, we should be able to question them.'

The Prime Minister seemed uncomfortable and he shuffled in his chair.

'I hope you won't let this escalate into an international incident, Helena,' he frowned. 'This isn't a good time to be upsetting the Russians.'

'But it *is* an international incident, Prime Minister,' Helena said. 'And a very serious one. It's outrageous that the Kremlin has poisoned, de-fenestrated and, by any number of other unpleasant means, assassinated a number of individuals on UK soil in recent years, yet their actions have gone unchallenged. Countries have gone to war for less.'

'Yes,' Sir Henry Mortimer agreed. 'Wasn't there that *War of Jenkins' Ear* that we once fought with the Spanish?'

Ivan Thompson suppressed a cough but said nothing. In the ensuing silence, the MI6 Chief loudly crunched off another section of his custard cream, licked his lips appreciatively and grinned with all the self-satisfaction and mischief of the proverbial dog in the manger.

'Well, um, keep an eye on the situation, will you, Helena. And keep me informed,' the PM said, as he cast a covetous eye towards the MI6 Chief's biscuit.

Half an hour later, as they left the meeting, Vanbrugge offered Helena a lift back to Thames House but suggested that, before he summoned his driver, they might take a short stroll in nearby St James' Park in order to discuss the import of the Hammersmith Broadway incident. The day was cold but dry and they spotted a quiet bench in an almost deserted park and sat down.

'This is a bit worrying, isn't it?' the MI6 Chief asked. 'GRU assassins normally head home as soon as possible after an assassination. Sometimes, they're back in Moscow before their handiwork has even been discovered. D'you think they have more targets?'

'I'm not sure, Bob. It's odd that they were taken to the airport and checked in but didn't embark.'

'Maybe that was just to put any surveillance off the scent, to make your people think they'd left,' Vanbrugge suggested.

'I have a feeling it was more about deceiving their Kremlin masters than trying to give us the slip. Annoyingly, we'd missed their arrival in the UK. We should have had eyes on them but we didn't.'

'Well, it happens. I'm more concerned, though, that that this chap Edelman had knowledge of the SCG's locally engaged staff still operating in the Ukraine. Our intelligence suggests the Russians are actively hunting them down. Whilst they're lying low, and if the Russians don't know exactly who they are, they might be safe. But if Moscow's got hold of their identities and whereabouts, they'll be compromised. They'll likely be caught and tortured.'

Helena considered this for a moment or two and a thought struck her.

'Bob. Are some of those monitors working for you?'

Vanbrugge said nothing. He simply shrugged and smiled. He glanced around to check they were not being watched or overheard. The fact that the park's trees and shrubs had lost most of their foliage to the recent storms made it easy to see for some distance around and to ensure they were indeed completely unobserved. Only some curious hungry pigeons approached. The MI6 chief put his hand in his pocket and withdrew half a dozen custard creams. He began to break them up and he threw bits to the pigeons who instantly pounced on the crumbs.

'Bob!' Helena exclaimed. 'Did you snaffle the Prime Minister's bickies?'

'Of course. Someone's got to save the PM from himself, the fat bastard,' Vanbrugge chuckled.

'I didn't think you liked custard creams?'

'You're right, Helena. Can't stand them.'

CHAPTER EIGHT

On Verona's arrival at her embassy the following Monday morning, there had clearly been some unusual developments. There seemed to be a general atmosphere of panic about the place. People were rushing around rather than ambling, and there seemed to be much making and taking of phone calls. The Security Officer on reception was speaking on the phone and seemed too busy even to wish her his usual cheery 'Good morning'. Verona found the DHM's office suite empty. She noticed that the waste paper bins had not been emptied, but she logged on to her computer and was soon busy. She presumed her boss was upstairs attending the usual Monday morning audience the heads of section had with the Ambassador, or, as Peter Cross usually called it, the 'call to prayers'. By ten-thirty, he had not yet returned and Verona was busy typing up one of his drafts when Daisy Rogers popped her head around the door.

'You have heard what's happened, haven't you?' she asked.

'No. What?'

She stepped inside and sat down on the chair in front of Verona's desk.

'One of the SOs decided to hold a random search of the office cleaners as they were leaving at eight-thirty this morning. Apparently, the SOs are supposed to conduct routine searches every now and again. Well, he found one of the women had some classified documents stuffed in the pocket of her overall.'

Verona's jaw dropped, 'goodness! So, what'll happen to her?'

'Well, they suspect she might have been stealing stuff for a while now. They immediately checked some of the folio sheets in the files the classified documents came from and it seems more of the documents listed on the folio sheets are missing from the file. They can't have her arrested though.'

'Why ever not?'

'Because the Russian police would want to take the documents found on her as evidence, and we couldn't allow that. They're too sensitive. But we've terminated the cleaning company's contract immediately. We'll have to put it out to tender again now.'

'They weren't documents from my office, were they?' Verona asked, fearful in case that was why Cross's attendance upstairs had gone on longer than usual.

'No. They were Defence's papers. Tiff's in trouble. They're putting the blame on her, as it was her responsibility to ensure everything was locked away.'

'Oh dear,' Verona groaned.

'She's also supposed to keep an eye on the cleaners whilst they're cleaning her office. She's saying the DA must have left the file sitting in his in-tray after she'd gone home on Friday.

Trouble is, she was a bit late getting in this morning as we'd all been out clubbing last night. But the cleaners are always in before seven each morning anyway, so it's not entirely fair to blame Tiff. Anyway, there's a right hue and cry going on. The Ambassador's doing his nut. I'd best be off. See you at lunch.'

Daisy disappeared as suddenly as she had arrived. Verona sat back to consider what she'd been told. She gave silent thanks to that past generation of administration ladies who had trained her in how to be the perfect diplomatic PA. She couldn't remember ever having been late for work, not once in all her years of service. Indeed, she prided herself on always having arrived before her boss each morning in every single post in which she'd served. This morning was different, however, and she guessed Peter must have been called in early because of the early morning discovery of the document theft.

In Verona's previous posts, it was often the case that her boss would be working late, especially if there was some on-going 'situation' to require his attention, and so she had often left work ahead of him, but, before leaving, she had always made a point of reminding her boss to put his documents in the safe. Of course, some diplomats would get tetchy about having the bleeping obvious pointed out to them, but the reminders were intended to cover her back as much as theirs.

So, Tiffany was in trouble? Verona's first thought was that it couldn't happen to a nicer person. Then she checked her feelings and realised how bad the Defence Attaché's assistant must be feeling. After all, it was the girl's first posting, and nobody wants to mess up their first posting. The import of a classified document being taken from the DA's section, of all sections, and at a time when Russia was at war with its neighbouring state and when, moreover, the UK was providing arms to that neighbouring state, wasn't lost on Verona. She guessed the fallout would be immense. There would be telegrams going back and to between the embassy and London – not that they were actual telegrams, these days. In Foreign Office parlance, secure e-mail communications were still referred to, quaintly enough, as telegrams. As she considered the seriousness of the situation, she could guess just how upset Tiffany Munro must be feeling right now.

Taking care to lock down her keyboard, she went along to the DA's office suite and popped her head around the door. The DA, Robin Harewood, was not there, and Verona guessed he, too, was upstairs making his confession to the Ambassador at the 'morning prayers'. Tiffany Munro was seated at her desk, head in hands. Verona thought she appeared the very picture of misery.

'Oh, Tiffany. I just heard. How awful. How are you?' she said, gently.

'I suppose you've come to gloat,' Tiffany spat.

'Not at all,' Verona assured her, as she entered and took a seat. 'I came to see if there was anything I could do to help.'

'It wasn't my fault, you know. I didn't leave any damned documents lying around.'

'I'm sure you didn't. Don't let them make you the scape-goat, though.'

'I never even *saw* the bloody documents. Robin must have left them out.'

Verona could see the PA was in tears. Tiffany's cheeks were streaked with mascara and, clearly, she was in sore need of some words of consolation.

'The thing is, though, Harewood's position is more important than yours,' Verona suggested. 'He has more to lose than you do. There's his rank, and his military pension. I imagine he has a wife to support. His children will be in private schools, all paid for by MOD. He won't want to be sent home or sacked. But that's what's likely to happen with a security breach as serious as this one. So, you see, he can't do anything other than put the blame on you.'

'What can I do, though?'

'Well, if he really was the last person to handle the document, presumably he'll have been doing something with it. He'll probably have been drafting something on his computer in connection with that document. He may have referred to it in an e-mail he wrote, or in whatever else he might have been drafting. Alternatively, he might have written a minute or a report on the file to which the document was attached.'

'Yes, so ...?'

'So, you need to find that file. If he's minuted it, and if the minute he wrote is dated, which it should be, then that would help.'

'I see what you mean.'

'If you find he *has* minuted the file, make sure you photocopy that minute sheet, in case he decides to alter or destroy it. Then, when they come to give you the third degree, you should urge them to check the file. It might show them who was the last person to handle the file and when. But if, by then, he's removed his minutes, you'll have a copy to show them.'

'What if he didn't minute the file?'

'Then urge them also to check his computer, to see whether he drafted anything which referred to the subject matter in that file. They can check the times and dates of his e mails and the creation times of his drafts. You did sign out of the building when you left the embassy ahead of him, didn't you?'

'Yes, I did.'

'And he would have signed out after you, wouldn't he? And he would have signed his office keys into the SO's keep. If they check the timelines, it should put you in the clear.'

'Oh, Verona. You're right. I hadn't thought of all that. Thank you.'

'I may be a bit old-fashioned – some might even say ... 'prissy' – but I've been around long enough to have learned a few tricks. In future, you'll know how important it is to cover your back. So, there's no need for you worry just yet.'

Back at her own desk, Verona sat, trying to work but she was distracted by contemplating the seriousness of Tiffany's situation. Soon, however, the DHM returned.

'Difficult prayer meeting?' she asked.

'You've heard?'

'Yes. Awful business. I suppose the cleaning company employees had been vetted?'

'As much as one can vet anyone without the co-operation of hostile local authorities. Trouble is, cleaners are paid so little, especially in Moscow. And we always have to have them in and gone before the day's business begins, which means there aren't enough of us dip staff around to keep an eye on them. Anyway, responsibility for cleaning will be down to you, now.'

'You mean you want me to draft a tender notice to put out to other cleaning companies?'

'No. Accommodation section will do that. I mean you'll have to undertake the cleaning of our office suite *pro tem*.'

Verona was shocked at the suggestion.

'Me? But cleaning's not in my job description. I'm an experienced personal assistant, Peter, not a char lady.'

'It'll only mean giving our desks a bit of a tickle with a duster every couple of days, and running the vacuum cleaner around a bit.'

'And emptying the waste bins and taking the confidential waste paper to the shredder,' Verona said, horrified.

'Yes. Oh, and as the tea station for this floor is situated nearest to our offices, I've agreed you'll keep that clean, too.'

'But everyone on this floor just dumps their mugs and plates in the sink. It'll mean washing all that lot up by hand. There's no dishwasher.'

'Isn't there? Well, it's just a few cups, isn't it?'

'It's the cups and plates of everyone on our floor. And there's the food waste bin to sort out. That only gets emptied once a week and it stinks. Are you seriously asking me to do that?'

'Well, the PAs in all the other sections will be doing their office cleaning, too. In an emergency it's what we do in the Foreign Office, isn't it? We all have to pull together?'

'We? Does that mean you'll be doing some of the cleaning, too?'

'Now, look here, Verona, don't be difficult,' he snapped with sudden irritation. 'Your predecessor wouldn't have made such a fuss. Just knuckle down and get on with it, will you? Now, if anyone needs me, I'll be up in the DA's office. Robin and I have to work out a damage limitation strategy.'

Verona was both shocked and disappointed. In all her previous postings, she had indeed 'pulled together'. She had undertaken lots of things which hadn't formed part of her job description. She had shopped for last minute birthday and anniversary gifts for bosses' wives. On occasions in Pakistan, she had babysat her boss's children. She had cooked and served buffet lunches for important visitors from London when an embassy club's kitchens had been closed for fumigation. On one painfully embarrassing occasion, she had even been required to enter a lap-dancing club to book a table for some visiting Turkish VIPs who had demanded some sleazy post-business entertainment. Yes, Verona recalled she had undertaken a great number of extra-curricular tasks over the years in order to oil the wheels of the diplomatic business process, but cleaning offices and washing dishes, somehow seemed beyond the pale.

She tried to look at it dispassionately. If every section had to do their bit of cleaning, perhaps it was unreasonable of her to baulk at doing her share. However, the more she thought about it, especially the stinky tea station bin, the more affronted she felt. Cross could at least have set up a rota with the other staff on this floor who used and abused the shared tea station. He shouldn't have been so quick to volunteer his PA for such a task. Maybe it would have seemed less of an imposition if she were actually happy in her post. Maybe, if people had been a little kinder, a little more welcoming, she told herself, she wouldn't feel quite so affronted.

Perhaps, if she'd been given an apartment within the embassy complex, she might have felt more included, more inclined to 'pull together'. But that was just it, she didn't feel included. She felt isolated, out in the cold – literally. She'd tried to tell the DHM how horrible her flat was, but he hadn't wanted to hear her complaints. It hadn't mattered to him that she was unhappy, that she felt lonely and unappreciated. And now this. It really was too much. To her personal disappointment, she actually felt close to tears.

Suddenly, a smiling face appeared at the door. It was Grant, one of the young messengers who collected and distributed everyone's mail and who undertook all kinds of odd tasks around the mission. To Verona's surprise, she saw he was wearing a frilly apron and the legs of his trousers were rolled up to the knees. He also wore bright red lipstick and a woman's headscarf wrapped around his head, turban-style. He looked rather like a badly costumed pantomime fairy as he waved a feather duster at her.

'Ooh, mornin' Miss Brooks,' he chirped in a falsetto voice. 'Can I do you now, Dear?'

He strode in, hopped about a bit and pirouetted in front of her desk. Verona couldn't help laughing.

'Oh, Grant. That's hysterical.'

'Just trying to make a point, Miss B., me and my diplomatic duster,' his voice now reverted to its normal pitch. 'Ridiculous state of affairs, isn't it?'

'It is indeed, Grant. Oh, but look out, your duster's shedding feathers onto my carpet. I'll have to get the vacuum cleaner out now.'

'I dunno. A woman's work is never done,' he chirped. Stooping, he scooped up the feathers, then he was gone.

CHAPTER NINE

Marina Ivanova awoke to the sound of birdsong. For a moment, she couldn't remember where she was. She had slept in so many different places that week, mainly in bombed out ruins, sometimes in beds, sometimes just sitting up with her back against a wall, but always fully dressed in case the Russians came. She had been dreaming about clean beds, hot showers and having clean, shining hair. Hot water was in very short supply, however, and clean bedlinen was just a distant memory. Usually, what awoke her was the sound of gunfire or the frightening explosion as a shell would land somewhere nearby. This morning, however, all was peaceful. She wondered why.

How she longed for a freshly brewed coffee. A warm pastry wouldn't go amiss, either. Suddenly, however, the thought of food made the nausea rise in her gorge. Placing her hand against the wall of the ruined building which had given her shelter, she bent forward and vomited. She decided it was time she consulted a doctor. If the reason for her sickness really was what she thought it was, a test should confirm this. She vowed to seek medical advice as soon as she could find a doctor.

She glanced around. It did seem odd that everything was so quiet. Taking her water bottle from her canvas holdall, she unscrewed the cap and rinsed her mouth. Taking a long drink of the water, she climbed gingerly over piles of bricks and rubble, shaded her eyes with her hand and scanned the horizon. Soon, she heard a familiar noise. It was the combination of a diesel engine and the squeaking tracks of an armoured tank approaching. She shrank back against the partly demolished wall of what she guessed had once been a warehouse, and she peered cautiously around the corner.

To her great surprise and utter delight, she saw that the tank was flying the distinctive blue and yellow Ukrainian flag. She wanted to rush forward, waving and shouting at her compatriots, but distrust made her hang back. It could be a Russian trick. She waited until the tank came nearer and she could hear the navigator shouting to the tank driver over the sound of the engine. Her heart leapt as she realised he was speaking Ukrainian. This was no trick. This was liberation! Rushing out from her hiding place, she waved her hands in the air and greeted the soldier.

'*Pryvit*!' she greeted him. '*Dobrohu ranku*!'

The tank's navigator waved at her but did not slow down.

'*Slava Ukraini*!' he called out, thrusting a victorious fist in the air as the tank rumbled past.

'*Slava Ukraini!*' she shouted back, '*Heroyam slava!*'

Glory to Ukraine, indeed, and glory to the heroes who had clearly freed her city. She felt an overwhelming sense of relief flooding through her veins as she realised the Russians had fled. Kherson had been liberated and the Russians had gone.

She had survived. Overcome with emotion, she suddenly felt the need to sit down. She perched on the nearest pile of rubble and she began to cry.

The following day, over a thousand kilometres away in Moscow, Verona had decided crying over her present predicament wasn't an option. She started the morning off by giving the office carpets a desultory vacuuming and had flicked a cotton duster over the DHM's desktop before emptying his waste-paper bin and her own, and then making a start on her e-mails. It was almost ten thirty before Peter Cross appeared, which surprised her as he wasn't usually that late in arriving. To her even greater surprise, she saw he had his right arm in a sling. His head was bent sharply to one side and his expression was pained as he slumped heavily into his chair.

'Goodness, what's happened to you, Peter?' she enquired.

'Out rather late last night. Had a few drinks. Walking back to the car, I slipped on the ice. Put my hand out to save myself. Broke my wrist and my collar bone. Hurts like the devil.'

With his left hand, he produced a small, brown plastic bottle of pills from his pocket and deposited them on his desk.

'Spent most of the night waiting around in casualty. They gave me these heavy-duty pain killers. I could really use a coffee to wash them down. Make me a strong one, would you.'

'I'm afraid you'll have to make do with water. The coffee mugs were in a truly disgraceful state this morning – sticky and mouldy. You wouldn't want to drink out of any of them. I've left them in the sink, soaking in bleach.'

'Damn! I've got a conference call in half an hour, too. The Old Man and I have to explain to London how the security breach happened and assure them of what steps we're taking to make sure it doesn't happen again. I also promised Simon Harris I'd help him conduct a full security sweep later today, too.'

'The Old Man' was, of course, how many referred to the Ambassador, whom Verona hadn't yet met, but nor had she met, or heard of Harris.

'Who's Simon Harris?''

'He's, you know, the embassy *spook*.'

'Ah. That's a bit ironic, then, isn't it? I'm doing the vacuuming and you're doing the sweeping,' she said, pointedly. 'I'll get you that glass of water.'

As she filled up a glass at the sink, she noticed the cups were already sparkling clean. It didn't actually take long to get them like that with the application of a little bleach. However, she decided she would make him wait for his coffee. She still hadn't forgiven him for volunteering her to do the washing up for the entire floor in the first place. Co-operation was a two-way street, she told herself.

It was some forty-five minutes later when Cross returned from the Ambassador's suite, following their conference call with London. He went into his inner office and switched on his computer. Verona heard him cursing as he struggled to type on his keyboard using just his left hand.

'Verona!' he called out. 'I've got an urgent briefing I really must make a start on today. Would you get me out the SCG file.'

She had no trouble locating the file, which was marked *'SCG: Security Co-operation Group'* and took it into his office.

'Is this the one?'

'Yes, but look, I won't be able to draft the brief with one

hand. It'd take me all morning. I'll have to dictate it to you and you type it up. Okay?'

'Okay. You'd better let me sit in your chair then.'

Cross gave up his desk chair and seated himself to one side on the spare chair. He had a quick glance through the file whilst he swilled back another pain killer.

'Right,' Verona said, 'I've opened a fresh word document. Where do you want me to save it?'

'Scroll down my list of files on the left-hand side. Save it in the one marked 'SCG'. Now then, put a centred heading in caps: '*Special Monitoring Group*'. Now, leave two line spaces and put '*Background*' in lower-case as another heading, and make it left-justified.'

Verona did as bid and began typing as Cross dictated his draft.

'*The background to this briefing note concerns the* ... um ... *situation relating to the locally engaged staff of the SMG in the occupied territories of Ukraine*. Okay, now put another lower-case heading, again left justified: *Lines to Take*. Now do the next bit in bullet points.'

'Indented?'

'No. First bullet point: *The LE staff's employment was terminated mainly as a measure to give them deniability, with a view to* ... um ... *to ensuring their own personal safety. If they were to be interrogated by the Russians about their employment, they could, in all honesty deny being employed by the SCG*. You got all that?'

'Yes,' she confirmed.

'Second bullet point: *The significant saving on the LE's pay and future pension payments* ... um ... *may be diverted into more urgently needed areas, such as defence items for use in Ukraine.*'

Cross paused before continuing: 'And for the third and final bullet, put: *The international community was unable to assist the escape* ... no, make that ... *the evacuation of LE staff from the region owing to the Ukrainian authorities' ban on men of fighting age leaving the country' Therefore the SCG may not be held culpable in the event of any reprisals the Russians might take against those local staff. It is not currently possible to ascertain the fate of the LE staff, owing to the on-going hostilities in the occupied territories, although intelligence suggests that several dozen of those based in Kherson, Luhansk and Donetsk have been executed as spies. However, where any of them do manage to escape the war zone, we are assured they will be offered every assistance by the Ukrainian authorities.* Now, let me have a look.'

Cross squinted at the typed draft.

'Hmm. Looks a bit small. Put it in font size twelve.'

Just then a man whom Verona did not recognise knocked and entered. He was a very good-looking man, dark-haired, well-groomed and in his late thirties.

'Ah, Simon,' Cross said. 'I'm just coming. Okay,' he turned to Verona, 'just add my name and designation at the bottom, will you, then hit 'save' and log out for me. I'll have another look at the draft after lunch.'

Simon Harris walked across to the desk, offered Verona his hand and introduced himself.

'Hi, so you're the new Alice. It's Verona, isn't it? I'm Simon. I hide out in the political section.'

'Good morning. Pleased to meet you,' she said, and she meant it, as she was impressed that he had at least taken the trouble to ascertain her name.

'So, Verona, how are you settling in?' he smiled pleasantly.

'Oh, so-so,' was her lacklustre reply.

Simon seemed a little taken aback by her answer. He

looked directly at her. His dark brows knitted together and she saw a kind of sympathetic warmth in his eyes – the kind of warmth she had not so far seen in Peter Cross.

'Right, Simon, let's crack on,' the DHM urged as he headed for the door.

'Catch you later,' Simon smiled pleasantly at Verona, and the two men left.

Verona added Cross's name and designation to the draft and saved it, but curiosity made her have a look at the SCG file. Cross having mentioned people being executed as spies had surprised her. She'd never heard of the Security Co-operation Group and, glancing through the file, she could see this was because the most recent countries in which she had served were not SCG members. She noted that Russia had been a member, until the invasion of Ukraine had begun, at which the other fifty plus states had voted to expel the aggressor.

As she browsed the various notes on the file, she saw that Peter Cross was a regular delegate at the SCG meetings which took place mainly in London and Vienna. She found herself growing even more curious about the SCG's Special Monitoring Group. She wondered what might have become of the members of that group who, it seemed, had been abandoned to their fate in those areas of Ukraine which had been seized by the Russians.

The more of the file she read, the more taken aback she was by its contents. From her reading of the various reports, the SCG's member states seemed to have a callous disregard for the Ukrainian men and women of the SMG who, for the best part of a year, had been risking their lives to observe and report back from increasingly dangerous parts of their besieged homeland. Despite the risks the local staff had taken, it appeared that this international group who employed them had decided to wash their hands of them. The reports on the file suggested that, in the very earliest days of the Russian invasion of Ukraine, some of the locally engaged staff may have deserted their posts and joined the massive hordes of refugees leaving the country, yet it was clear that most of them had either elected to stay or had been forced to remain by circumstances, and they had been continuing to send out reports from the occupied zones.

There were numerous reports filed from these monitors, which listed incidents of arrests, executions, rape and torture of civilians. The reports and signed witness statement had been submitted for onward transmission to the War Crimes Commission. The monitors providing the reports also expressed their fear of being caught in possession of such documents or of being caught in the act of transmitting them. They had asked for guidance on this but, as far as Verona could see from the papers, no guidance had been agreed or provided.

What Verona found even more shocking than these detailed reports, however, was a submission by her own boss who, in his capacity as the Moscow-based senior British delegate to the SCG, had recommended that those besieged local staff should have their contracts terminated. Furthermore, Cross had urged that the SCG in general, and the UK in particular, should deny the very existence of the Special Monitoring Group. His reasoning was that this might be construed by the Russians as interference in areas which they considered to be Russian territories. The Russians, he had argued, would almost certainly consider the monitoring staff to be spies and might decide to execute all of them. Worse still, they might use this as a pretext to mount a nuclear attack on Ukraine and perhaps also on its western allies.

It all made difficult but compelling reading, and Verona was quite relieved when Daisy suddenly appeared to ask if she was lunching in the canteen. Verona quickly logged out of the DHM's computer and, mindful of recent events, rather than leave the SCG file in his in-tray, she put it back in the appropriate drawer and locked the filing cabinet before heading off with Daisy.

As usual, she and Daisy sat with the other PAs, although Verona didn't feel she had much of an appetite. Her head was still full of the troubling information she had just absorbed from the SCG file. The talk amongst the PAs was all about the incident involving the cleaner, naturally enough but, to spare Tiffany any further depression over the incident, Verona, thoughtfully, quickly changed the subject.

'I met your boss this morning, Caroline.'

'Did you swoon?' Daisy asked. 'Most of us do.'

'Well, I can see why,' Verona agreed. 'He's quite a dish.'

'A *dish*?' Tiffany spluttered. 'Who says *dish* these days?'

Once again, Verona felt her attempt to be kind to Tiffany was thrown back in her face.

'Would you like me to translate?' she bristled, 'or to speak more slowly so you can follow?'

'He's a very thoughtful boss, too,' Caroline tactfully intervened.

'Care to swap?' Verona asked.

'No way, sorry,' Caroline smiled.

'Oh, Verona,' Daisy remembered. 'We're putting on a performance of 'Cats' instead of a Christmas pantomime this year. You must come and see us rehearse. It's terrific fun.'

'Oh, I'd love to,' Verona enthused. 'I love musicals. My sister and I usually try and see a musical whenever I'm home at Christmas.'

'Will you be taking leave this Christmas, then?' Caroline asked.

'No, unfortunately not. Because of the situation in Ukraine, Peter says he'll have to remain in post over Christmas, which means I'm required to stay, too. I share a house with my sister back in Dulwich. And, since I'm not going to be home for Christmas this year, she's swung an invite from one of her old school friends to spend the festive period in Scotland. So, I'll certainly be here to see you in 'Cats'. Are you all in it?'

'Yes, we are,' Daisy nodded enthusiastically. 'Come along tonight at six-thirty and see how we're doing.'

'Have all the parts been cast?' Verona asked. 'Only I've done quite a bit of am-dram myself over the years, and I can sing, too.'

Tiffany suddenly snorted.

'Sorry, Verona. It's definitely a young person's production. I can't see you in a cat costume, somehow.'

It seemed to Verona to be a savagely unkind comment. Clearly, Tiffany's gratitude for the advice Verona had given her had soon evaporated.

'Really? Well Judi Dench played the part of Old Deuteronomy in the film version, didn't she?' Verona countered. 'And she's, what, thirty years older than me?'

'Well,' Tiffany shrugged, 'I suppose it depends what one feels one can bring to the part.'

'In your case, I suppose, that would be claws,' Verona retorted.

Daisy and Caroline spluttered with laughter.

'Actually,' Verona continued, 'I was a cast member for a different kind of 'Cats'. 'It was KATS with a 'K' – Karachi Amateur Theatrical Society.'

'Really?' Daisy asked. 'What kind of productions were you involved in?'

'Oh, all sorts. We put on Gilbert and Sullivan light operas, and the odd suspense play. But the largely diplomatic audiences mostly preferred the Whitehall type farces. The Americans, in particular, liked coming to see those. They liked what they considered to be typically British humour. You know, English chaps caught with their trousers down. That sort of thing.'

Verona now spotted Cross on the far side of the canteen. He had obviously been lunching with Simon Harris and the DA, Robin Harewood, and the three men now stood to leave.

'Oh-oh. The boss is heading back to the office. I'd better follow. Not only has he got me cleaning for him, but I'm now doing his typing, too, and I've locked his papers away. He'll get grumpy if he has to unlock the cabinets himself, especially one-handed.'

'Ah, yes,' Daisy said. 'You know what they say about the DHM? Cross by name, cross by nature. See you in the hall at six-thirty, then.'

Verona rose, grabbed her lunch tray and deposited it by the serving hatch before taking off after her boss.

'I'm sure we could find *something* for her to do in 'Cats', you know,' Caroline said as she watched Verona depart.

'Hmmph,' Tiffany scoffed. 'I doubt it. I imagine Verona Brooks is the woman who put the 'dull' into Dulwich.'

Back in the DHM's office, Verona unlocked the cabinet and brought out the SCG file again for Cross. He was clearly pleased that she had thought to lock it away whilst they were both out at lunch. She knew that because, under his breath, he grunted something that sounded remotely like a 'well done'.

'I'll have another read of that draft,' he said. 'If I need anything added or amended, I'll give you a shout. Oh, and by the way, I've got some good news for you. There's an urgent SCG meeting been scheduled in London for the twenty-first of December, *vis-a-viz* the latest developments in Ukraine. I'll have to attend, and there seems little point in my coming back before the New Year, so I'll be taking the missus home for Christmas after all.'

'You will?'

'Yes. So, that means you can have Christmas off, too. I expect your family will be glad to have you home.'

'Well, there won't actually be any family at home at Christmas, now. Since I wasn't expecting to be home, my sister's going to be away staying in Scotland with a friend. I think it's a bit too late for me to make alternative arrangements. It'll either be Christmas alone in Dulwich, or Christmas alone in Moscow.'

'Ah. Oh well. I'm sure you'll have a nice time anyway. Christmas is fun wherever we are, isn't it?'

'You bastard!' Verona thought, *'you utter bastard!'*

CHAPTER TEN

HARRY EDWARDS AND JO LASKA ALIGHTED AT EAST CROYDON RAIL station in south London and headed the short distance to the Home Office's Immigration Asylum Intake Unit in the new Ruskin Square HQ. Once in the building, they were met by the section's Senior Executive officer Hailey Simmons. They produced their warrant cards, although she was expecting them.

'Actually, I'm glad you're here,' Hailey smiled. 'Business is brisk at the moment and we're grossly understaffed, as always. Your being here has saved us the cost of calling in a Russian interrupter, too. Most of the applicants in our backlog require Albanian interpretation. It's rare that we need a Russian speaker.'

Harry smiled at the officer referring to interpreters as 'interrupters'. He supposed that was part of the asylum staff's banter. As he surveyed the packed waiting area, he guessed the screening of the thousands of asylum applicants who arrived in the UK each month must be a most tedious process. He imagined one would need a sense of humour to cope with it.

'Don't you find all this dispiriting?' he asked. 'I mean coming in every day to a full waiting room, and, I guess, asking hundreds of applicants the same set of standard questions.'

'We don't actually conduct full interviews here. Our job here is just to book them into the system. The interviews come later, but even then, they don't get asked a lot of questions. Most of the applicants have already been briefed by their legal reps on the answers they're to give. Some of them just hand over the typed briefing notes they've been given. They don't even bother to memorise the stories they're supposed to tell. Their accounts are all the same.'

'Do you get any useful intelligence from the interviews, such as who organised their illegal travel across Europe?' Jo asked.

'Not really. Not unless you actually believe that just *one* man, allegedly a 'Mister Artem', is responsible for pushing *all* the clandestines into *all* the small boats on the French coast *every* day.'

'So, what kind of screening do you actually do here?' Harry asked. 'Do you check with CRO, Interpol, that kind of thing?'

'We do, but few of the asylum applicants have any identity documents. We've no way of knowing if they're giving us their real names.'

'So, how do you know they aren't murderers or even terrorists?' Jo asked.

'We don't,' Hailey shrugged. 'Of course, we fingerprint them and check their dabs against the major databases. But we only get a hit if they've been convicted of something serious somewhere. If they're wanted on suspicion of an offence, we won't know right away. Anyway, let me find you a desk so you can have a read of the files before you interview Messrs Ignatiev and Cherny.'

'We don't believe those are their real names, by the way,' Jo informed her.

'No shit?' Hailey exclaimed with more than a hint of weary sarcasm.

Once they had perused the scant information on the case files, Jo and Harry escorted the two Russians into one of the small interview rooms. Their faces were familiar and the colleagues had no doubt these were the two suspected killers whom they'd spotted on the CCTV images. Jo kicked off in Russian.

'*Dobroe utro*,' she greeted them.

'It's okay,' the bearded man smiled, somewhat patronisingly, Jo thought. 'We both speak English fluently. I'm Igor Ignatiev and my friend here is Zoltan Cherny.'

'*Glavnoye Razvedyvatelnoye Upravlenie*?' Jo asked.

She observed Ignatiev's face drop slightly.

'Yes,' he said. 'We are GRU. How did you ...'

'We and the Americans want you for the murder of Walter Edelman in Hammersmith on the twenty-fourth of November,' she said, cutting straight to the chase.

'What? He's dead? We didn't intend to kill him,' Ignatiev protested, his patronising expression rapidly turning to one of concern.

'And Moscow will want you for desertion and defection,' Jo added. 'You are seeking to defect, aren't you?'

Ignatiev glanced sideways at his compatriot, who shrugged.

'Yes,' Ignatiev conceded. 'We wish to defect.'

'But what makes you think we would want two Russian

killers roaming free on British soil? You aren't high value government men or scientists.'

'No,' Cherny piped up. 'But we have knowledge which will be very valuable to you, and to the Americans.'

'What sort of knowledge?' Harry asked.

'We have information about people the Kremlin have placed at the heart of the American administration. They are, how do you call them, *spyashchikh agentov*? They are betraying the west.'

'Sleeper agents,' Jo translated for Harry's benefit. 'And why would you want to tell us about those?'

'For money,' Ignatiev said. 'And for a new life here. Or in America. We don't mind which.'

'Oh, you don't mind, do you?' Jo replied. 'That's very accommodating of you. And how would two cheap thugs like you even know about the Kremlin's sleepers?'

'We just know. If we give you the information and you check it out, you will see it is genuine.'

'And why would you give us that information? Why would you betray your country?' she asked.

'Because our country has betrayed us,' Cherny spat. 'We did everything we were asked to do. We risked our lives for our country. Then we were recalled from ... from where we were based, and they sent us to a barracks. It was like a *gulag*. They made us live in a pigsty. They cut our pay and, when we complained and threatened to resign, our general said 'you can get yourself a motorbike and go deliver pizza'. *Suvohj*!'

'Yes. He's an asshole!' Ignatiev agreed. 'He has no loyalty to us, so why should we be loyal to him?'

Jo looked at Harry and raised her eyebrows. She got it that they were disaffected, but they were, indeed, low-level operatives. She wouldn't have expected them to have any great information to barter. But still, if there was the slightest chance they really did know of a serious threat to the west posed by embedded Russian agents, then the Security Service couldn't afford to ignore what they might have to say.

'Okay,' Harry nodded. 'We'll give you a chance to tell us whatever it is you're burning to tell us, but not here. We'll need to take you to a safe place. A secure place. It won't be a *gulag*, though. I can promise you that.'

Ignatiev sat back in his chair and gave a self-satisfied smirk. Harry and Jo left them in the interview room and, once out in the corridor, Harry took out his phone and called Adrian to request a car to convey the two Russians to a safe house.

CHAPTER ELEVEN

On Friday evening, as Verona trudged up the stone steps of her apartment block, laden with more grocery shopping, and let herself into the communal hallway, she saw Aleksandr coming out of the Petrenkos' ground floor apartment. He was wearing his outdoor clothes and clearly was just heading off out somewhere.

'Good evening, Miss Brooks,' he grinned.

'Hello Aleks. Going somewhere nice?' she enquired.

'Yes. I'm going to see a play at the University.'

'Oh, what's the production?'

'It's *The Government Inspector* by Nikolai Gogol. Are you familiar with it?'

'No. I've heard of Gogol, of course, but I'm ashamed to say I'm not familiar with his work.'

'He was Ukrainian, you know. Have you heard of his short story *Nevsky Prospekt*?'

'No. I haven't.'

'Well, it was called *Nevsky Prospekt* because it was set in the avenue of that name in St Petersburg. So, the story was named after the street. But here in Moscow, our own *Nevsky Prospekt* was named after Gogol's story.'

'How funny. Well, since I find myself living on *Nevsky Prospekt*, I suppose I should read the story sometime.'

'I have a copy of the play in English translation. I will lend it to you. Do you like the theatre?'

'I absolutely love it. The theatre, musicals, opera, ballet, anything like that.'

'Then you must come and see one of the plays our university puts on. They sometimes have performances in English. Next week, they're putting on an Agatha Christie, but I'm not sure which one it is. Would you like me to get you a ticket?'

'Oh, yes, I would love that – so long as you let me pay. You and your mother have been so kind to me since I arrived. I mustn't take advantage of your kindness.'

'Oh, and my mother asked if you are doing anything tomorrow morning, only she would like to take you to a very nice coffee shop for coffee and cake. She would like to introduce you to some more Russian cakes, and maybe Ukrainian ones, too. My parents and I are Ukrainian, you see.'

'Oh, I didn't know that. How kind of her to invite me. Please tell her I would love to go. The play you are going to see, will that be in Ukrainian?'

'Sadly, no. It's in Russian. The Ukrainian language is not encouraged in Russia. But we speak it at home mostly. Well, I must go. So, ten o'clock tomorrow morning. Would that be okay for you?'

'Yes. And please thank your mother for me. That will be most convivial.'

'Convivial. That's another nice word. I shall use it. Good evening, Miss Brooks.'

'Good evening, Aleks.'

Verona climbed the stairs and let herself into her little apartment. It was no longer hot and stuffy now, thanks to Aleks' adjustment of the radiators. And now she had an invite to go out for coffee and cake, tomorrow. How nice was that? It seemed ironic that the locals were showing her such kindness, when, apparently, her own compatriots couldn't care less.

The next morning, Verona was agonising over what to wear. Although it was just an invitation to coffee with Olga, it was the only outing she had been on since arriving in Moscow. The occasion probably called for something casual, but she actually had some nice clothes which she hadn't yet had an opportunity of wearing. For all she knew, she might never get the opportunity to wear them in Moscow. She wasn't exactly overwhelmed with invitations.

She recalled how, in the first week of her posting to Delhi, she'd had had printed invitations lined up on her bookcase. There were dinner parties, supper buffets, charades evenings, and cocktails at 2KG – as the embassy staff called the High Commissioner's residence. They called it that because it was located at 2 King George's Avenue. Even though that street had long since had its name changed to *Rajaji Marg*, the official residence was still referred to as 2KG. Moscow was very dull indeed by comparison. She eventually decided to wear one of the silk blouses she'd had made up in Delhi. They were such pretty colours and she settled on the emerald green one. Of course, she would have to wear a sweater over it, and several more outdoor layers over that, since it was bitterly cold outside. Yes, she decided the nice green blouse would cheer her up.

At ten o'clock precisely, there was a knock at her door. Throwing on her big coat and slipping her feet into her boots, she grabbed her handbag and went to answer the door. It wasn't Olga who stood there, however, but Aleks.

'Miss Brooks, unfortunately, my mother has met with a small accident. She dropped the ... er ... what do you call it?'

He made a gesture with his hands, as if he were pressing clothes.

'Oh, the iron?'

'Yes, she dropped the iron on her foot. I don't think it's serious, but it hurts her to walk.'

'Oh dear. I'm sorry to hear that. We can make it another time for coffee.'

'Oh no. I will take you.'

'Oh, you needn't ...'

'But it will be a pleasure to have coffee with you. You will learn about our wonderful cakes and I will get to practice my English. Please say you will come.'

'Well, if you're sure ...'

The coffee shop, *Konditeskaia Kafé*, was just a few blocks' walk away in one of the city's *fin-de-siècle* buildings, and the interior was pleasantly old-fashioned. They managed to get a table for two quite near the counter, so Verona could see the cakes. Aleks pointed out the different types of cake, most of which seemed to be named after cities. The layer cakes had names such as Moskva, or Moscow cake, and there was a

Prague cake and a Kyiv Cake. Aleks informed her that, in his household, the name of the Ukrainian capital was pronounced the Ukrainian way, 'Keev'. Verona was intrigued by a confection which went by the strange name of 'Bird's Milk Cake' and which looked rather like a bar of marshmallow coated in chocolate, but in deference to Aleks' heritage, she opted for a slice of the 'Keev' cake. Aleks ordered the same and also two coffees.

'This is a lovely café,' she declared, as she noticed the ornately plastered ceilings and the cheerful tablecloths.

'In the evenings it becomes a wine bar, and they serve traditional Russian meals to eat in or take away. Sometimes, they have live music as well.'

When their coffee and generous slices of cake arrived, Verona found the Kyiv or 'Keev' cake consisted of feather-light layers of sponge, sandwiched with buttercream and hazelnuts and it had a chocolate topping. It was very rich and deliciously indulgent. As they tucked into the confection their conversation halted temporarily and Verona took a long look at Aleks. She hadn't really done so previously. She now noticed how good looking he was. He had perfect white teeth and a ready smile. He also had an unusual combination of very blond hair and pale, grey eyes. He didn't look very much like his mother, since Olga had dark hair and brown eyes. She imagined he must favour his father, Olga's husband, whom she hadn't yet met.

'So, Miss Brooks ...,' Aleks began.

'Verona, please,' she insisted.

'Verona? Oh, what an unusual name. Unusual and beautiful. Is it Italian?'

'Yes, it is. My parents loved Italy. They spent their honeymoon in the lovely city of Verona. In fact, ...' she broke off and blushed slightly.

'Yes?'

'Well, I was actually conceived during that honeymoon in Verona – hence the name.'

'How very romantic. Has that given you a love of all things Italian?'

'Well, I love Italian opera, and Italian food, of course. Everyone loves Italian food.'

'And do you have brothers and sisters?'

'Just a sister. Apparently, she was conceived three years later, also in Italy. It was during a holiday in Florence.'

'So, let me guess what they named your sister,' he grinned. 'Was it ... Florence?'

'No. Funnily enough, they called her Romola. That's the title of a novel by George Elliot. It's set in Florence during the Renaissance.'

'Well, that's a pretty name, too.'

'She hates it, though. You see, the trouble is, everyone mispronounces it. People tend to put the emphasis on the second syllable instead of the first. Romola is supposed to be pronounced like Pamela, you see, but most people say it so it rhymes with tombola.'

'What is tombola?'

'Tombola is ... well, it's a kind of fairground lucky dip. You pay a small amount and you choose a ticket from inside a sort of revolving drum and if the number on your ticket corresponds with the number on one of the prizes, you win that prize. It's very popular at English summer fetes.'

'It does sound like an Englishman's name though – Tom Bowler. As for me, I was named after my grandfather. Not so very original, is it? I don't know where I was conceived. My parents had a honeymoon of sorts by the Black Sea. I suppose they could have called me Odessa. That would be a funny name for a twenty-five-year-old. Doesn't sound as romantic as Verona.'

'Twenty-five? You're only twenty-five? Goodness me, there must be many more exciting things a twenty-five-year-old could be doing on a Saturday morning than having coffee with someone twi ... someone almost his mother's age.'

'With a beautiful lady named Verona, you mean? A lady with a romantic Italian name and green eyes – green like the Adriatic. You know, green eyes are quite rare in Russia. Many Russians have blue eyes, or grey or brown, but you rarely see green eyes. And I just noticed, your eyes are the same colour as your shirt.'

Verona blushed. *She* certainly didn't have anything more exciting to do that Saturday morning than to sit drinking coffee with someone young enough to be her son and as handsome as hell. It occurred to her that there was no possibility she would ever have a son of her own. Olga was lucky, she thought. Verona and Aleks continued to chat and she found him surprisingly easy to talk to. They conversed mostly about Russian theatre and the arts. He suggested a number of galleries and theatres she should visit and she told him about the various roles she'd played in amateur theatrical productions. All too soon, their coffee was finished and only a few cake crumbs remained on their plates. She had really enjoyed their little outing. Aleks was undeniably charming company. He made to take out his wallet, but immediately, Verona was on her feet.

'Oh no, I'm paying. Please put your wallet away.'

It was still cold as they left the café, but the air was pleasantly crisp and fresh. Aleks seemed to be leading her a different way back to *Nevsky Prospekt.*

'We didn't come this way, did we?' she asked.

'No, but there's a very nice little park just up here. It's a lovely place to sit and watch the world go by. Unless you're in a hurry to get back?'

'No. No hurry at all. I haven't been along here before. Usually, I just walk from the apartment block to the embassy, then home again via that little deli and supermarket. That's all I've seen so far.'

'Oh, but there is much to see and enjoy in Moscow. You must let me show you some of the sights. Next weekend, perhaps.'

'That's very sweet of you, Aleks, but I'm sure you don't want to be stuck showing me around. You must have friends to see. A girlfriend to spend time with. I'm sure.'

'No girlfriend. During the week I spend a great deal of time studying. Girls don't like that. They want to go out to parties and to be treated to meals in restaurants. I don't have the money for that. I want to get my degree and then get a good job. Then there will be time later for girlfriends. Maybe I'll leave Russia and work in Europe. Who knows?'

They came to the park and it was indeed a pretty spot. Aleks found a bench which overlooked the lake and they sat down. There were lots of families in the park. Children were feeding the ducks and there were teenagers kicking footballs about. Verona was impressed that the Muscovites didn't let the cold weather stop them enjoying life. On days when it was scarcely this cold back in Dulwich, most folks would be at home, watching the football on television.

'Would you really leave Russia?' she asked. 'It sounds as though you love Moscow.'

'Well, I do. Moscow is my home. But things are getting difficult nowadays, especially for those of us with Ukrainian heritage. The economy is really bad right now, because of the sanctions and the cost of the war.'

He glanced over his shoulder to ensure no-one was close enough to hear, before he continued.

'Of course, we're not supposed to call it a war. It's a 'special military operation'. Anyone with Ukrainian connections is looked on with suspicion by the authorities, and the Russian people blame the Ukrainians for the fact that prices are going up and the economy is suffering. My biggest fear, though, is that I might be conscripted into the army.'

'Is that a possibility?' Verona was shocked.

'I don't know. They're mainly conscripting men from outside Moscow, especially from the ethnic minorities. There have been many protests against the war in the cities. That's why they're not opening recruitment centres here in the capital. It would lead to more protests, and with foreign press correspondents being based in Moscow, the world would see. Putin can't take criticism. If people protest in the villages, though, there's no-one to see.'

'But if they're mainly recruiting ethnic minorities ...'

'Yes, but, technically, I am an ethnic minority. I'm not considered properly Russian.'

'What would you do if you got called up?'

'I don't know. There's no way I'd go to fight Ukrainians. It would be a betrayal of my parents. I suppose I'd go to prison.'

'That's quite a dilemma. I'm sorry to hear that.'

It suddenly felt even colder. Verona shivered involuntarily.

'Oh, you're cold. We should get back before the temperature drops even more.'

Aleks stood up and gave a dramatic bow from the waist.

'Miss Brooks, your date will now walk you home.'

'My date, indeed!' she laughed, as she took his arm.

CHAPTER TWELVE

DECEMBER ARRIVED ALL TOO SOON, BRINGING WITH IT THE PROSPECT of a dull and quiet Christmas for Verona. Aleks kept his promise, however, and brought Verona a ticket for his university's production of Agatha Christie's 'And Then There Were None'. He took her to see the production at the Institute of Theatre Arts. It wasn't intended to be a comedy, but several things went wrong during the performance, causing unintended mirth amongst the mixed audience. Verona and Aleks were still laughing as they left the university's auditorium.

'I can understand that they wanted to save on the cost of breaking statues during each performance,' Verona remarked, 'and the idea of portraying the figurines as shadows on the wall was quite a novel one, but they should have found a stage hand who could keep count. First, there were ten little Indians, then nine, then eight, then ten again ...'

'Then six' Aleks added. 'I thought it funniest when we saw the shadow of a giant hand moving the little statues. I don't think we were meant to see that. I'm so sorry it was so ... how would you say ... amateurish?'

'Oh, not at all. After all, that's what amateur dramatics is all about – amateurs doing their best and putting their own interpretation on a standard piece. It was delightfully entertaining, although perhaps not exactly in the way the director intended. And, you know, it's the first time I've laughed since I arrived in Moscow.'

'Are you not happy in Moscow, then?' Aleks asked, as they left the institute and walked across towards the taxi rank at *Nikinsky Boulevard.*

'I'm happy to have met you and your mother, Aleks. But I can't say I've found the embassy a very happy place.'

'I'm sorry to hear that. But in three weeks it will be Christmas. Everyone is happy at Christmas, no?'

'Oh yes, everyone looks forward to a happy Christmas.'

'But you will be going home to England for Christmas, no? And Aleks will have no-one to speak English with.'

'Strictly speaking, one should say 'with whom one might speak English'. As my English teacher back in my school days used to joke 'a preposition is a very bad thing to end a sentence *with*'. Of course, it only really matters in writing, not so much in spoken English. And no, I'm not going home for Christmas.'

'Oh, is your sister, Tombola, coming to Moscow to spend Christmas with you?'

'Romola,' Verona chuckled as she corrected him. 'No. She's going to Scotland. You see, my boss said I couldn't take time off because he had to stay in Moscow and he'd need me to be here. Then he changed his plans and said I could take leave at Christmas after all. But it was too late for me to change my plans. No point in flying home just to celebrate on my own. Still, as he says, Christmas is Christmas wherever you are. Anyway, look, next week, there's a production of

'Cats' at our embassy. You and your parents must come and see it.'

Aleks' face was a picture of delight.

'Cats? Oh, Verona, we'd love to come. And we'd love to see your embassy.'

By comparison with Moscow University's production of Christie's drama, the UK embassy's production of the musical 'Cats' the following week was surprisingly professional. Verona regretted having arrived in post too late to audition for a part in it, but she enjoyed it nonetheless. She particularly enjoyed Grant's interpretation of the role of Rumpleteazer. Daisy, too, played the part of Mungojerrie to perfection, and Verona was surprised to see Simon Harris playing the piano to accompany the cast. She felt he played as competently as any professional musician. Seemingly, he wasn't just the most handsome man in the embassy but he was quite cultured, too. He was very different from Peter Cross, she decided.

She made notes of her impressions of the performance on the back of her programme because Daisy had asked if she would write a little critique of the production for inclusion in the embassy's newsletter. She thought that was a kind gesture on Daisy's part. It was a nice way of including her, since there wasn't a stage role for her. Verona decided she wouldn't comment on Tiffany's gaffe in fluffing her lines in the second act. To be fair, the part of Old Deuteronomy was a major one, with an awful lot of lines to be learned, and Tiffany was no Judi Dench.

Aleks and his mother attended the Saturday night performance as Verona's guests and they seemed to enjoy the show enormously. In the interval, over a glass of Prosecco, Olga expressed her delight also at having been included with so many important invitees. The guest list included various Heads of Mission and other local and foreign dignitaries. Olga declared, in her very basic English, that she would never normally have the opportunity of rubbing shoulders with such an esteemed gathering of people. Verona had invited Olga's husband Vitaly, too, but Olga had declined the invitation on his behalf, saying he wouldn't understand a word of it, and he was prone to falling asleep in front of the television most evenings, so she couldn't trust him not to drop off and start snoring during the performance.

There were drinks after the show, too, and Verona fetched more Prosecco for each of her guests.

'Are you not drinking, Verona?' Aleks asked.

'No. I'm not much of a drinker. I'll have a nice cup of hot chocolate when I get home. But how did you enjoy the show?'

'It was wonderful, Verona,' Olga enthused. 'Thank you so much for the inviting.'

'It was enormously enjoyable,' Aleks agreed. 'A most ... convivial evening.'

Aleks seemed enormously pleased with himself that he had digested and regurgitated an appropriately elegant word which Verona had taught him earlier. Verona thought that was boyishly endearing of him. The disappointment she had felt at not having been given a role in the production was forgotten now, as she enjoyed the company of her neighbours. She was pleased to have the other embassy staff see she had made friends of her own and wasn't reliant upon them for a social life.

The cast members soon appeared and joined the assembly

of guests. Verona glimpsed Daisy, Caroline and Tiffany, now out of costume, standing by the bar. Tiffany gestured in Verona's direction and seemed to be interrogating Daisy. It was fairly obvious to Verona that she was demanding to know who Verona's guests were, since Daisy had been in charge of the guest list and had issued the written invitations. Verona guessed it wasn't the presence of Olga which was causing Tiffany some consternation, but that of her very handsome son. Verona imagined Tiffany's interrogation would be along the lines of 'who is *he*, and what's he doing with *her*?' Aleks was, after all, far and away the most beautiful person in the room. It pleased Verona to be the subject of Tiffany's envy for a change. In fact, it pleased her very much indeed.

Arguably the second most handsome man at the event was Simon Harris, and he came over to ask how Verona was enjoying the show. Naturally, she complemented him on his piano playing. She introduced him to her neighbours, Olga and Aleks, and was most impressed when Simon addressed them in fluent Russian. She explained, however, that her neighbours were ethnically Ukrainian. Undaunted, Simon uttered a greeting in Ukrainian also, to Olga's evident surprise and delight. When he moved off to continue circulating, Olga, her cheeks flushed, said something to her son in her own language.

'My mother is honoured to have met such a charming British diplomat,' Aleks translated. 'Especially one who has taken the trouble to learn our language. She will not forget tonight in a hurry. Thank you so much for inviting us, Verona. You have made my mother very happy.'

Verona felt her own cheeks flushing now, too. It seemed such a small thing to have invited her neighbours to the show, but the fact that they had enjoyed it so very much gave her a warm inner glow of satisfaction. Despite the various disappointments her posting had brought her thus far, this evening at least, Verona actually felt happy.

The following weekend, it snowed heavily. On the Saturday morning, Verona had planned to try and find a little antiques market in the neighbourhood which Daisy Rogers had told her about. She hoped to find some nice small *objet* which she could send home as a Christmas gift for Romola. However, when she climbed out of bed and looked out of the window at what seemed to be a blizzard, she immediately decided against going out, and she climbed back into bed again. She dozed for another couple of hours, only surfacing again around lunchtime. She ran herself a hot bath and treated herself to a long soak. Whilst languishing in the hot water, she reflected on all that had happened lately.

She hadn't entirely abandoned her idea of asking to be short-toured. There were days when she felt decidedly homesick, especially as Christmas approached. Yet, although there had been a few disappointments, there had also been some pleasant moments. The time spent with Aleks, for example, had really cheered her up. She thought it must be rare for a young man of his age to actually enjoy the company of someone her age. Then again, he was obviously quite attached to his mother. Perhaps young Russian men had more love and respect for their mothers. Or perhaps this was a Ukrainian attitude.

After her bath, she dressed and decided to finally empty the small trunk which had arrived as her unaccompanied air freight. Of her heavy baggage, which had been despatched by road, there was still no news. She had packed only clothes and a few extra toiletries in her air freight and she lamented the delay in the arrival of her domestic items in the heavy baggage. She always included in the latter such things as framed pictures and colourful cushions, her books, some of her favourite English blue and white china and her Scandinavian glassware. She hoped that the eventual arrival of all these items would suddenly transform the dismal apartment into a home from home. Of course, the situation in Ukraine meant her baggage had to come to Moscow via a hastily arranged alternative route. She had no idea where it was currently.

She knew the war in Ukraine was affecting many people in many different ways. She chided herself for missing her goods and chattels when many Russian and Ukrainian women were missing their sons and husbands. She imagined Olga must be tormenting herself at the prospect that Aleks could be called up to fight. Verona's own worries seemed trivial by comparison. She reminded herself that it was always a bit difficult settling into a new post, but that she was used to her own company and to making do in difficult locations. On reflection, she felt she should give the place a bit more time. She had borrowed a few English novels from the selection available at the embassy club and she planned to spend the day having a good read.

It was the ideal sort of day for reading. The snow had brought that rare kind of silence to the neighbourhood. There was virtually no traffic passing on *Nevsky Prospekt*, and few people were venturing out onto the streets. She made herself some toast and coffee and hunkered down on her sofa to enjoy a quiet read. In the afternoon, she called her sister and told her of the DHM's change of plans for Christmas. She hadn't told her until now, just in case the DHM should change his mind yet again.

'Honestly, Rom, it's just too bad of him,' she complained.

'What will you do then?' Romola asked.

'Strangle him, possibly.'

'No, I mean about Christmas.'

'Well, there's little point flying home just to spend time on my own. I'll probably stay here and make Christmas dinner for one. I don't even know if you can buy turkey here. I'll send you a gift via the diplomatic bag, though heaven knows when I'll get to go Christmas shopping. The snow's keeping everyone indoors today. I hope it doesn't get much worse than this.'

'Are you still in that poky little flat?'

'Yes, unfortunately. Still, I've got some nice neighbours downstairs. They've been very kind and helpful. So far, they're the only saving grace about Moscow.'

'Well, do try and keep your chin up, Rona. I might come and visit you in the spring. That's if they've moved you to a bigger flat and you've got room for me. Got to go now, though, Darling. Church choir carol rehearsal in half an hour.'

'Okay. Bye, Rom.'

She felt quite flat after her brief call to her sister. She wished they could have chatted for longer, but Romola had so many pleasant things to do in the run up to Christmas. Verona wished she had, too. She had always enjoyed her local church's carol service. She doubted she'd be singing carols in Moscow this Christmas. The afternoon passed very slowly. She had read one of the books and had also ploughed through an old copy of *The Times*. She missed the internet access to the BBC and other news media which she had enjoyed in previous postings. Since the internet in Moscow was heavily controlled and censored by the Russians, the diplomats had to rely on brief news summaries circulated on the Foreign Office e-mail network or on printed copies of newspapers sent out via the diplomatic bag. A limited number of copies of *The Times* were circulated amongst the diplomatic staff but, because Verona was a recent arrival and thus very low down in the pecking order, she was last on the distribution list, so this particular copy of *The Times* was almost two weeks old. She would have loved to complete *The Times* crossword but someone ahead of her on the distribution list had already done so.

The temperature in the apartment was pleasantly warm, but, thanks to Aleks, not excessively so, and, before long, she found herself dozing on the sofa. At six o'clock, however, there was a knock at her door. Surprised, she ran a hand through her tousled hair, picked her books up off the rug and placed them and the newspaper tidily on the coffee table, then rushed to answer the door. Aleks stood there with a bottle of red wine in one hand and some paperwork in the other. He seemed excited and his cheeks were flushed.

'Aleks?' she said. 'Is everything all right?'

'Everything is not all right, Verona. Everything is *wonderful*. I got this letter this morning. My mother was upset at first, as she thought it might be my call-up papers for the army. But it isn't. It's my end of term exam results. Verona, I came top in my whole year.'

He thrust the letter at her, but she couldn't actually read it since it was in Russian.

'Oh, Aleks. Well done, you. That *is* wonderful.'

'Anyway, we must celebrate. Look, I have wine. May I come in?'

'Oh, well, I ..., I mean, aren't you going to celebrate with your parents?'

'I already did. But now, I wish to celebrate with the lovely English lady who told me all about tombola.'

'Tombola?' she laughed.

'Yes. I wrote an essay about English village life – about which I know very little, of course – but I wrote of village greens with fairgrounds; of coconut shies and tombola, and how it was all typically English and very ... convivial. My English tutor really liked my essay. She said it was 'evocative'. So, I want to thank you. Please may I come in?'

Verona could hardly refuse. She suspected Aleks had already downed a glass or two of wine, since his face was a little rosy and his eyes sparkled. Although she wasn't much of a drinker herself, his joy was so great and so infectious, that she felt it would be churlish to turn him away. She got two wine glasses from the kitchen. Since they'd been provided from the embassy's float, naturally, they were mis-matched and of different sizes, but Aleks didn't seem to notice. He sat on her sofa, unscrewed the cap from the bottle and filled both glasses, gallantly handing Verona the larger of the two. She sat down next to him.

'*Nahzdrovhyeh!*' he raised his glass to her and drank.

'Cheers!' she raised her own and sipped at the wine. 'Oh, this is actually very nice.'

They chatted, mainly about Aleks' future options and plans, as they drank the wine. Once again, she found Aleks easy to chat to. His smile was warm and ever present, and his big, grey eyes rarely left hers. He seemed truly excited about his future options and she was reminded of the time when she had been about Aleks' age and equally excited to leave the dull world of insurance and join the Foreign and Commonwealth Office, as it then was, to head off on her first overseas adventure. Although almost three decades had passed since then, and the romance of working for the Foreign, Commonwealth and Development Office, as it now was, had worn off a little, she could still recall how wonderful it had felt to be on the threshold of a career. Aleks laughed a lot, and he made her laugh, too. His laughter was almost musical and quite infectious.

'Verona,' he suddenly demanded, 'you are so lovely. Why have you never married?'

'Oh!' she spluttered into her wine, as she found his question unexpectedly forthright. 'Well, I suppose I was never in one place long enough to get to know anyone well enough. There are always lots of single women in UK diplomatic missions, you see, but not so many single men. That limits one's options. And I suppose I was married to my job.'

She put her wine glass down onto the coffee table. His question seemed to have injected a note of seriousness into the conversation. He topped up both their glasses, raised hers and handed it back to her.

'Oh, now I see your crest has fallen,' he said, and he pulled a comically sad face.

She laughed.

'You mean I *look* crestfallen. Goodness, how does anyone cope with learning English? It really is the most peculiar language.'

'Are you sad?' he asked. 'Have I made you sad? Tonight, I want you to be happy, like me.'

'Aleks, I'm very happy *for* you. If I look sad sometimes, it's just because, well, I'm not very happy at work. I'm not very happy in this flat, either. But I'm sure things will improve – in time.'

'My mother says you must not sit up here alone in your flat. You must come downstairs and have Sunday lunch with us. Are you free for lunch tomorrow?'

'Well, yes, I am free. Of course, I am. My social calendar is disappointingly empty. I would love to come. That's very kind of your mother. Do thank Olga for me.'

Aleks went to pour some more wine, but the bottle was empty. To her surprise, they had finished it between them.

'I know,' he stood up. 'We need more wine. I will go downstairs and fetch more wine.'

'Oh, no, Aleks. I'm quite squiffy already.'

'Oh, yes, Dear Lady. We need more wine so we can be happy.'

It was clear to her that Aleks was a bit squiffy, too.

'No need to go downstairs,' she said. 'I have a couple of bottles of red wine in the kitchen. I got them in, just in case the girls from the embassy should visit. Of course, they didn't.'

'I'll get one,' Aleks said and he headed into her little kitchen. 'Where are they?'

'On top of the fridge.'

He opened a fresh bottle, filled their glasses up once more and sat down beside her again.

'So, now, tell Aleks what is making you unhappy?'

She felt so easy in his company, and, of course, there was no-one else she could talk to. It didn't feel right speaking to Romola on the telephone about how things were at work, especially as there was always the possibility some Russian official might be listening in. She found herself telling Aleks that Lauren, Daisy and Caroline, who were three of the other

PAs and were the girls she usually lunched with, were actually quite nice, even if they didn't have much time for her outside of their busy schedule of rehearsals and nightclubbing. However, she confided, there was a fourth girl who was actually quite a bitch. She giggled and put her fingers to her lips, as she asked him to excuse her language. She assured him she wouldn't normally use such a word. It must be the wine speaking, but, yes, Tiffany Munro was a bitch of the first order. There was no other word for her.

'Tiffany Munro? So, she's not a beautiful person. Not like Marilyn Monroe?'

'No, not at all like Marilyn Monroe. Ironically, she works in the Defense section. Maybe that's why she's always on the attack,' Verona giggled at her own pun. 'And as for my boss, well, he can be an utter bastard, too.'

'Who is your boss?' Aleks demanded. 'I will come and punch his nose.'

She giggled again.

'He's the number two in the embassy, Aleks. It would create a diplomatic incident.'

'But how does he make you unhappy? Does he speak unkindly to you?'

She found herself telling him about being made to clean the office, washing everyone's dirty dishes and emptying the bins. She told him about the cleaner's security breach which had led to her virtual demotion to the role of a cleaner. That breach was probably down to Tiffany Munro, too, she explained, and she had tried to make Tiffany feel better about it, but would you believe, the bitch had thrown it back in her face. And then there was the fact that she was now taking dictation and having to type up the boss's drafts, all because he'd had too much to drink and had fallen over and broken his wrist. And then, of course, there was the business over Christmas. She told him of the DHM's *volte face* over her Christmas leave.

'And that's another thing. His use of Latin phrases. He uses them all the time, and not always appropriately. It's just to show off that he did Latin at school. He probably gave it up after third year.'

'Latin?' Aleks queried, as he topped up her glass again. 'Why does he speak Latin? Why not English?'

'Well, exactly. He was dictating this draft to me the other day, all about the SMG, this Special Monitoring Group who got left behind in Ukraine and, well, he's giving London lines to take, you see, depending on whatever happens to those poor monitor people. So, he says his lines can be put to the Prime Minister, '*mutatis mutandis*' if necessary. I query his use of the Latin and he asks 'don't you know what that means?' I say, of course I do, it means 'suitably amended'. So why not say 'suitably amended'? And he gets cross, which is ironic, you see, because that's his name – Peter Cross – and he shouts at me, 'Who's writing this draft?' 'I am,' I tell him. Stupid sod!'

Verona chuckled again. How she would have loved to call Peter Cross a stupid sod to his face. It was only her civil service pension, she told Aleks, which prevented her from doing so.

'He does sound like a stupid sod,' Aleks agreed, 'Latin is a dead language. He is flogging the dead donkey.'

'Flogging a dead horse, you mean,' Verona snorted. 'That's the usual expression.'

'You are so right about English, Verona. It is a very strange language. I thought the phrase 'number two' meant ... um, you know ... shit. Now, you tell me your boss is a number two.'

'Yes, I suppose he is a little shit. I never thought of that,' Verona curled up with laughter.

Between fits of the giggles, she finished off the wine in her glass. Aleks promptly filled it up again. The wine had indeed made her feel happy – happy and relaxed. She could see the funny side of things now. She could even see the funny side of Peter Cross *viz a vis* his ridiculous insistence on using Latin wherever possible. What an arse!

After a few more gulps of the wine, however, the happy feeling seemed to dissipate. It now occurred to her that she was only happy because of the wine and because Aleks was here, trying to cheer her up. But she knew that, when the wine was finished and when Aleks left, she would be alone again in her dismal and dingy little apartment, and Peter Cross would still be Peter Cross. There would still be office bins to be emptied and cups to be washed and bleached, and she would still be facing Christmas alone. Her unhappy situation would be unchanged.

'He sounds like a very unkind man,' Aleks said as he slipped a consoling arm around her shoulder. 'Unkind and heartless. He doesn't deserve you.'

Verona rested her head on Aleks' shoulder.

'Oh, you don't know the half of it. He's not just heartless towards me. He's an utter bastard when it comes to those poor people in Ukraine.'

'There are many poor people in Ukraine at the moment,' Aleks said. 'Which ones do you mean, exactly.'

Verona found herself telling him all about the abandoned Ukrainians of the Special Monitoring Group, and how many of them had already been executed by the Russian authorities controlling Kherson, Luhansk and Donetsk. These were ordinary, decent people, who were risking their lives to ensure the truth came out about Russian war crimes. And she knew about them because she had seen some of their reports. And, what's more, there were more than five hundred of them, spread across two dozen different regions of Ukraine. Some were safe, but many were trapped in the occupied zones.

'Verona,' Aleks said solemnly. 'What you have told me breaks my heart – my Ukrainian heart. But I'm glad you told me this. Now, I must tell you something about myself.'

Verona looked up into his big, grey eyes. They looked troubled. She hoped she hadn't upset him, especially when he had been so happy about his test results. She hadn't wanted to dispel the optimism he clearly felt about his future, but he was just so easy to talk to. Too easy, perhaps. She felt he genuinely cared about her situation.

'I am part of a network of students and other young people who are opposed to the war in Ukraine. There are many of us. We are not just protestors, though. We started by raising money for Ukraine, to help the refugees. Then we started taking more direct action.'

'What sort of direct action?' Verona asked, surprised.

'Acts of sabotage. We have blown up munitions plants in several locations here in Russia. Some of the members of our network have even been going into occupied Ukraine to try and get people out of the war zones and into the regions which are still free. There are useful people who needed to leave the danger zones – academics, dissidents, humanitarians, people who are being hunted down and killed by the Russian military. We are helping them get out.'

'Oh, Aleks. That sounds very dangerous.'

'Yes, it is, but we all do what we can, when we can and

where we can. We also have links with a great many Russian soldiers who have deserted. They have formed their own legion which they call the *Freedom of Russia Legion*.'

'Really? And what do they do, these deserters?'

'They are fighting alongside the Ukrainian army. There are thousands of such men in the new legion.'

'Oh, Aleks, that's amazing. And you are in touch with them?'

'Yes. That is why I am fearful about being conscripted into the Russian army. If a member of our network should be captured and tortured and made to talk, we would all be arrested. Either I would be shot or I would be sent to the front as ... cannon fodder – that's the expression, isn't it? But it sounds as though those people you mentioned, the people on the monitoring group, they need our help, too.'

'Do you think your network could help them?'

'We would certainly try. But we would need to know who they are and where they might be. It is possible some of my network could go in and try to get them out. We could get them to safety.'

Verona began to look at Aleks with new eyes. This was a surprising and quite exciting side to him. For someone so young to be involved in something so dangerous, so reckless, was quite remarkable – if, indeed, it were true. She was suddenly beset by doubt.

'I'm not sure I should be discussing this with you, Aleks,' she said. 'This could get us both into trouble.'

'I understand. Then we will speak no more about it. It is an unhappy situation. And tonight, I want you to be happy.'

He cupped her chin in his hand and drew her face towards

his. Unexpectedly, his lips met hers. Despite the wine she had drunk, she pulled back.

'Oh, Aleks. I think maybe you'd better go, before we make fools of ourselves.'

'I'm not going before I have made you happy, Verona,' he said and he kissed her.

She placed her hand on his cheek. It felt so soft, so smooth, but she gently pushed his face away from hers.

'Aleks, you don't understand. I don't ..., I mean, I have never ...,' she broke off and she blushed fiercely.

'Ah. I see. Then it's time you did. My lovely English lady with the romantic Italian name and the beautiful green eyes, it is time that you did.'

CHAPTER THIRTEEN

THE TWO RUSSIANS LOOKED SLIGHTLY UNCOMFORTABLE AS THE MI5 driver conveyed them, Harry and Jo towards Heathrow Airport. Any fear they might have had that they would be forcibly returned to Moscow abated, however, when Jo produced her and Harry's passports and the new British passports in fictitious names which had been issued to Messrs Cherny and Ignatiev and she handed them to the British Airways staff at the domestic check-in desk for Belfast.

'We are going to Ireland? Ignatiev queried,

'Belfast – it's in Northern Ireland,' Jo said, indicating the front cover of her own British passport which proclaimed 'United Kingdom and Northern Ireland'.

'It's very beautiful, and your former employers won't think to look for you there,' Harry reassured them.

The Russians still looked a little uneasy as they walked down to Terminal One's departure gates, and it was only when they reached the gate lounge for the Belfast flight that they seemed to relax a little. Eventually, they were summoned to board and the defectors and their two escorts passed through the document check at the gate and headed down the ramp to the aircraft.

'Passports, please,' Jo held out her hand as they shuffled on board, and the Russians handed the freshly issued UK passports back. They were happy for Jo to hold onto them for safekeeping. Jo knew, however, that they would not be needing them again.

Ignatiev and Cherny slept on the flight, which persuaded their escorts that, whilst they may have been under stress to start with, they were now feeling more relaxed about the circumstances of their defection. On arrival at Belfast, a black people-carrier met them outside the terminal and drove them all the along the A2 north eastwards out of the city. At Holywood on the County Down coast they were driven in through the gates of the Palace Military Barracks, where the Russians were to spend the next three days being de-briefed in the relative comfort of MI5's Northern Ireland HQ.

The following morning, the two Russians were escorted down to the modern canteen where they were met by Harry and Jo.

'Did you sleep well?' Harry asked.

'Extremely well, thank you,' Ignatiev said. 'The accommodation is very good.'

'The food is very good, too,' Jo promised. 'Wait until you try the full Irish,'

'What is a full Irish?' Cherny asked.

'The breakfast. Irish bacon, sausage, black pudding, white pudding, eggs and potato farl. And you must have the soda bread with it. The local butter is so good, and the water here comes from the Mourne mountains. It makes the best cup of tea you've ever had.'

'So, the condemned men will eat a hearty breakfast,' Ignatiev said, 'and what's after that? A firing squad? I saw from my window there are many soldiers here.'

'No firing squad,' Harry laughed. 'I'd recommend a swim in the indoor pool, or maybe a game of squash. There are all sorts of facilities here. We want you comfortable and rested before your de-briefing this afternoon.'

Ignatiev glanced at his compatriot, who shrugged. His look reflected Ignatiev's thinking. If this was what defection meant, then, clearly, they had made a wise decision.

'Do all British soldiers enjoy these conditions?' Ignatiev asked. 'I mean, comfortable beds, leisure facilities and wonderful views of whatever that river is out there?'

'The Belfast Lough,' Jo advised him. 'Yes, of course they do. Our fighting men and women are looked after very well.'

Of course, this was the only barracks Jo had ever visited, and she knew it was far superior to any other UK military barracks, not least because, for obvious historic reasons, recruitment in Northern Ireland had always been problematic, and the government had spent a great deal of its defence budget on making Palace Barracks appealing to potential local recruits. Of course, the rooms in which the Russians had spent the night were not the usual barrack accommodation, but were in a block reserved for the Security Service's 'special guests'.

'What have you done with our phones?' Cherny asked.

'We have to check them over for tracking devices,' Harry said. 'Wouldn't want your former employers sending someone to look for you, would we? You'll get them back shortly.'

'How shortly?' Ignatiev asked.

Harry knew that 'shortly' meant as long as it would take for all the contacts, texts and images to be downloaded by tech ops staff.

'Shortly,' he repeated.

Back in London, Thames House's tech ops staff were already assessing the information downloaded from the Russian's phones. They were able to mine a seam of valuable intelligence in terms of the defectors' contacts, the calls and texts they had made and received and also their travel. In particular, the men's movements were traced from the point of their arrival at Heathrow, as recorded on a variety of phone masts along the way to Kensington Palace Gardens, then to the London venue where the SCG meeting had taken place, and from there on to Soho and, via the London Underground route, to Hammersmith, before returning, via Kensington Palace Gardens back to Heathrow once more. The day after their arrival, their phone signals had hit masts from west to south London as they made their way to Croydon to claim asylum at the Home Office's asylum screening unit.

Adrian Curtis sat in his office, studying Carol Murray's telephone analysis reports and the still photographs taken from the various CCTV images. The evidence against the two Russians was convincing enough for him. They had already confessed to Harry and Jo that they had attacked US diplomat Walter Edelman, but Adrian was pleased to have enough firm evidence to definitely put them at the scene at the precise time of Edelman's death. The only question was what he would do with that knowledge. He needed to decide how to use it to best advantage. He would see first what information the defectors had to share, but then he might use them either as a bargaining chip or perhaps to mend some bridges between the UK and the US. Yes, he would give careful consideration to what he would do next with Ignatiev and Cherny.

CHAPTER FOURTEEN

Monday morning found Verona at the tea station once more, washing the stack of tea-stained mugs and dirty plates which she had not felt like tackling on the Friday evening. This morning, though, she didn't feel quite so resentful about the task. This morning, things felt different. Of course, she told herself, this was nothing to do with her boss. She still felt justifiably aggrieved at having to do the menial stuff. This morning, however, it didn't seem to matter so much.

The weekend's events had somehow put things into a different perspective for her. As she stood at the sink, tipping desiccated teabags out of mugs into the stinky food waste bin, she found herself blushing fiercely at the thought of Aleks and of how their Saturday evening had ended up. Her young neighbour's joy at his exam results, and their celebration of his achievement, had ended a lifetime of celibacy for his middle-aged neighbour. Her cheeks burned at the recollection of her own joy and the ways in which she had expressed it. Indeed, she had surprised herself at how freely she had expressed it – all Saturday night and again on Sunday morning.

So far, her Sundays in Moscow had been extremely dull, but yesterday had been very different. She had accepted the invitation to share the Petrenko family lunch, and Olga and her husband had been most hospitable. The meal had been good and Vitaly Petrenko, although unable to speak English, had been a most assiduous host and had topped up Verona's wine glass each time she had emptied it. She had begun to wonder whether this was a Ukrainian rule of hospitality, so she had slowed down her drinking a little. Vitaly had put away quite a bit of wine himself and had nodded off in his armchair after lunch. Verona wondered whether the Petrenkos knew their son had spent the night in her bed, but she suspected they did not. After lunch, she had left their apartment a little unsteadily, owing to the wine, and Aleks had gallantly walked her upstairs to her front door. He had kissed her goodnight but had acquiesced to her plea that she was exhausted and needed to get a good night's sleep as she had to be at the embassy extra early the following morning to tackle her cleaning duties before she even began her proper tasks. The memory of that kiss, however, had given her a kind of inner glow fit to melt the snow on her walk to work.

Her blissful reverie at the tea station sink was suddenly cut short by the arrival of the DHM. His arm was still in a sling, she noticed, as he barked a curt 'morning' at her and she followed him into their office. As he passed her desk, he noticed her weekend reading matter lying there.

'Ah, *The Times* is in. What's new? Anything?'

'Well, I see Mussolini's troops have invaded Abyssinia,' she said, hoping her sarcasm would register her dissatisfaction at being so far down the distribution list.

'Ah, yes. Very funny. So, clearly that's your copy, then.

Perhaps you'd pop your head around Robin Harewood's door this morning and see if he's finished with his copy. You can read it after me, if you like. Nobody really takes much notice of the attached distribution list, you know. If you see a recent paper sitting in someone's dip, you can just nab it, read it and put it back later.'

Verona didn't know that's what one did. She wished she'd known that earlier. If she had, she'd have probably nabbed the DA's copy before now from his 'dip', as the embassy staff members' individual pigeon holes were called, and that would have left Tiffany to explain its disappearance.

'Oh, before I forget,' she told him, 'Simon Harris phoned. He asks if you'd kindly pop along and see him this morning. At your convenience, of course.'

'Right. Well, I see all the cups are still being bleached,' he said, peevishly, 'so I'll see if *his* PA's got some coffee on the go.'

Further along the corridor, in the political section, Cross followed the aroma of freshly brewed coffee. Simon's PA, Caroline, rose to pour him a cup, as he headed into Harris's office.

'You wanted to see me, Old Boy?'

'Yes, Peter,' Harris stood up, took the cup of coffee from his PA and closed the door between his office and hers before presenting the coffee to Cross.

'Thanks for coming. Do take a seat. I wanted to discuss a little matter which is a bit sensitive. It concerns your PA.'

'Verona? Why, what's she done?'

'Oh, nothing, so far as I know. No, it's just that Caroline tells me she thinks Verona's not very happy.'

'Oh, did she say why?'

'Well, for starters, she's stuck in that poky little transit flat down in *Nevsky Prospekt.* It's the one-bedroom flat that we normally use to accommodate the King's Messengers, when they stay overnight after dropping off the diplomatic bags. But it's not really suitable for long-term occupation.'

'But it's only *pro tem*, isn't it? I mean, she'll get the next apartment that comes available within the embassy complex.'

'Does she know that, though?'

'I would have thought so. I mean, the old girl's a seasoned trooper. She's been with FCO for years. She'll know how these things work.'

'Well, it might cheer her up if you remind her that it's just temporary. Mind you, with the current security situation in this region, our ... temporarily expanded staff complement isn't likely to shrink any time soon, and we've still got the Canadians as room-mates. She might have a long wait.'

'I'm sure she'll understand. My impression is that she's a fairly self-contained person. She's had postings in some pretty far-flung places, including at least one Islamic country. From what I remember of her personnel details, she's considered to be someone who fares well in hardship posts. I guess that's why they sent her here.'

'Yes, Peter, but you and I both know that the social life in most hardship posts tends to compensate for the difficulties staff might have in getting out and about, or for the taboos on making friends outside the embassy. European posts are different, of course. No-one really puts themselves out to create social activities in our embassies in Europe, simply because it's Europe, and because it's easier for us to pop home to visit UK, or to have friends and relatives come to stay.'

'Yes, I suppose you're right.'

'And, of course, Moscow may be in Europe and only four hours from home, but it has its own particular challenges. Plus, she's arrived at the worst time of the year. Not only has the bad weather begun to set in, which keeps us all indoors and grumpy with cabin fever, but everyone's either been tied up with rehearsals for the musical, or they've been busy making plans for Christmas – too busy to take the time to help a new staff member settle in.'

'Yes, I suppose so,' Cross agreed.

'She's also quite a bit older than the other PAs, so I can't see her socialising much with the girls. And she's single. So, there's no partner to go home to.'

'Yes, that's true. But I imagine she's single by choice.'

'I gather she's also feeling the requirement to clean the office is a bit of an imposition. She is, after all, quite senior and experienced. And I hear she's been stuffed over the arrangements for Christmas leave, too. Got a lot of factors going on there to make her unhappy.'

'Well, yes, but all unavoidable, what with the Ukraine situation. And your girl, Caroline, she doesn't seem too put out about the dusting and vacuuming.'

'No, but that's because I've cut her some slack in other areas. I tell her to take a two-hour lunch break on occasions, or I send her home two hours' early on a Friday, and that sort of thing. Don't forget, you and I have non-working wives who have plenty of opportunities during the week to get grocery shopping done, or to visit the hairdressers, or whatever. The PAs have to fit all that in after work or at weekends.'

'Yes, fair enough, I suppose. I take your point, Simon.'

'Good. Well, I think we all need to be mindful of the possibility that a member of staff who feels lonely could find themselves being cultivated by hostile intelligence agencies. You remember the Security Service briefings we all had on the sort of issues which might motivate staff to betray secrets?'

'Yes. The motivation acronym was MICE, wasn't it? Money, ideology, coercion or, what was the last one, ego? But I haven't heard Verona express any dubious political opinions. And I've no reason to think she's short of money. I can't see her causing any problems.'

'Well, personally, I've always felt that MICE acronym was a bit outdated. And I'm not sure it absolutely applies to women.'

'How do you mean?'

'I suspect when women betray secrets it's for a different set of reasons. Take Mata Hari, for instance. She was a pure fantasist. She was a pint-sized, mixed-race woman whose only asset was a good body. She believed her exotic dancing gave her some influence and control over men that she wouldn't otherwise have. She thought she could use her powers of seduction to induce men to part with secrets. Unfortunately, her ambitions ended in front of a firing squad.'

'True,' Cross agreed, 'but I can't see Verona Brooks as any kind of Mata Hari.'

'No, but then there was Dolly O'Grady.'

'Who the Dickens is Dolly O'Grady?'

'Dolly O'Grady was a plain, middle-aged housewife, a seaside landlady on the Isle of Wight during World War Two. She was no *femme fatale*, but she was lonely when wartime restrictions put the island off limits to visitors. She was so desperate for excitement and adventure in her life she fantasised about spying for the Nazis. She tried to bribe an army sentry to draw her plans of his camp so she could send them to the Germans. She also tried to pay a couple of schoolboys to shin up a telegraph pole and cut the phone wires. She was arrested, tried and condemned to death.'

'Good God! Did they hang her, then?'

'No, eventually the sentence was commuted to imprisonment. You and I know most men are susceptible to pretty young women, and that's why the Russians have a whole flock of 'swallows' – pretty girls who'll seduce a chap and get a few secrets out of him, either through pillow talk or blackmail.'

'Hmmm, yes, I've had all the briefings on that,' Cross agreed. 'If you're going to sleep around, sleep NATO. Isn't that the guidance?'

'Yes, and although, so far as I know, it's unheard of for any of our female colleagues to have fallen under the spell of a trained *gigolo* – the Russians call their male seducers 'ravens', by the way – if one did betray her country, it would probably be for love. Anyway, looking at the examples of mesdames Mata Hari and Dolly O'Grady, I've always thought a better acronym for the motivation of women traitors should be LIFE – love, infatuation, fantasy or just plain excitement.'

'Well, Verona's only been here five minutes. Not long enough to fall in love. And I haven't seen her reading any romantic literature, or anything soppy like that.'

'Don't forget, though, that, for all their shortcomings, the Russians are especially good at reading people. They're good at spotting someone's vulnerabilities – loneliness, for example. D'you remember the case of that young comms chap from Hanslope Park who was sent out here back in the Cold War era? He was lonely and he just didn't fit in. He was miserable, until some nice Russian sugar daddy started taking him to the opera and buying him dinners. When he was back in England, the sugar daddy's friend took over. The lad was caught handing the man his Hanslope code book.'

'But Verona doesn't have access to anything particularly sensitive. Not really.'

'Maybe not, but if she's feeling isolated or side-lined and unappreciated, she could be still be susceptible to approaches. In the past, traitors have been motivated simply by virtue of the fact that they felt under-valued. And some perfectly decent people have been tricked into revealing things they shouldn't. And it doesn't have to be top secret stuff. The Russians like all kinds of inside information – details of diplomats' movements, the Ambassador's travel plans, tidbits of overheard gossip. You know the sort of thing – so and so's a drunk, such a one's got debts.'

'Okay. I see what you mean. I'll have a little word with her on the QT.'

'Great. Thanks, Peter. It's part of my responsibility to ensure none of our staff gets compromised in any way. Once the furore over the Defence Section's security breach dies down a bit, I'll arrange a little refresher briefing for the admin grades, just to remind them of the specific challenges of being in Moscow.'

On his return to his own corridor, Cross found Verona putting the vacuum cleaner away in the cleaner's cupboard by the tea station. Entering his own office, he spotted a sparkling clean mug sitting on his dust-free desk. Having taken in what his colleague in the political section had just told him, he made a point of thanking Verona.

'Splendid job you've made of the dusting and washing up this morning, Verona. Much appreciated.'

'Oh, you're welcome,' Verona said, taken aback by this unaccustomed praise.

'Look, I know these little tasks must seem a bit ... *infra dig* and all that, but I really do appreciate you doing them. I know we've been asking a lot of our admin staff just lately, and I know Monday mornings are busy, but why don't you take an extra-long lunch hour today? Why not hang out with the other girls, or go shopping or something?'

'Well, thank you, Peter. I'd like that.'

'Oh, and I've heard a whisper that one of the flats here in the embassy might be coming available, soon. I'll make sure it has your name on it.'

'Well, thanks again, but, you know, I'm getting used to my poky little flat now. Once my heavy baggage arrives with my nice bits and bobs, it might make the flat feel more homely. And I've met some of the neighbours now and they seem awfully nice. They fixed my central heating for me, and they cooked me a splendid roast lunch yesterday.'

'Did they? Yes, well, just make sure you don't get *too* friendly with the locals. They might not have your best interests at heart. Right, would you get me that SCG file out again, please? When you've got a minute, Dear. No rush.'

CHAPTER FIFTEEN

VERONA DETECTED A SOFTER TONE IN THE DHM'S VOICE THE following morning. She wasn't accustomed to this and wondered what had prompted it. Cross was on the phone when she approached his desk and put the SCG file, which he had again requested, in his in-tray. It was obvious he was speaking to his wife.

'Darling, so sorry, but I'm going to be working late again tonight. Big rush job on. Got to get briefings done for the SCG's December meeting... Oh, not until ten thirty, maybe eleven o'clock. Don't hold dinner for me, Darling. See you later.'

Verona's heart sank. If the DHM was going to be working late that evening, then he'd almost certainly need her to work late, too, especially if he had briefings to be word processed. Damn! So much for having an extended lunch hour yesterday. It seemed today would be a long working day. This was especially disappointing because she had promised to cook supper for Aleks at eight. She had wanted to be home promptly to prepare some food and to get herself ready, too. She had hopes that the evening would end the same way last night had – in her bed, with Aleks alongside her.

Back at her own desk, she quickly checked the staff contacts list for the telephone number of her flat. She wasn't familiar with the number as she'd had no reason until now to call her own flat. She had left Aleks sleeping in her bed when she had left home that morning and she hoped he would still be there. She needed to catch him before he left for the university. As she listened to the ringing tone, she pictured her last sight of him as she had slipped out of bed, trying not to wake him. She pictured his long back, his narrow waist and the curve of his slim hips, as she had gently placed the covers back over his naked body. Once again, she felt a warm glow rising within her and she closed her eyes to preserve the image of him. Suddenly, the phone was picked up and she heard his voice.

'Hello?'

'Oh, Aleks, it's me,' she whispered, conspiratorially. 'Look, I'm so sorry, but it looks like he'll want me to work late this evening. I probably won't get away till ten-thirty or even eleven tonight. I'll have to postpone our dinner. Can we make it tomorrow night?'

His sleepy voice told her that was fine.

'No problem. I'll see you tomorrow evening, then, Lovely Lady,' he breathed, sleepily.

Verona put down the phone and glanced towards her boss's office door, to reassure herself he could not have overheard. 'Lovely Lady'? No-one had ever called her that before. She was disappointed not to be seeing Aleks after work, but soon she was distracted by an avalanche of e-mails.

Half an hour later, Cross emerged from his office.

'Verona, I hear you've taken on Alice Bartram's car.'

'Yes. I haven't used it yet, though. Haven't actually needed it. Why do you ask?'

'Well, since I'm *hors de combat* with this blasted broken wrist, I can't drive, and I've got a meeting after work this evening. D'you think you could drive me there?'

'Um, yes, but I don't know my way around the city just yet. Where is it?'

'Oh, it's not far. It's here in the *Arbat* district. Just a few roads away, in the old quarter.'

'Okay, well, I'd better pop down to the car pool and check that it still starts and that Alice has left fuel in it. Will you want me at the meeting, too?'

'No. You can just drop me off over there, if you would. I'll get a taxi home after.'

As Verona walked to the embassy's garage and car pool area, she wondered why Cross couldn't have got a taxi *to* his meeting, as well as taking one home from there. This was just another thing which made her feel he was taking advantage of her. It now seemed she could have made dinner with Aleks this evening after all. It really was too bad of Cross, she felt. However, she also felt she hadn't really got her feet under the table sufficiently as yet to even think about asserting herself. She didn't think she could refuse to drive him. At least the car wasn't exactly an old banger, as Tiffany Munro had led her to believe, but, nevertheless, it was a rather basic saloon in a most unappealing shade of tan.

Verona guessed her predecessor must have bought the car in Moscow, possibly from another member of the diplomatic community. Alice wouldn't have been able to benefit from the FCDO's interest-free loan scheme to purchase a second-hand foreign car. Such loans were only available against the purchase of new British-made vehicles. That meant the car would now be third-hand at least. As she had expected, the car wouldn't start first time. It had been standing in the cold for a month now. However, she persevered and, eventually, the engine spluttered reluctantly into life, and the fuel gauge showed the petrol tank was two thirds full. She let the engine run for a while to warm everything up.

Back in the office, she tried ringing the flat again to tell Aleks she would be home on time after all, but the phone rang unanswered. Obviously, he had already left for the university. She decided she might as well leave things as they were, especially since she didn't know how long it would take her to drop off her boss and to get back home afterwards. She had a look at the Moscow guide book her predecessor had also kindly left for her. She was surprised Alice hadn't kept the book. Perhaps she had decided she wouldn't need it again as she didn't intend ever returning to Moscow. This reinforced her suspicion that Alice, too, had been unhappy working for Peter. She looked up *Arbat* in the guide and saw it extended from the embankment where their embassy was situated, further inland from the river. Apparently, it included one of Moscow's smarter, historic quarters.

At five-thirty, Cross emerged from his office, his coat on and his briefcase in hand. Clearly, he was ready to go. Verona logged out of her computer, made sure everything was locked away, and grabbed her own coat. They headed out to her car. Once again, the car took a little persuasion to start. She found it quite annoying that Cross kept looking at his watch until, eventually, the engine coughed into life. He directed her to head north and away from the river. In the car's confined interior, Verona was aware of her boss's rather overpowering after-shave or cologne. She didn't think he'd been wearing it earlier in the day. She supposed his business meeting must be with someone important, someone he wished to impress, but she didn't think it appropriate to ask.

Soon they came to a wide avenue, where Cross indicated she should pull up. Although it was already getting dark, she could see this was a very smart boulevard. Indeed, much of the *Arbat* district seemed very elegant. The impressively ornate, three-branched streetlights illuminated the broad avenues, as did the neon signs outside a variety of up-market restaurants and cafes. They had stopped on the opposite side of the road from a rather grand apartment block. With a little difficulty, since he was clutching his briefcase and had only one good arm, he wrenched open the rather reluctant passenger door of the car and climbed out.

'You'll find your way back okay from here, won't you?' he asked.

'I expect so,' Verona said, though she didn't imagine it would make any difference to him if she didn't.

'Well, many thanks, Verona. See you in the morning.'

Verona watched him enter the apartment building, then she gazed up and down the elegant Avenue. She promised herself she would come here again one day soon, but in daylight, as it looked like a really interesting part of the city to explore. She switched on the car's interior light and took out the guide book to confirm exactly where she was. The book showed several places nearby that were worth seeing, such as the Pushkin Museum. She was surprised that Aleks hadn't mentioned that, as he loved anything to do with poetry and plays, and the guide book described the poet and playwright Alexander Pushkin as being the father of Russian literature.

The apartment building which had swallowed up her boss looked expensive. Most of the apartments were in darkness. This wasn't surprising as she knew that most Muscovites didn't leave work before half past six. Her attention was suddenly drawn to one of the large balconied windows up on the first-floor of the block, where a light had just come on. She saw a blonde woman at the window, drawing one of the curtains closed. Suddenly, a male figure appeared behind the woman and, slipping one arm around her waist, he drew her to him and they kissed. Seconds later, the woman drew the other curtain shut, but not before Verona had recognised the man. To her surprise, it was her boss, Peter Cross.

Shocked, she paused for a moment to think. She realised the woman wouldn't be Mrs Cross, since Peter had earlier called his wife and told her he would be home very late and not to hold dinner for him. In any case, she knew the Crosses didn't live around here. Like all the other UK staff in her embassy – with the exception of herself, of course – they lived in an apartment within the embassy complex. So, who was the woman the DHM was kissing? It hadn't been a chaste kiss on the cheek, such as one might expect between diplomatic acquaintances. It had been a fairly protracted kiss on the lips, and their bodies had been close enough to suggest intimacy.

As her surprise gave way to embarrassment at having caught out her boss in what seemed to be an illicit affair, she told herself she ought to drive away. That would be the diplomatic thing to do, the considerate thing to do. Then again, Peter Cross hadn't exactly been considerate towards her. Curiosity now got the better of her. On impulse, she stepped out of the car and crossed the street to see what the address of the apartment block might be. She clocked the street name which was elegantly inscribed on the side of the building – *Nikitskaya Ulitsa.*

Venturing into the empty lobby of the apartment building, she saw a unit of wooden mail boxes ranged along one wall. Each one was labelled with the apartment number and the name of the occupant. She glanced along the row of boxes relating to the first-floor apartments and all the residents' names appeared to be men's names – all save one. Amongst the Ivanovs and Stepanovs and Lavrovs, there was a Natalie Schoen in apartment three. Making a mental note of the name and the apartment number, though she didn't really know why she did so, she headed back to her car.

Suddenly, it became clear to her why Cross hadn't wanted to call a taxi to take him to the apartment of someone who was obviously his mistress. Others in the embassy might have seen him leave in a taxi and might have wondered why he did so, since he lived within the embassy complex. Also, the taxi company might keep a record of where someone from the British embassy had gone and might have reported it to the Russian authorities. She had heard that sort of thing went on. Russian intelligence liked to know what foreign diplomats were up to and which of their nationals were fraternising with them.

Of course, Verona herself was fraternising with Aleks, but she told herself that was different. Some might be shocked at the age difference between them, but at least they were both single, unlike Peter Cross. Verona told herself *she* could not be blackmailed into giving away her country's secrets, even if she knew any. But Peter Cross could. The phrase which suddenly came to her mind was the old adage that 'knowledge is power'. She had no intention of doing anything with the knowledge she had just acquired about her boss's extra-marital activities. Of course, she hadn't. But it was intriguing, nonetheless. She wondered whether other men in the UK's diplomatic mission had mistresses, too.

She remembered the mantra which was routinely drummed into every diplomat during a security briefing on her induction course some thirty years before: 'if you are going to sleep around, sleep NATO'. Back then, she'd had no intention of sleeping around at all. In fact, during the intervening three decades, she'd had neither the intention nor the opportunity of sleeping with anyone. During her numerous overseas postings, with so many new beginnings and new environments to explore, the years had passed by quickly, and opportunities for romance had passed her by also. As her youth had given way to middle-age, so her virginal status had morphed into spinsterhood.

Spinster – how she hated that word! Romance wasn't for spinsters, at least that was what she had thought. That was why her sudden awakening to the joy of a physical relationship had taken her completely by surprise. Aleks was, to all intents and purposes, a Ukrainian, of course. And, by all accounts, Ukraine was about to be granted membership of NATO, so, she told herself, she *was* 'sleeping NATO' – well, almost. She wondered whether this woman with whom she presumed her boss was sleeping, this Natalie Schoen, was NATO. The name didn't sound particularly Russian, at any rate.

It was around six-thirty when she arrived back at her own flat. This pre-war, utilitarian building was a far cry from the elegant apartment block where the DHM housed his mistress.

Somehow, that fact caused her even more resentment. She was surprised to find her flat in darkness. She had expected to find Aleks there. Perhaps, though, believing she would be working late, he had gone downstairs to have dinner with his parents. She looked in the fridge and saw the food she had planned to cook for herself and Aleks. Well, there was no point in cooking just for herself. In any case, she was weary and she didn't feel like cooking at all, although she was hungry.

If she had known Peter's plan to 'work late' would not involve her, she could have been eating a nice meal with Aleks right now. Just as with the Christmas arrangements, her boss had scuppered her personal plans. The dismal little flat had seemed much less dismal for Alek's presence during the weekend. Now, it seemed more depressing than ever for his absence. She recalled the nice coffee shop Aleks had taken her to for coffee and cake, the *Konditeskaia*. She remembered him saying that, in the evenings, it became a bar which served meals and also provided take-away food. The idea of picking up a ready-cooked hot meal, something typically Russian perhaps, appealed to her. If she had to eat alone, she might as well eat something nice. It would be a sort of consolation for the evening she had planned but which, disappointingly, had been put on hold.

Putting her coat and boots back on, she headed outside and walked the several blocks to the café. Moscow looked different at night, she thought. The street lights seemed to be crowned with blue haloes caused by the frosty air. The café, too, looked different at night, with a pink neon sign illuminating the window, and dimmed lights within. Glancing in through the window, she could see there were candles in bottles on each of the tables, and the diners seemed to be enjoying their meals. She stopped short, however, on seeing one of the couples seated at one of the tables, their heads together, laughing. The young woman was attractive, with long dark hair and long, slim legs. The young blond-haired man with her was equally attractive and his features were all too familiar. It was Aleks.

Verona's heart sank as she stepped back away from the window, lest she be seen, but she continued to observe the couple. They were sharing a bottle of wine and seemed to be enjoying each other's company. Seated too close, she felt, to be mere acquaintances, they seemed at ease with each other. The way they interacted suggested shared intimacy. Aleks had told her he had no time or inclination for girlfriends. However, it appeared that wasn't absolutely true. She suddenly felt betrayed. Then she felt foolish. She told herself that Aleks had every right to have a girlfriend. A fifty-year-old spinster wasn't going to be the love of his life. She wasn't going to be the love of *any* man's life. Why, though, she wondered, had he chosen to spend a weekend in Verona's bed, when he could have been sleeping with the girl with the lovely hair and the long legs?

For the second time that evening, she felt she had witnessed a relationship she wasn't supposed to see. Seeing her boss with another woman had been a surprise. Seeing Aleks with another woman was a shock. Disappointment stabbed at her heart. She was confused. She also felt more than a little stupid, but she no longer felt hungry. She turned and walked away.

Back in her empty flat, she consoled herself with a cup of hot chocolate and decided to have an early night.

'Thank you, Peter Cross,' she said to herself, as she climbed into bed alone that night. 'Thanks a bloody bunch!'

CHAPTER SIXTEEN

NATURALLY ENOUGH, VERONA WASN'T FEELING PARTICULARLY WELL disposed towards her boss the following morning. Her response to his 'good morning' was a grudging 'mmh'. However, she was surprised when, instead of stomping past her desk as he usually did and heading into his own office to begin his morning routine of unlocking his desk drawers, logging on to his computer and resorting to Anglo-Saxon rather than Latin to curse his full inbox, Cross stopped by her desk, produced an envelope and handed it to her.

'What's this?' she asked.

'Dinner party invite for you,' he smiled. 'The Missus and I are having a few people over for dinner on Saturday evening and we wondered if you'd care to come.'

Verona half expected him to follow this up with 'and would you mind doing the washing-up afterwards?' but, thankfully, he didn't.

'Oh, thank you, Peter. I'd love to come.'

Over lunch in the staff canteen, Verona learned that Lauren and Tiffany would be at the Cross's for dinner that Saturday, too. Daisy now reminded Verona that, before that, they had cinema night to look forward to on Wednesday.

'It looks like the bag's going to be delayed again this week,' she said. 'Still, we've got that box set of DVDs we can watch. It's a TV drama series. It's supposed to be very good. *Doctor Foster – A Woman Scorned*. It's a revenge story. Have you seen it, Verona? It was on TV in the UK not that long ago.'

Verona said she had seen it, and it was very good, she assured them, so good, she wouldn't mind seeing it again. Her heart wasn't really in the conversation, though, and her thoughts were elsewhere. Having seen Aleks with someone who seemed to be a girlfriend, she determined she would try and avoid bumping into him for the next few days if possible. She felt she needed time to think about what had happened between her and Aleks, and to work out how she felt about it. Never having had any kind of romantic relationship before, she realised she didn't really know how these things worked. She had no idea of the rules, if, indeed, there were any rules. Yes, she would certainly stay behind after work for Wednesday's curry supper and the cinema night.

Tiffany was late joining her fellow PAs for lunch and, when she did appear, she seemed to be in an angry mood.

'What's up, Tiff?' Lauren asked.

'The DA's still trying to pin the blame on me over those missing documents. Seems they're a lot more sensitive than we'd thought. The Ambassador's going to hold some sort of internal inquiry.'

'Well, if it wasn't your fault,' Daisy reassured her, 'you've got nothing to worry about.'

'Unless it's made to look like it was my fault,' Tiffany sulked.

'Well, just remember what I told you,' Verona added, kindly, 'and cover your back.'

Tiffany's expression seemed to suggest something else might be eating away at her.

'Oh, yes, Verona, I meant to ask you about the guests you invited to the performance last week. Who were they?'

'Why?' Verona was puzzled.

'I just wondered who they were, that's all.'

'They're my neighbours. From my apartment building. Olga has been very kind to me. Bringing them along seemed a nice way to repay their kindness.'

'Yes, but who's the hunk?'

'The hunk? Who says 'hunk' nowadays?' Verona asked, pointedly.

'The fit-looking guy who came with your neighbour.'

'Oh, Aleksandr? Yes, he's quite a ... a dish, isn't he?'

'Yes, but *who* is he?' Tiffany demanded.

'He's ..., oh, well, if you must know, he's my clandestine lover,' Verona teased.

'Your lover?' Tiffany gasped.

'Yes. Oh, look, Peter's on the move. I'd better go, too. See you later,' she breezed and, having deliberately given Tiffany something to gossip about, smiling mischievously to herself, she hurried off after her boss.

That afternoon, Simon Harris emerged from his office, clutching mail for the outbound diplomatic bag, and saw the Defence Attaché's PA sitting alongside his PA in the outer office. The two were chatting earnestly.

'Well, Ladies,' he smiled pleasantly. 'What's the *goss*?'

'We were just talking about Verona Brooks,' Tiffany

informed him. 'Unlikely as it seems, she says she's got a boyfriend.'

'A boyfriend?' Harris sounded impressed.

'Yes. He must be half her age. She says he's her ... what did she call him, her *candelstein* lover?'

Caroline burst out laughing at Tiffany's gaffe.

'Ah, a nice Jewish boy, eh? Good,' Harris joked.

'Oh, Tiff,' Caroline chided her. 'The word is 'clandestine'. She was just winding you up, though. She knows what a gossip you are. She hasn't got a secret lover. He's her neighbour's son. She asked Daisy to invite her Ukrainian neighbours Olga and Vitaly to the performance, but Olga's husband didn't want to come as he speaks no English, so her son came instead. He's studying English at university. Her neighbours have been very kind to Verona. She had some trouble with the central heating in her flat. Aleks just popped up and sorted out her pipes for her. That's all.'

At this, it was Harris's turn to burst out laughing and, shaking his head with mirth, he left the girls to their gossip and disappeared back into his own office.

Verona had hoped to avoid Aleks and she made the effort to slip in and out of the building as quickly and quietly as possible over the next few days. She felt embarrassed at having seen him with the young woman. She felt even more embarrassed about that than she had felt at seeing her boss in a clinch with his mistress, although both incidents made her feel like some kind of *voyeur*. If she should bump into Aleks in the hallway, she wondered how she should react, what she would say. She would most likely be stuck for words.

As it happened, things seemed very quiet in the Petrenkos' apartment. Usually, she could hear their television as she passed their door, but this week, all was quiet. She began to wonder if they might even have gone away for a week. Or perhaps it was the case that Aleks was avoiding her, too. Surely, he hadn't seen her outside the café, looking in at him? No, she was fairly sure he hadn't. Maybe he had tired of her already. Perhaps he had only just met the girl, and perhaps the brief interlude with his middle-aged neighbour was nothing more than that. Perhaps she was just a stop-gap. She consoled herself with the fact that, even if that were the case, and if her intimacy with Aleks were not to be repeated, at least she had the memory of their brief liaison to bring her pleasure.

When Thursday evening came around and she quietly let herself into the apartment block, Aleks suddenly appeared in the hallway. Pulling the door of the Petrenkos' apartment closed behind him, he strode across to her and took her in his arms.

'Hello, Lovely Lady. I have missed you so much this week. May I come up and see you tonight?'

'Oh, I'm not sure. I mean, well, for one thing, I haven't got any food in. I'd need to go out again and get us something,'

'Not necessary, Verona,' he smiled and he kissed her on the cheek. 'I will cook supper for us both and bring it up to you. And I will bring wine. What time should I come?'

'Oh, I don't know, Aleks. I'm not sure it's a good idea,' she protested.

'I will come up at eight o'clock,' he insisted and he released her from his embrace, just in time, for, suddenly, his mother emerged from their apartment. She was carrying what seemed to be a bundle of cloth. Her face lit up when she saw Verona.

'Ah, Verona. Good evening. These are for you,' she grinned as she thrust the bundle at Verona.

'Oh, what's this?' Verona asked.

'I saw your curtings is horrible. These my old curtings but still very good. Your windows same like mine. Should be fitting. You take and if you like, you put these at your windows.'

'Oh, Olga, how thoughtful. Yes, I'll see how they look. Thank you.'

Olga grinned her gold-toothed smile again and then she was gone.

Aleks laughed and Verona laughed too.

'Oh, how sweet of your mother.'

'Well, if you don't like them don't be polite,' he urged. 'I can bring them back down again. Mother won't be offended.'

'She's absolutely right, though. My curtains are truly frightful. These are bound to be nicer,'

'Okay, well, I'll see you later. Eight o'clock.'

Verona hurried up the stairs. Although she was annoyed with herself that she hadn't felt able to say no to Aleks, she was secretly glad that he clearly wanted to resume their relationship. Perhaps relationship was too strong a word. Relations might be more apt, she thought. Well, what had she to lose, other than that which was already lost but didn't feel like any kind of loss? She realised she desperately wanted him to be with her again. Did it really matter if she were not the only woman in his life? Perhaps she should feel flattered that, although he had a beautiful young girlfriend, he still felt inclined to spend time with his middle-aged paramour.

With each step she climbed, she felt the cares of the week being shed one by one. She felt happy. It was an unaccustomed kind of happiness, and Aleks was the cause of it. The Moscow chill didn't matter. Her poky apartment didn't matter. Peter Cross didn't matter, and nor did Tiffany. Nothing mattered. She hurried inside her flat, threw off her coat and boots then quickly tidied up. She opened the bundle of curtains. They gave off a pleasant scent of fabric conditioner, by which she guessed they had been freshly laundered. She spread them out on the sofa and they were indeed much nicer than the curtains which already hung at the lounge windows.

The existing curtains had a pattern which was far too big and imposing for the small living room, and the colours were nightmare-inducing shades of forest green, deep violet and yellow. The King's Messengers who would have stopped over in the flat for a night or two after dropping off the embassy's diplomatic mail, probably wouldn't have cared a jot what the curtains looked like. However, having lived with them for a few weeks now, Verona found them quite oppressive.

By contrast, Olga's carefully pressed cast-offs were cream with a delightfully tasteful small floral sprig design. Verona felt the pattern was more like the kind of design she would have chosen for herself. It wasn't too different from the pattern on her lovely Laura Ashley curtains in her bedroom back home in south London. Once she had taken down the offending curtains and replaced them with Olga's, not only did the room suddenly feel bigger and smell fresher, but the curtains gave the windows the look of an English country cottage. She bundled up the embassy curtains and stowed them on top of her wardrobe, then she ran herself a warm bath.

As she waited for it to fill, she threw off her dressing gown and stood naked before the bathroom's full-length mirror. Running a hand through her hair, she saw how much grey there was these days. It had appeared so gradually that she hadn't really noticed. Her hair could only be described as 'mousey', she thought. Indeed, her late father's nickname for her had been 'Mouse'. By contrast, her younger sister had fair hair, and it seemed to Verona that grey locks were less visible in fair hair. She ran a hand over her cheek. Her skin felt dry, but she didn't think she had wrinkles yet – laughter lines, perhaps, but not exactly wrinkles. She looked herself up and down critically. There was still some bounce in her breasts, though by no means could they be described as 'perky'. Her abdomen was no longer taut, but some men liked a woman to have a curvaceous belly and hips. Aleks had said he did. However, as she gazed at herself in the mirror, she wondered what it was that attracted Aleks to her, especially when he clearly had such a young and attractive girlfriend.

At eight o'clock on the dot, there was a knock at the door. Verona rushed to open it and a smiling Aleks entered, carrying a tray with several dishes on it and two bottles of red wine. He took them straight into the kitchen. He wore slim-fitting denim jeans and a crisp white cotton shirt with the top few buttons undone. She thought he looked very handsome indeed and she now felt glad she had agreed to have dinner with him. Suddenly, it didn't seem to matter who he might be seeing when he wasn't with her. This evening, he would be here with her, and that made her happy. Once he had deposited the dishes on the kitchen worktop, he turned and took her in his arms again.

'Verona, you are looking especially beautiful tonight. And that perfume, it is very sexy.'

She laughed, embarrassed at his unbridled show of affection. Did he really mean the things he said, she wondered, or was this just a young man's flattery as a prelude to sex? Well, she had no illusions about her looks, and if he only wanted her for an occasional and convenient sex partner, then she told herself that, probably, she was okay with that. No-one had ever said such nice seductive things to her before and, even if it was nothing more than empty flattery, well, she didn't care. Aleks had made her feel good about herself. He had aroused feelings in her that she had never felt before. She told herself that, even if, tomorrow, he should decide he no longer wanted to sleep with her, well, so what? It had been utterly wonderful this far. She hadn't known this sort of excitement before and it might not last, but whilst it did, she would embrace it with fervour.

'Thank you, Aleks,' she breathed, 'and you look ...well, wonderful.'

'Let's eat,' he said. 'Do you have plates?'

She removed the plates from the oven where she had placed them to keep them warm. Taking them into the living room, she set them on the table which she had already laid for supper. Aleks brought his serving dishes through and put them in the centre of the table.

'It is a special veal stew,' he announced, 'and sautéed potatoes and beans. I hope you'll like it. I'll open the wine.'

Verona lit the candle she had pushed into the neck of one of the wine bottles she had kept from the previous weekend. Suddenly, with the candlelight and the paler backdrop of Olga's curtains, the whole room took on a much more pleasant ambience. Aleks opened the wine and filled their glasses.

'Here's to you, my beautiful English lady,' he raised his glass to her, and she did likewise to him.

The first draught of the wine relaxed her immediately.

'So, how was your week?' she asked. 'I haven't seen much of you. I thought you must have been busy.'

'I was. On Monday, I met with Anna, a woman I know. She's one of the members of my network. Remember I told you about the network?'

'Yes, I remember.'

'I mentioned to her what you had told me about those special monitoring people, and that so many of them are trapped in Russian-occupied Ukraine.'

'Ah, yes, well I probably shouldn't have told you that,' Verona said, surprised, as she didn't actually recall having mentioned the subject at all.

She realised she must have really been in her cups the previous weekend. It alarmed her to think she had discussed so sensitive a subject with Aleks. Okay, so she had entrusted him with her heart, but perhaps she shouldn't have been so free with information about the monitors. Maybe she shouldn't drink so much wine tonight, she thought.

'No, it's okay for you to tell me, and for me to tell Anna. You see she has a cousin who is one of those special monitors.'

'Has she?'

'Yes, her cousin, Marina Ivanova. She worked for that organisation in the city of Kherson until they sacked all the local staff. She was trapped there. When my friend last heard from her, Marina was hiding in the basement of her apartment block with a lot of other people and she was passing on information about the Russian troop movements in and around the city. Then the apartment building was attacked and Marina had to flee.'

'Oh, goodness!' Verona exclaimed.

'The electricity generators in the city were deliberately

destroyed by the Russian troops, too, so then there was no electricity there. They couldn't charge their phones or use their computers and the landline exchanges weren't working either. Since then, Anna hasn't heard from her cousin at all.'

'Oh, I'm sorry to hear that, Aleks. Poor Anna. She must be very worried.'

'She is. That's why some members of the network are going to go to Kherson to try to find her cousin.'

'But it's under Russian occupation, isn't it? How will they get in?' Verona asked, alarmed to hear about what sounded like a suicide mission.

'Actually, the news from Kherson is good. They don't announce such things on Russian television, but Ukrainian forces re-took the city this week. Anna doesn't know if Marina survived, but she and others will go and try to find her. I will go part of the way with them and wait until they come back. But don't say anything to anyone about this, will you? In Moscow, you never know who you can trust.'

'Of course, Aleks. I won't tell a soul.'

'With the grace of God, we will find Marina Ivanova. But, if we should fail, well, maybe there will be other people in Kherson that need our help.'

'You think there may be other monitors there?'

'Yes. At least Anna believes Marina worked in the SCG office in downtown Kherson. Some of her colleagues from that office may still be living in the ruins of the city. They will have no money and no food. If the Russians have captured them already, then they will have killed them, but we need to know. Anna needs to know.'

'But, if you don't find Marina, how will you know where to

find her colleagues? Do you know who they are and where they are?'

'No. That's a problem. If we don't find Marina, then she won't be able to tell us who her colleagues are and where they might be.'

Verona reflected on what Aleks had just told her. The network's plan to help the SCG's locally engaged staff was certainly very daring and also very dangerous. But, for Verona, the key thing which stood out in what Aleks had said was that the young woman she had seen him with in the café, the beautiful young woman with the lovely dark hair and the long, slim legs, was not his lover, but his friend, his fellow networker. The sensitivity of the topic they had clearly been discussing probably explained why they had their heads together. Verona suddenly felt relieved about that. In fact, she felt the relief flood through her. She quickly dismissed thoughts of the young woman, however, since the more pressing issue, surely, was the plight of the SCG staff. She now remembered Peter Cross's SCG file.

'Oh, but I believe that information may be on file at our embassy,' she told him.

'Is it? Oh, but, Verona, I wouldn't want you to get into any trouble. Maybe you should ask your boss if it's okay to disclose it?'

Verona thought back to the recommendations the DHM had made on that file. He hadn't given a thought to the safety of those brave Ukrainians. He had recommended deniability. He clearly didn't give a damn about those people. And, in the light of the current security breach in the DA's office, she very much doubted Cross would be agreeable to any information being disclosed. Of course, he didn't have to know.

‘When are you setting off?’ she asked.

‘Five of us are going on Sunday.’

‘That soon?’

‘Yes, well Sunday is a good day to travel. Russian forces are always hungover on a Sunday. We will travel by train to Sochi on the Black Sea. Others will meet Anna and our friends there and take them by sea to Kherson.’

‘Listen, I’ll have to think about this. But if I could find details of the SCG staff, if I could get hold of a list tomorrow, I might be able to get you the information by late on Saturday night.’

‘That would be wonderful. It would be great if we could help some of those brave people. But, please, Lovely Lady, don’t take any risks. I wouldn’t want you to get into trouble.’

‘Just let me think about it. Okay?’

‘Okay. And now, please, let’s eat. And let me pour you some more wine.’

CHAPTER SEVENTEEN

Two days later, on the Saturday morning, Verona awoke late. Aleks had slipped away from her bed a couple of hours earlier. She had heard him leave and she had expected him to, for he had said he had much to do to prepare for his trip to Sochi the following day. She had hardly slept during the night, and it wasn't just due to the fervour of Aleks' love-making. She had agonised over her decision regarding whether or not to give him the list of the SCC's Ukrainian staff. Supposing she was wrong about Aleks? What if he were lying to her? Would she be helping the stranded monitors or would she be endangering them? Yet she had no cause to doubt Aleks or his intentions. Conversely, Peter Cross's attitude to them was abhorrent to her. Still, she had tossed and turned for most of the night as she had mulled things over in her head.

She was expected at the Cross household by seven-thirty that evening for an eight o'clock dinner. She was dressed and ready by six thirty and she set off walking to the embassy. The snow was still fairly thick on the ground, so she wore her boots and carried a pair of indoor shoes in a canvas shopping bag.

She also had a bottle of wine in the bag. Rather than heading into the residential block, however, she used her swipe pass to let herself into the main embassy building. The security guard was surprised to see her arrive, given that it was a Saturday evening. He put down the paperback book he had been reading.

'Good evening, Miss Brooks,' he greeted her quizzically.

'On my way to dinner at the DHM's,' she told him. 'I picked up a nice bottle of wine yesterday to take along, but stupidly, I left it on my desk. May I have our office key from the keep?'

He nodded and went to fetch the key, which, in common with all internal embassy door keys, had to be signed out of the keep at the start of each working day and handed back in at the end. Having handed Verona the key, the SO picked up his paperback book once more, so Verona headed confidently towards the lifts. Once in the office, she switched on her desk lamp. She had no need of the cabinet keys from the keep, and nor did she need the SCG file, for she had already photocopied the required list the previous day, and she had left it in her own personal desk drawer until needed.

Cross had unwittingly assisted her in this, due to his own vagueness. All documents which were photocopied in the embassy had to be listed and numbered in a log, and the total number of documents logged had to correspond with the document counter on the photocopier itself. But Cross had asked her for 'two or three' copies of the recently updated staff telephone directory, one for his desk, one for hers and one for him to keep at home. Verona had given him just two copies. The third document she had photocopied had been the SCG list.

She noticed the handwritten annotation across the top of

the list, written in thick black ink in Cross's handwriting. It stated simply: *'Nota Bene: Not to be issued with visas'*. She glanced at the long list of names. This was the first opportunity she had had to peruse those names. They did not have home addresses next to each employee's name, but they were grouped according to the local offices in which the staff were based. There were several hundred names on the list and she had to keep an eye on the office clock, in case the security guard became suspicious as to why it was taking her so long to collect a bottle of wine, so she quickly ran her eye down the pages until she found the names of staff attached to the Kherson office. There was indeed a Marina Ivanova listed there. That persuaded her that Aleks must be telling her the truth. After all, how else could he possibly know that someone of that name worked in the Kherson office of the Security Co-operation Group?

As she sat looking at the list, at the names of all those brave, trapped, frightened Ukrainians, she knew she was doing the right thing. Peter Cross might not care what happened to them, but she did. If she could do any little thing to ensure that those people might be brought out to safety, then she must do it. Her heart was beating fast as she stuffed the list into her canvas bag, along with the shoes. Turning off the desk lamp, she exited the office and locked the door behind her.

'Found it,' she called out to the security guard, though her heart was in her mouth as she raised the canvas shopper in his direction to give the impression she had stowed the wine in the bag, which she had of course, but earlier back at the flat. She handed him the office key then strode quickly towards the exit.

'Oh, Miss Brooks,' the guard called out.

Her heart stopped and she froze in her tracks. She turned around and it suddenly crossed her mind that there might be internal security cameras up on their floor. He might have seen her on camera as she had retrieved the document. She could have kicked herself for not having checked that. Or maybe, if she was lucky, he was simply going to ask her to show that she really did have a bottle of wine in her bag.

'Yes,' she faltered.

'Have a nice evening,' he smiled.

'Oh, thanks,' she said, and her heart began beating once again.

The apartment occupied by the Deputy Head of Mission was modern and tastefully arranged. It was the first time Verona had met Sarah Cross, and the boss's wife was more attractive than Verona had expected. Sarah, a slim and well-dressed woman in her mid-forties, welcomed Verona warmly. Verona handed her the wine and her hostess offered to relieve her of the bag into which she had stuffed her boots before entering the flat. This was another heart-stopping moment, for, of course, the copied documents were in the bag, too, tucked inside one of her boots, but she realised it would look odd if she sat clutching a shopping bag all evening, so she handed over her coat and the bag and Sarah hung them both in the hall cupboard, before ushering her into the lounge and asking if she would like a glass of wine. Verona would normally have stuck to water, but, in view of the stressful operation she had just completed, she felt she needed something to steady her nerves.

The other PAs had already arrived, as had the Harrises. Simon Harris rose to his feet gallantly as she entered and introduced Verona to his wife, Ruth. Verona decided that Ruth

Harris must surely be the most attractive of the embassy wives, although, to be fair, she had not met the others. Taking a seat, Verona took in her surroundings. She supposed that the choice of pictures and other tasteful ornamentation in the apartment would be down to Mrs Cross rather than to her husband. The blonde Russian she had seen kissing Peter Cross was certainly no more attractive than his wife. Somehow, that made his infidelity seem all the more baffling and unforgivable to Verona.

'So, how are you settling in?' Sarah Cross asked her, as she handed her a glass of red wine.

'She's in the transit flat,' Tiffany Munro answered, before Verona had a chance to respond.

'Oh, that doesn't sound very nice,' Sarah sympathised. 'Are you okay over there?'

'Well, it's a bit poky, but I'm getting used to it. Once my heavy baggage arrives it'll begin to feel more homely, I'm sure.'

'Well, if you need to borrow anything, any books or some nice cushions or lamps to brighten the place, do let me know.'

'Thank you, Mrs Cross That's very kind of you.'

'Sarah, please,'

'Sarah. Thanks. Actually, a neighbour gave me some really pretty curtains and that's already made quite a difference.'

Sarah excused herself and headed off to the kitchen to see to the dinner. The conversation moved on and Verona was pleased that the spotlight was no longer on her. She could feel her nerves beginning to settle down. The wine helped. She had never seen the point of wine before but, just lately, she had been discovering its potential to reduce tension and to make her feel at ease with new situations. A sudden vision of Aleks swept across her thoughts and a warm glow began to suffuse all through her. It occurred to her that Aleks was a warm and delicious secret. She had never had a personal secret before and that thought made her smile to herself.

'A penny for them,' Ruth Harris interrupted her reverie.

'Pardon? Oh, I see. I don't think my thoughts are worth a penny,' she laughed.

'It's a shame you've arrived at such a dreadful time of the year,' Ruth said. 'The Moscow winter can be quite a shock, even for someone from Yorkshire, like me. Where do you live in the UK?'

'Me? Oh, Dulwich in south London. So, you're from the north, Mrs Harris?'

'Ruth, please. Yes, Leeds. Christmas in Leeds is lovely. We have a German Christmas market there, these days, and the big stores are all lit up. The atmosphere's great.'

'Yes, Dulwich Village has a lovely Christmas market, too, with a puppet theatre and lots of craft stalls. I shall miss all that,' Verona lamented.

'Aren't you going home for Christmas, then?' Ruth asked.

Verona shot a reproachful glance across the table at Peter Cross.

'Apparently not,' she said. 'How about you?'

Ruth Harris exchanged a glance with her husband.

'Yes. We'll be having our usual Yorkshire Christmas with the family,' Ruth confirmed.

'Verona,' Simon Harris joined in, 'did you know that, in Yorkshire, they eat Yorkshire pudding with *everything*?'

Verona guessed from Simon's accent that he hailed from the south of England somewhere.

'I understand it's traditional to have it with roast beef,' Verona said.

'Yes, but Ruth's family are weird. They serve up the Yorkshire pudding before the meal, as a starter.'

'That's because, in days gone by, there wouldn't have been a lot of beef, so the Yorkie pud would fill up hungry bellies before the beef was served,' Ruth explained.

'Ah, the roast beef of old England,' Verona sighed. 'I wonder what I'll be eating for Christmas lunch this year. Borsht and a bit of old goose, perhaps. Can one find goose in Moscow?'

'I've seen a few of them strutting about in the park,' Simon replied, unhelpfully.

Soon, they were summoned into the dining room and Sarah Cross directed everyone to their seats.

'I'm afraid we're overbalanced towards the distaff side this evening,' she said, 'so I can't arrange you boy-girl-boy-girl.'

Verona was pleased to find herself seated between Simon Harris and Caroline Howard, and opposite Ruth Harris and Sarah Cross. She was grateful not to have to spend the evening sitting next to Tiffany. Simon Harris was most solicitous and asked her again how she was settling in and what she had seen of Moscow thus far. She told him of the local café, recommended by Olga, and the sumptuous offering of cakes, and she said how much she had enjoyed wandering around the elegant boulevards of *Arbat*. She also told him she had attended an amusing production of an Agatha Christie play at the university.

Harris seemed genuinely interested in her well-being and he told her that, if she ever felt in any way isolated over at the transit apartment, she should come and see him immediately and he would try and pull a few strings to get her accommodated within the embassy complex. He apologised that the co-location of the staff from the Canadian Embassy, together with the arrival of the temporary staff from London, had put undue strain on their available accommodation. Verona assured him she felt a lot more settled now than she had when first she had arrived, and she told him of Olga's kindness, bringing her cake and curtains. Naturally, she didn't think it appropriate to mention Olga's son and the wonderful things he had done for her. However, Harris seemed genuinely pleased for her. Ruth Harris, too, seemed friendly, and she promised she and Simon would invite Verona to dinner soon, too.

As it turned out, Sarah Cross was a first rate cook and the meal she had prepared was delicious. Verona felt a lot more relaxed now, especially after her third glass of wine. Over dessert, Caroline raised the subject of the Wednesday film show, and the regular delays in the arrival of the diplomatic mailbags which included the films from London. The box set of the BBC television drama, however, had been well received, she said. Sarah Cross said she regretted she hadn't been able to get along to the cinema night but wanted to know what the drama had been about. Caroline and Tiffany, between them, gave a blow-by-blow account of the first couple of episodes of the revenge drama. Verona remembered the dark-haired, dark-eyed actress who had played the vengeful, cheated wife in the drama. She felt she had looked not unlike Aleks' friend, Anna.

The conversation continued without Verona's participation. She was once again lost in her thoughts. She continued to harbour some doubts about Aleks' relationship with that most attractive young woman. She could still picture them sitting, heads together, laughing and chatting so intimately in that café. It had looked at first as though they were flirting. But if, as Aleks suggested, they were plotting Anna's trip to Ukraine, then perhaps that explained the necessity for keeping their conversation so close and intimate. Somehow, though, she had regarded the café as her and Aleks' special place, so it had thrown her to see Aleks there with another woman. In some small way, it had spoilt the café for Verona. It had made it less special. Tiffany was now going into details about the BBC drama. Verona still couldn't help wondering whether, like the woman in the drama, she herself was being cheated on. It still bothered her.

'It does make you wonder what you would do if you found out your partner was having an affair,' Verona declared suddenly.

The moment she said it, she realised she hadn't actually meant to say out loud what she had been thinking. In fact, she had spoken those words a little louder than she had intended to.

Peter Cross suddenly coughed and dropped his dessert fork. In fact, he seemed to be having something of a coughing fit. Verona realised he was glaring at her. *'Oh, God,'* she thought, *'he thinks I'm referring to him!'*

'I mean, the main character,' Verona added, quickly. 'She's taking it very badly, isn't she? The wife, played by Suranne Jones, that is. I don't want to give the plot away but it's obvious she's going to do something particularly evil.'

'Oh yes,' Tiffany chipped in. 'It's going to get really nasty. You can feel the tension building up.'

'Well, I'm sorry I missed this,' Sarah Cross said. 'It sounds rather gripping.'

'Oh, it is,' Caroline assured her. 'We watched two episodes.

Can't wait for next Wednesday. I, for one, don't care if next week's film doesn't turn up at all. I want to watch more of *Dr Foster.*

Verona risked a glance down the table at her boss. He seemed to have recovered his composure now and he was no longer glaring at her. He could not have known that Verona had spoken as she did because she was worried about her own affair of the heart, and not his. How typical of Peter Cross, she thought. The arrogant sod thought the world revolved around him. He had little regard for Verona, or for his wife, or, so it seemed, for anyone else. If she had earlier harboured doubts about giving Aleks the names of the Ukrainian monitors who were in hiding, she now looked at her boss's smug features and she decided it was the right thing to do. Yes, it was absolutely the right thing to do.

CHAPTER EIGHTEEN

MONDAY AND TUESDAY CAME AND WENT WITH NO WORD FROM ALEKS. Verona prayed he had been successful on his mission. Not knowing was killing her, yet she could hardly call at the Petrenkos' apartment and ask Olga. She didn't even know whether Aleks' parents were aware of his network and their activities. Of course, Aleks wasn't going to be crossing over into Ukraine himself, he was just assisting the others on their journey. Yet, if they were caught, Aleks might be implicated.

At ten o'clock on the Wednesday morning, Verona received a call from the embassy Security Officer, asking her to call in at his office on the ground floor as soon as possible. He didn't say what it was about, and she didn't like to ask. When she got there, she saw it was the same SO who'd been on duty the previous Saturday evening when she had called in, ostensibly to collect a bottle of wine but intending to retrieve the photocopied list of SCG staff for Aleks.

'Ah, Miss Brooks,' he said as she entered. 'I've been meaning to catch up with you.'

She blanched slightly, wondering if she had been found

out. However, he opened a log book and thrust it in her direction.

'I'll need your signature, please.'

'What for?' she asked timidly.

'For this,' he lobbed an envelope onto the log book. 'It's your diplomatic pass. I told you it would take some time. The wheels of Russian bureaucracy turn very slowly, you know.'

She breathed a sigh of relief as she removed the newly-issued pass from the envelope, took the pen the SO proffered and signed the book.

'You won't need to wear it on a lanyard like you do your embassy pass, he informed her. Just keep it with you when you're out and about. It'll stop you getting arrested,' he grinned.

She very much doubted it would stop her from getting arrested, though it might not be the Russians who would be after her. She was having second thoughts now about having handed over the list to Aleks – or were they third thoughts? Supposing she had misjudged him?

Back upstairs, she found a handwritten note on her desk. She recognised Caroline's handwriting. The note invited her to attend a security briefing in the Political Section at ten thirty. She went into Peter Cross's office to let him know she'd be gone for an hour or so.

'Any chance you could rustle me up a cup of coffee before you head off?' Cross asked.

'Of course. When's the plaster coming off, by the way? she asked, pointing to his right wrist.

'Tomorrow, thank goodness. Then I've got to have some physio. They say I'll be able to write a little again, but they don't recommend pounding a keyboard just yet. Meantime,

I've another draft I need you to type. Ideally, if you could do it right after lunch, I could get it off soonest. And if you could drop me off at a meeting after work again, as well, I'd be very grateful.'

'Sure. Will that be in Arbat again, only I'll need to bring my guide book so I can find my way back?'

'Yes,' Cross said, avoiding her gaze. 'Same place as before. Thanks.'

Verona smiled to herself, knowingly.

The briefing was delivered by Simon Harris. His small audience comprised all the PAs, the admin assistants, receptionists and a couple of messengers. Thoughtfully, he provided a cake, which Caroline duly sliced and handed around with cups of decent coffee. Before Simon got started, Lauren announced that a new company had been awarded the contract to clean the embassy and would be starting next Monday.

'Well, thank heavens!' Grant, the messenger, declared. 'I can hang up my pinny at last.'

'And I can put away my marigolds,' Harris joked. 'But we'll all have to be vigilant again with strangers in the building. All the usual guidance and instructions apply. No documents, however insignificant, are to be left lying around. All drawers, cupboards and safes are to be locked and computers shut down, not just at the end of the day, but whenever you have to leave your room unattended.'

Everyone nodded. Some glanced at Tiffany. She reddened and chewed the inside of her lip. Simon kicked off with his briefing. He uttered the usual warnings about making injudicious comments in local bars or restaurants. Even something as innocuous as commenting that the Ambassador would be spending the weekend out of town, or just simply exchanging some trivial gossip about a fellow staff member in a place where one might be overheard, could be dangerous. All of this Verona had heard before, naturally. Keeping her own counsel had always been second nature to her, at least until she had met Aleks. But that was different, as she trusted Aleks.

Simon also related some fascinating anecdotes which Verona hadn't heard before; salutary tales of Foreign Office staff who, when overseas, had allowed themselves to be compromised by locals pretending to be their friends. Simon expressed his personal view that men were more likely than women to be conned by an unlikely admirer, leading them to a situation where they might be, as he put it, 'punching above their weight'. By that, he explained he meant that a middle-aged man with middle-aged spread should be suspicious when an attractive younger woman made a play for him. Of course, that didn't mean that women were completely immune to the attention of foreign spies, only that, in his opinion, they might apply a bit of sensible assessment to the situation using a different part of their anatomy than would their male colleagues. Grant thought this hugely amusing and he chortled.

Harris went on to explain that the Russians employed highly trained seducers to wheedle secrets out of diplomats and other important officials. The female seducers were known as 'swallows' and the male seducers as 'ravens'. 'Sexpionage' was what Harris called the process of espionage using sex as an inducement.

'If an offer, *any* kind of offer, seems too good to be true,'

Simon warned, 'it probably is. Here in Moscow, it almost certainly will be.'

Verona hoped Simon's warning wasn't being aimed at her, though she couldn't imagine it was. She didn't see how he would even know about her and Aleks. Of course, everyone had seen Aleks with her in the bar after the embassy's performance of 'Cats', but she had made a point of ensuring Olga stood between them. She also felt sure that Tiffany would have taken her joke about Aleks being her lover as just that – a joke. Simon's general words of wisdom were well-meant and not pointed at any individual, she had no doubt. She did wonder, however, whether Peter Cross had ever been to one of Simon's briefings.

Harris pointed out something new, something Verona hadn't previously considered.

'The Russian state has always been suspicious of its own people who forge friendships with westerners. That means that any Russian befriending one of us will be taking a risk. Whilst, on one level, Russians are very hospitable people by nature, you have to ask yourself why any individual would risk attracting the attention of internal security in order to be your friend.'

That gave Verona cause to consider Aleks' motives yet again. But then, he was Ukrainian, wasn't he? He would be under suspicion anyway, and he seemed genuinely concerned about the fate of the monitors in Russian occupied Ukraine. And his parents were open and naturally hospitable people, too. The briefing ended with the usual exhortation: 'when in doubt, give the benefit of the doubt to your country'.

If Tiffany had remembered Verona's comment about Aleks, she certainly didn't mention it over lunch. Clearly, she was still preoccupied with the possible outcome of the Ambassador's review regarding culpability relating to the theft of the defence documents, and so this was all she could talk about. Despite Tiffany's indisputably catty nature, Verona still felt a degree of sympathy for her. The young woman was clearly fearful of the cloud which was hovering over her head. It was noticeable that she ate very little that lunchtime.

That afternoon, Verona was seated at the DHM's desk once more as he sat alongside her and dictated a draft report for London. This time, it was not connected with the SCG but with the security incident in their embassy. The gist of the report was that procedures within the Moscow mission had been tightened up and that there would be greater supervision of the new cleaning contractors who had, in any case, been subjected to as rigorous a security check as was possible, this being Moscow. There was little doubt that at least one member of the new cleaning staff would be under instructions to take advantage of their embassy access to glean whatever information they could to pass on to the Russian authorities. However, assurances were given that such an individual would not find themselves alone and in a position to access anything sensitive.

The report further stated that an internal enquiry had confirmed that a junior member of the Defence Staff – and that staff member alone – bore responsibility for the stolen documents being accessible to the cleaner. Disciplinary action of that staff member was already in hand, the report went on, although it didn't suggest what such action would entail. Verona was disappointed for Tiffany. She wondered how much longer they would leave Tiffany in the dark about this before they told her what her fate was to be.

Verona glanced at Cross. He didn't seem to think it at all injudicious or indiscreet to have dictated this to Verona, knowing that she could pass it on to her fellow PA, not that she would. Verona felt as she imagined one of those Victorian servants must have felt whose employers considered them so inconsequential that they had no qualms about discussing intimate matters in front of them. However, given that Cross would have her delivering him into the arms of his mistress again that evening after work, it was clear that discretion was not one of his virtues.

At half-past four that afternoon, earlier than usual, Verona heard Cross locking his office drawers and putting on his coat. Obviously, he was ready to be chauffeured to his regular assignation with the blonde in the elegant apartment. She shut down her own computer and locked her desk drawers. By the time she had put on her own coat, Cross was hovering by her desk, his briefcase in hand, and looking at his wristwatch. How she hated it when he did that! They headed downstairs and made for the car pool. Having had so little use, once again the car took a few attempts to start and, once again, irritatingly, Cross kept checking his wristwatch, as if that would somehow coax the engine into co-operating. Eventually, the engine did, with spluttering reluctance, fire into life.

Verona pulled up outside the apartment block which housed her boss's mistress. Since it was not yet dark, there were no lights on in the apartment. Verona watched Cross head in and make for the stairs, but no light came on in the apartment and no curtains were drawn. It was an earlier rendezvous than last time, however. She rolled down her window to allow the cloying scent of Cross's aftershave to dissipate, and she waited a while with her engine switched off, just in case his paramour should be out and he might need a lift back to the embassy again. But Cross didn't reappear. Wearily, she drove back to the embassy and parked her vehicle back in the car pool.

She passed a large, wooden packing crate which she had noticed each day tucked in beside the parked cars. It bore the marking 'Bartram – UK' on the side, by which she guessed this was her predecessor's heavy baggage. The fact that it had not yet been despatched back to England suggested the land routes were still problematic, given the security situation on the Russian border and beyond. That told Verona that her own heavy baggage would not be arriving any time soon. That thought depressed her. As she walked the few blocks home to *Nevsky Prospekt*. She wondered what sort of Russian hospitality Cross was enjoying in that elegant apartment block with his blonde Russian. Wondering also when she would see her own lover next, she trudged up the stairs and let herself into the quiet, lonely little apartment.

CHAPTER NINETEEN

Forty-year-old Denys Danyluk let himself into the small, one-bedroomed local authority flat in east London's Stepney Green. He didn't really like his drab fourth-floor flat in the nineteen-fifties' block, and nor did he like the neighbourhood very much, but he told himself that he was lucky to have escaped Ukraine. He assured himself he wouldn't be living here too long, and so the accommodation would do for now. It was just until he could establish himself. It was just four days until Christmas and he wasn't looking forward to spending the festive season alone, but at least he was safe.

He made himself a cup of strong tea, sat down wearily on the sofa and opened up the laptop on the coffee table. He pulled up the draft of the letter to the local constituency MP and read over what he had written. He assumed the MP would have some knowledge already of the Security Co-operation Group and might feel as aggrieved as Danyluk did that he and so many of his fellow Ukrainian monitoring group members had been dismissed and left to fend for themselves. Having addressed the recent SCG meeting in London with what he felt was genuine and emotional supplication, he wasn't sure what else he could do, but seeking the intervention of the local MP couldn't hurt.

He glanced at the array of international business cards he had collected at the meeting and he picked up the one the American had given him. He had been pleased to find Walter Edelman sympathetic. At least Edelman had heard him out and had spoken up for him, unlike the British representative. Edelman had also agreed to inform Washington of the many former SCG employees trapped in Russian-occupied territory to see if the Americans could do anything to get them out, or at least to get funds to them. Danyluk had no hesitation in giving Edelman a list of who the monitors were and of their last known whereabouts. Those brave souls were, after all, providing useful intelligence on what the Russians were doing in the occupied zones, and now they needed help.

He recalled how visibly shocked Edelman had been to read the reports from Bucha of the torture and executions of citizens. The photos Danyluk had acquired of the aftermath, of the bodies buried in shallow graves with their hands still tied behind their backs, and of the blood-spattered schoolrooms used as places of torture, had persuaded Edelman to take up his cause. Edelman had promised to forward the original photos and hand written witness statements to the War Crimes Commission. Danyluk had e-mailed Edelman a couple of times since the meeting, and was disappointed not to have had any reply as yet. Nor was he getting any news out of Ukraine regarding his former colleagues. He imagined they were in hiding. He hoped they were safe and weren't starving.

Having finished the draft e-mail, he read it several times over before hitting 'send'. Then, draining his tea, he took his cup back into the kitchen and tipped the tea bag into the plastic pail he used for kitchen waste. The pail was overfull. He decided he ought to empty it before he began to prepare food for his evening meal, so he took it outside onto the communal walkway, intending to take it down to the communal bins on the ground floor. Mindful of his own personal security, he first glanced over the balustrade. Small groups of school children were making their way home now and the usual mob of unruly teenagers was beginning to congregate on the playground swings on the green four floors below.

As he made his way towards the steps, two men appeared on the walkway, coming in his direction. He didn't recognise them as residents on his landing, but he stood to one side to let them pass. As they drew level with him, however, they did not pass but suddenly grabbed hold of him and propelled him towards the balustrade. Before he could react, they had launched him out over the balcony and he was hurtling towards the ground, his arms and legs flailing in a hopeless attempt to try and slow his descent. He landed heavily on the concrete just in front of the playground. The plastic pail landed a second after him and disgorged its contents of tea bags, vegetable peelings and other garbage all over him. He never heard the children's horrified screams.

Later that evening, and five hundred miles away, it was pitch dark when Harry and Jo ushered the Russian defectors into the black SUV once more and they headed out of Holywood and back towards Belfast.

'Where are we going? Ignatiev asked.

'To the place you'll be staying longer term. Somewhere

even more comfortable than the barracks,' Harry told them. 'It's a rural farm house, and it's just a couple of hours' drive away.'

Crossing the city of Belfast again, they next headed out along the A6. Unable to see much of the scenery, the Russians sat back in their seats and dozed. Cherny opened his eyes at one point and glimpsed an illuminated sign indicating they were heading for someplace he thought he had heard of. The sign said 'Derry/Londonderry'. Satisfied, he closed his eyes again. Neither Russian awoke again until the vehicle pulled up outside the stone farmhouse. Jo remained in the vehicle as Harry invited the Russians to step out and check out their new accommodation.

'So, now where are we?' Ignatiev asked wearily.

'We're in a village just outside the pleasant town of Lifford,' Harry advised him. 'And these gentlemen are your new hosts. They'll take care of you.'

If Ignatiev and Cherny had expected a female housekeeper and a butler to take care of them, they were to be disappointed. If they thought they were still in the UK, they were to be even more disappointed, though they wouldn't discover this just yet. Harry supposed the beautiful County Donegal countryside the Russians would see around them in the morning wouldn't look a great deal different from the scenery in County Down. The Russians would have no idea they were now in the Irish Republic, nor what that might mean for their safety. They were to stay here in this remote Irish farmhouse until such time as a decision was taken as to what would be done with them. Harry consigned his charges to their new hosts, two thick-set, unsmiling Irishmen, then he rejoined Jo in the vehicle. As the two Russians watched their MI5 escorts depart, Harry wound down the window of their vehicle and called out: 'Have a good Christmas.'

'It isn't their Christmas,' Jo informed him. 'The Russians don't celebrate Christmas till the end of the first week in January.'

'Don't they?' Harry asked. 'Well, maybe they'll get to celebrate two Christmases. Of course, that depends on whether or not we decide to hand them over to the Yanks and how soon. I don't think the US plan for them would include happy holidays.'

Harry put his foot down and he and Jo took off, heading back towards Belfast to spend the night back at the barracks. Tomorrow, they would catch a flight back to London to be home in good time to celebrate Christmas themselves.

CHAPTER TWENTY

In Moscow's Nevsky Prospekt the following day, contrary to her earlier expectations, Verona was looking forward to Christmas. She was making mince pies. She had picked up a jar of imported mincemeat at the embassy's commissary and had made her own shortcrust pastry. She was rolling this out whilst the oven heated up. Ruth Harris had thoughtfully lent her a bun tin, having no need of it herself, since she and Simon were spending their Christmas with family in Yorkshire. Verona didn't have a fluted edge pastry cutter but she made do with a tea cup and an egg cup to cut out the pastry circles.

As she rolled and cut out the pastry, she remembered the many times in different overseas locations where she had managed to create Christmas using local implements and local foods. Given more time and access to her own kitchen equipment, she would have made her own mincemeat mixture weeks earlier. She would also have baked and iced a richly fruited Christmas cake, but the *batterie de cuisine* included in the embassy's float was woefully inadequate, consisting mainly of assorted crockery, glassware, cutlery, a rotary whisk and a corkscrew. There was a chipped glass gravy boat, but Verona hadn't managed to find anything to roast which might provide the basis for gravy. In any case, there didn't seem much point in trying to produce anything remotely resembling Christmas dinner when she would be the only one there to eat it. At least, she consoled herself, she could have a mince pie with a glass of wine this Christmas Eve.

Her thoughts were interrupted by a knock at the door. She half-hoped it might be Olga, inviting her to come downstairs for some Ukrainian hospitality. Smacking the flour from her hands, she went to answer the door. To her delight, however, Aleks was standing there.

'I'm back,' he announced, and he held up a bottle of red wine. 'May I come in?'

'Oh, Aleks, of course. Come in. How did it go? Did you find them? Tell me all about it.'

Aleks placed the bottle down on the coffee table and immediately took her in his arms and kissed her. Verona's disappointment at the prospect of a solitary Christmas now turned to excitement. This was better than Christmas. She drew him to the sofa and they sat down so Aleks could recount details of his trip.

'Anna managed to get to Kherson. She went to Marina's apartment block. It's half destroyed, of course, and Marina was no longer there, but the neighbours said she's okay. She had left and gone south when the Russians came looking for her, but at least she was still alive when they saw her last. Anna had to come back without her, but the good news is that the city of Kherson is now fully in the control of the Ukrainians again. The Russians have retreated. That's something to celebrate.'

'Oh, that is good news. But let me quickly finish making my mince pies and I'll put them in the oven. We can have hot mince pies with your wine.'

'May I watch how you do it? I've never had mince pies.'

Aleks accompanied her into the kitchen, found the corkscrew in the kitchen drawer and opened the wine. He left it to breathe whist he watched Verona filling her pies. She offered him a teaspoon of the mincemeat to taste.

'Oh, it's not meat at all,' he declared. 'It's fruit. And it's very good.'

'I expect Olga and Vitaly are delighted you are home safe and sound?' she asked.

'Yes, they are. And they want you to join us for Christmas lunch tomorrow. Will you come down at around twelve?'

'Oh, but I thought Christmas was celebrated in January here?'

'It is – for the Russians. Traditionally, though, it was celebrated in December in Ukraine. Then, when Ukraine was made part of the Soviet Union, the Russian Orthodox Church said all the people of the Union must celebrate in January. Following Putin's invasion of Crimea, however, Volodymyr Zelenski has decreed all Ukrainians should celebrate Christmas on the twenty-fifth of December again, just as they do in the west. So, for the past seven years, that is what my family does. We have a traditional Ukrainian Christmas, not a Russian one.'

'Oh, how wonderful. Yes, I should be delighted to come. Thank you. In my family, we always have the first mince pies on Christmas Eve. These will be ready in around fifteen minutes.'

Aleks poured out two glasses of wine and they drank to the partial success of the operation. Verona's face glowed, partly due to the effects of the wine but also to her happiness and relief at Aleks' return. She would enjoy her little festive fare so much more for having Aleks there to share it with her. She now felt a special kind of excitement, the same kind of excitement she had always experienced as a child on Christmas Eve. She realised she hadn't felt like this on any Christmas Eve since her parents had passed away. It was a mixture of happiness, excitement and anticipation. She now had a Ukrainian Christmas dinner to look forward to the following day. And it would be especially wonderful, she thought, if Aleks decided to spend tonight with her, that was, if the lovely Anna really wasn't his lover. She wished he would stay. She wished it with all her heart. Happily, Verona's only Christmas wish was to come true.

The following morning, Aleks left her flat early in order to help his mother prepare food. He explained that there were to be twelve different dishes on the table and that each dish had a religious or superstitious significance. Verona passed her Christmas morning getting herself bathed and dressed, then she called Romola to wish her 'Happy Christmas', to thank her for her Christmas present, and to reassure her sister that she would not be alone this Christmas Day but was to be the guest of her neighbours at their Ukrainian feast. At midday, she took a bottle of wine and a tray of mince pies downstairs to the Petrenko's apartment where she was warmly welcomed in.

Verona offered to help Olga in the kitchen, but Olga would have none of it, insisting she was their guest and should make herself comfortable. There were to have been twelve different dishes, just as Aleks had said, but on seeing Verona's mince pies, Olga said she would keep one back, since she believed having thirteen dishes on the table would be unlucky. The Petrenkos' feast included the Ukrainian version of *borscht* – a beetroot soup with prunes and mushrooms – and fried carp in soured cream sauce with rice-stuffed cabbage rolls, and a whole variety of sweet dishes, including dried fruit compote, jam-filled *pampushky* donuts, pancakes and bowls of *kutia* – boiled wheat with nuts, seeds, dried fruit, and honey. There were also little berry-stuffed dumplings, called *varenyky*, and Verona was warned that one of these would contain a coin, so she must bite into hers carefully. Either by happy accident or by Olga's design, it was the one Verona was given which turned out to be the one with the coin, which Olga assured her meant she would enjoy wealth for at least the coming year.

As Vitaly topped up Verona's wine glass, which he did every time she emptied it, she reflected that it had been some years since she had experienced a warm family Christmas. She and her sister usually had a fairly scaled-down Christmas celebration. At the Petrenkos' table, there was not a turkey leg in sight, and many of the dishes and flavours were new to her, but the lunch was excellent, and the company was delightful. Verona's mince pies seemed to be well received by her hosts, who insisted on serenading her with some traditional songs, not one word of which she could understand. By ten-thirty that Christmas night, and feeling quite squiffy, Verona made her way up the stairs, escorted by Aleks. She invited him to come in, but he declined, explaining that, as they were Catholics, it was his family's custom to attend midnight mass. Verona said she understood.

As she climbed into her bed, she was both happy and relieved. Any reservations she had previously about Aleks being trustworthy, and any doubts that she had done the right thing in giving him such critical information, were now well and truly dispelled. She did, indeed, trust him. She trusted him and she loved him. As ridiculous as that might seem to outsiders, she loved this young man and, moreover, she felt he loved her, too.

CHAPTER TWENTY-ONE

VERONA RETURNED TO WORK THE DAY AFTER NEW YEAR'S DAY, though her boss had taken both Christmas week and the first week in January as leave and he was still in the UK. Verona quite enjoyed his absence that week. She preferred her own company anyway, and without Cross around, she could take the minimum lunch break and then finish work early in order to get home and prepare supper for herself and Aleks. Naturally, she would never work fewer hours than she should. That would be dishonest. It was enough that she had far less work than if Cross had been there. The office was also calmer for his absence, and she did not have to put up with him standing over her, dictating his reports and e-mails for her to type. The weather was still bitterly cold but at least she didn't have to struggle to get the car started in order to drive Cross to his assignations at his mistress's apartment.

Whenever she bumped into Simon Harris or his PA Caroline, they would express their apologies that there was still no prospect of an apartment in the compound becoming available for her occupation. She assured them that, actually, she had got quite used to her pokey little transit flat and was fine there for the time being. She rather hoped no apartment would become free, as she knew she wouldn't be able to entertain Aleks in a flat within the embassy complex. Even if she were able to sign him in through security, which in any case was most unlikely, how people would talk if he didn't sign out again until the following morning. Life within the embassy's residential enclave might be more comfortable, but there her every move would be seen. Dismal though it was, Nevsky Prospekt afforded her a considerable amount of independence and privacy.

Peter Cross returned to work on the Monday of the following week and found Verona in good spirits, not least because the new cleaning company, in hoping to make a good impression, were doing a very thorough job. The dirty, tea-stained cups which Verona had been tackling for the past few weeks were all squeaky clean each morning when she arrived, and the stinky food waste bin no longer stank, and this process did not involve her but was entirely due to the cleaners' efforts. She felt her status as a senior PA had been restored.

'Did you have a good Christmas, Peter?' she asked.

'Oh, so-so,' he told her. 'Sarah's mother was with us. The old dear's stone deaf, so conversation was difficult and we had to listen to the King's speech at two hundred decibels. Then she sank a pint of egg nogg and snored all the way through 'Die Hard'.'

'How's the wrist?' she asked, noting that he wasn't the slightest bit interested in whether or not she had enjoyed her Christmas.

'Less painful, but still pretty stiff. I've got some scribbled notes from the December SCG meeting. I'd be grateful if you'd type them up for me. No hurry.'

Cross headed upstairs for the usual Monday morning meeting between the section heads and the Ambassador, so Verona made herself a coffee, retrieved the SCG file and began to transcribe his notes. She was surprised to read that the chair of the meeting had asked for a minute's silence out of respect for one of the US delegates to the committee who had, unfortunately passed away following the previous meeting in London last November. Verona read how Walt Edelman had suffered a tragic accident, a fall which proved fatal, just hours after that meeting, whilst alighting from a tube train at Hammersmith Broadway station. Verona told herself it wasn't just Peter Cross who was prone to falling over.

As she ploughed through the DHM's handwritten notes and processed them into print, she found herself typing up an account of the fate of more of the special monitors in Ukraine. It had been reported to the committee that many more of the five hundred or so monitors trapped in the Russian-occupied areas of Ukraine had been hunted down and were believed to have been tortured and killed. There had been rumours of unmarked mass graves and local registrars being forbidden from issuing death certificates so that the mass killings would go unrecorded. At this, Verona stopped typing and she began reading the notes. It was further reported that the monitors' names and their whereabouts were believed to have been disclosed to the Russians by an unknown source. Enquiries were still ongoing into how their identities and last known places of residence had been leaked to the Russians.

Verona's blood suddenly ran cold. She had given the list of monitors and their last known locations to Aleks. But that had been so he could arrange for others in his network to try to rescue them. Could someone in that network have betrayed them? Surely, Aleks would not have done so? He was Ukrainian himself, and so were his parents. They were devout Catholics, too, and she trusted them. She trusted Aleks completely. In any case, she remembered that Aleks had already known the name of one of those monitors – Marina somebody. Marina was Anna's cousin. Aleks would surely not betray Anna's cousin. He wouldn't have let Anna go there to rescue Marina if he intended betraying Marina to the Russians. At least, he wouldn't, if ... if what he had said was true. Of course, she only had Aleks' word for it that the network even existed and that he was part of it.

Verona sat, motionless, for quite a while, deep in thought. Swallowing hard, she struggled to go over everything Aleks had said to her about the network and their missions. She had believed everything he had told her because she had trusted him. She had trusted him, because she loved him, and because she believed that he loved her too, although he had not said as much. She trusted her instincts about him, though. Of course she did. Otherwise, she would never have parted with such sensitive information. But ... what if she'd been wrong? What if her feelings for him had blinded her and had led her to accept everything he said as the truth, when perhaps it wasn't? Had she been wrong to trust Aleks? Had she simply been naïve and gullible?

Simon Harris's warning in his security briefing came back to her. He had warned about those situations where a diplomat might be seduced by someone who was younger and more attractive than they. He had mentioned situations where a member of the embassy staff, drawn into such a relationship, might be described as 'punching above their weight', which ought to make them suspicious. Was she punching above her weight? Was she too trusting? Had Aleks really found her attractive, or had this been a triumph of hope over expectation on her part? Could a young and handsome man like Aleks really be in love with a middle-aged woman like herself? Never having been in love before, she had no way of judging her own attractiveness to men. She knew she fell short in terms of looks compared to Anna. Once again, she pictured Aleks and Anna, seated in that café, their heads together in conspiracy, or was it intimacy?

So many questions and so many doubts began once more to circle in her head. There were small things. The evening Alex had prepared a meal for them both and had brought it up on a tray to her flat, what had he told his parents? Had he told them he was taking the food to his middle-aged neighbour? Wouldn't Olga and Vitaly have thought that odd? Did they even know that, on the nights he didn't return to their flat, he was sleeping upstairs with Verona? Did they approve? Surely, if they did know but didn't approve, they wouldn't have invited her to spend Christmas Day with them? Could they possibly not know? Were they turning a blind eye to their son's relationship with an older woman? Maybe they believed Aleks was simply benefiting from English conversation lessons with Verona? Could they really be that naïve?

These were doubts she had entertained previously but had dismissed. Had she been wrong to do so? She now began to feel rather stupid. Had she been deceived? Was she just a sad, middle-aged woman who had fallen for the charms of a ... what had Simon called them during his briefing? A *voron* – a raven, a seducer employed by the Russian state to extract secrets from sad, lonely women employees like herself? Had her actions contributed to the torture and deaths of those poor Ukrainian monitors? Surely not, and yet, how likely was it that someone else had also disclosed that list? Was there another traitor besides herself who had access to that list? Was that possible? She suddenly felt sick.

She wondered what she ought to do. Should she go and see Simon Harris and confess what she had done? But, if she did, she would certainly lose her job – her career. She would find herself back in Dulwich and maybe back in an insurance office again. In fact, she wouldn't be surprised if she were arrested. She had, after all, signed the Official Secrets Act, and now she had revealed a major official secret. What she had done could be seen as an act of treachery. She could go to prison. She really felt sick now. She leapt up from her desk and headed out into the corridor. Once in the ladies' room, which thankfully was empty, she dived into a cubicle, sank to her knees and vomited into the toilet bowl. She knelt there for some time, clutching the toilet seat and trying to think. She tried to look dispassionately at her relationship with Aleks, to try to see it as others might. There was no escaping the fact that, however noble her intentions had been, she had committed an act of treason.

Eventually, she arose and left the cubicle. Splashing cold water on her face, she headed back to her office, aware that she was shaking, but determined not to confess anything until she might be found out. Cross was standing by her desk as she entered. He was perusing the notes he had given her.

'Oh dear, Verona,' he tutted. 'You've been a very naughty girl.'

'What?' she faltered.

'You've committed a serious security breach, haven't you?'

'What do you mean?'

'You forgot to lock your computer and lock away the file when you left your desk. Naughty, naughty,' he waggled a finger at her.

'Oh, sorry. Had to go the loo in a bit of a hurry. Got a bit of a tummy upset.'

'Well, get me a coffee and we'll say no more about it.'

Relieved, she went to the tea station, selected a couple of the sparkling clean mugs and made them both a coffee.

That evening, she walked home via the deli where she picked up a couple of bottles of wine. Entering the apartment building as silently as she could, she crept up the stairs to her flat. Inside, she hung up her coat, did the rounds of the lamps and checked the telephone receiver to ensure she had not been bugged then she fetched a wine glass from the kitchen and sat in semi darkness, determined to drink the wine alone.

At around eight that evening, there came a knock at her door. She heard Aleks whispering her name and asking to come in, but she sat, silent, pretending she was not there. She had already decided she wouldn't let him in. She had to think. She now regretted having trusted him, and she was fearful of the possible consequences. She knew that, if she did let him in, once she was in his arms and he was reassuring her that she could trust him, she would again lose all her inhibitions and would give in to him. She already felt she had lost all reason in trusting him and stealing secrets for him. She could not let it happen again. She didn't know how long she could avoid him, but she must try. She told herself she had indeed been stupid and naïve, but she hadn't yet been caught out. There was a chance she might get away with it, so long as she avoided

Aleks and didn't allow herself to be seduced into giving anything else away.

The following week, she popped upstairs to see Simon Cross. Caroline confirmed he was in his office. He looked up as she knocked and entered and he smiled at her.

'Verona, how are you? And how was your Christmas?' he asked.

'Oh, very quiet,' she replied. 'How was yours?'

He patted his stomach.

'Wonderful. Ate too much. Drank too much. The in-laws gave us a real Yorkshire welcome. What can I do for you?'

'You said you might be able to pull a few strings in getting me the next available apartment in the compound.'

'Yes, I did, and I will. But when last we spoke, you said you were getting used to the transit flat and you didn't find it so bad.'

'Yes, well, that was before I spent Christmas there, all on my own, with not a soul for company. I suppose it's starting to get to me now. It's dismal and claustrophobic. I'm not sure I can stand it much longer.'

'I can understand why you feel that way. You've done well to put up with the transit flat for this long. Let me have a word with the accommodation section. I see no reason why we couldn't arrange a swap with some of our temporary attachees from London. They'll argue that they need to be based within the complex for security reasons, but I'll see if I can persuade them to move out. If not, though, I'll certainly do my best to ensure you're at the top of the list for the next apartment that's vacated. I'll check with accommodation to see who's the next to leave post. Then at least I can give you a likely timescale for your move.'

'Thank you, Simon. I appreciate your help.'

'Not at all. You've served your country well all these years. It's time your country served you better. Leave it with me.'

'Thanks,' Verona said, and she turned to leave.

'Catch you later,' Simon said.

She knew that was just his usual turn of phrase but, today, it sounded somehow ... ominous.

CHAPTER TWENTY-TWO

Verona managed to avoid bumping into Aleks for the next ten days, whilst she prayed the offer of an embassy apartment might materialise. Peter Cross never once enquired whether she was still happy to be in the transit flat. She guessed it just wasn't in his nature to think of other peoples' welfare. The longer she knew him, the more she realised just how self-centred he was. Once again, she found herself regretting she had not asked to be sent home long before now. If she had done so, she could have been at home for Christmas, and she would not have betrayed any secrets. But it was probably too late now to ask, now that she was almost three months into her posting.

One morning, as Cross arrived for work, she sensed that he was a little uneasy, nervous even. He returned her greeting with a grunt and disappeared into his office. She imagined he might still be in some pain or discomfort from his wrist and this might be the cause of his ill humour. At one stage, he emerged from his office with a large envelope in his hand and, passing her desk, walked out into the corridor with it, but then he did an about turn and came back in again, only to disappear back into his office still clutching the envelope. He seemed to be pacing about aimlessly. That struck her as a little odd.

Although he still needed her to word process his work for him, he no longer dictated his reports and e-mails to her but had taken to handwriting drafts and leaving them in her in-tray. She preferred that to having him gazing over her shoulder as she typed. His distinctive large handwriting, in bold, black ink, would appear also on the front of files, as he marked them up either for her to despatch to London or to file away locally. She thought the boldness of his handwriting reflected his arrogance and self-importance. At midday, just as Verona was about to log off her computer, lock her drawer and head to the canteen for lunch, Cross emerged from his office once again. He placed on her desk the large envelope which he had been carrying earlier.

'I need you to deliver these papers for me,' he said.

'To whom?' Verona asked, assuming the recipient would be someone within the embassy.

'To an American, the US official, you know, where I go for meetings, in *Nikitskaya Ulitsa*.'

'Oh, can't one of the messengers take it for you? Grant is around somewhere.'

'I want *you* to take it, Verona,' the DHM snapped. 'It's quite important.'

'Well, all right. But it's lunchtime now. Is it okay if I take it after lunch?'

'Is it?' Cross glanced at his watch, clearly distracted and not keeping track of time. 'Okay. I mean, yes, please. If you would.'

He disappeared back into his office again. Verona picked up

the envelope and checked it over. It was addressed to 'Natalie Schoen'. The apartment number and street name, which were already familiar to her, were also written on the envelope. A US official, indeed! She realised it was meant for his lover. Verona considered it a bit of a cheek him asking her to deliver notes to his girlfriend, especially as she had to use her own petrol to do so. He had never once offered to reimburse her for the occasions on which she had driven him to his trysts with this Natalie Schoen. She supposed that, having previously asked her to act as office cleaner, he had no compunction about roping her in as an illicit go-between in his sordid little affair. However, she greatly resented being taken for granted. Maybe she ought to have had the courage to say something about it before now. She didn't really know why she hadn't. Perhaps it was because asking for petrol money might sound like begging. It might make her seem mercenary. It did seem wrong, though, that he should involve her in his adulterous assignations.

It occurred to her that maybe she should embarrass him by submitting an expenses claim for her mileage between the embassy and the apartment block on *Nikitskaya Ulitsa*. The embassy accountant would probably query why she made such regular trips there – often twice a week – and whether these were in fact official trips, and why, if it really were an official journey, she hadn't used an embassy driver and vehicle. Cross would be obliged to countersign the claims and then he would have to explain to the accountant why he had authorised them. Somebody in the embassy might then start asking questions about the *Nikitskaya Ulitsa* address and the purpose of his visits there. She dismissed this mischievous idea, however, since she had sinned herself and felt she wasn't in a position to cast stones. She also felt a sense of loyalty to the DHM, even though he didn't seem to care a jot about her welfare.

Of course, the envelope Cross had produced seemed rather large and bulky for a lover's *billet doux*. She wasn't sure why, but she suddenly felt uneasy about delivering it. She wondered why Cross couldn't take it himself. Obviously, he still wasn't comfortable driving, but why not ask her to drive him so he could present it in person, especially if it was that important? And why would he not trust the messenger to deliver it? After all, the messengers were entrusted with opening the diplomatic mail bags and distributing the mail around the embassy. She guessed he probably didn't want the messengers to see the name of the recipient, and yet he had no qualms about Verona knowing who the recipient was. Maybe he realised that, unlike Tiffany Munro, Verona was no gossip. Or perhaps it was because he saw her as some kind of servant, someone whose wellbeing and feelings counted for little.

She wasn't terribly hungry so she decided to forgo a cafeteria lunch and just make herself a coffee. Taking a break from her work, she sat at her desk and began browsing a week-old copy of *The Times*. Cross now closed his office door. She could hear him speaking on the telephone but could not hear what he was saying. As soon as she had finished her coffee, she glanced at the clock. It was twelve-thirty. She decided she might as well go and collect her car from the garage and deliver the envelope now. Then she could legitimately ask to go home a little early that evening. She needed to call at the little supermarket after work and pick up some food for the rest of the week. She could then get into her apartment building early, too, before Aleks came home from university. She had managed to avoid bumping into him or answering her door to him thus far. He had stopped knocking at her door, so perhaps he had got the message, that she no longer wished to see him. She realised she couldn't trust her own resolve to tell him in person.

Less than fifteen minutes later, she pulled up opposite the apartment block on *Nikitskaya Ulitsa*. She had hardly been aware of the short drive, so engrossed was she in her thoughts, and she had almost been on auto-pilot. She had certainly driven here often enough to drop off Peter Cross that she mused the car probably knew the way. The street was fairly busy with traffic and pedestrians that lunchtime, but she managed to park up without difficulty, though she had to wait a few minutes to cross the road. Heading into the lobby, she saw there was a reception desk but it was unmanned. If there were a concierge of any kind, they must be away having lunch somewhere. She saw again the block of wooden mail boxes and found the one with Natalie Schoen's name on it. Having no desire to meet or speak to her boss's lover in person, she pushed the envelope into the relevant mailbox. Being fairly large and stiff, however, it wouldn't go all the way in. She gave it a good push but a corner of the envelope remained sticking out. At least Ms Schoen would spot the fact that she had mail when she came downstairs, Verona thought.

As she made to leave, she passed another tall, attractive blonde woman who was entering the building. Verona supposed this particular blonde must be married to one of the Stepanov or Ivanov residents whose names appeared on the other mail boxes, since Schoen's was the only woman's name shown. She mused that the mail boxes were, in fact, mostly 'male' boxes, since only one was assigned to a female resident.

She hurried back across the road to her car, started up the engine and headed back to the embassy. As she entered the DHM's office suite, Cross emerged from his office and glanced at her in-tray where he had earlier left the envelope.

'It's okay,' she assured him. 'I just delivered it.'

'Great. Thanks,' he said, and he disappeared back into his office, closing the door behind him.

Verona unlocked her desk drawers again and spent the next hour transcribing Cross's drafts. She was contemplating making herself a cup of instant coffee when her phone rang. It was Caroline Howard calling from the political section upstairs.

'Verona, would you mind popping upstairs for a few minutes? Simon would like a word.'

'Sure,' Verona said, hoping he might have word of an apartment coming free. With any luck, she thought, he might even offer her a decent cup of coffee from the bean-to-cup machine in his office. She caught the aroma of freshly brewed coffee as she climbed the stairs. It was calming and reassuring. Caroline smiled as Verona arrived and indicated she should go straight into Harris's inner office. Harris was seated at his desk but he wasn't alone. Standing alongside him was a thirty-something, fair-haired man whom Verona did not recognise, and a tall blonde woman stood over by the window, gazing at the view out over the river. Both of Harris's visitors were drinking coffee. Harris smiled and beckoned Verona to take a seat. He did not offer her coffee and she noticed that the two visitors remained standing.

'Verona,' Harris began, amicably enough, 'where did you go this lunchtime?'

'I drove over to *Nikitskaya Ulitsa* to deliver a letter. Why? Is there a problem?'

'Was it this letter?' he asked, tapping a large opened envelope on his desk.

Verona glanced down and saw the familiar name and address on the envelope. Harris withdrew from the envelope a manilla folder. She saw it had a note attached to the front.

'Yes,' she said. 'That looks like it. But how ...?'

Baffled, Verona glanced at the strangers in the room and she realised the young woman was the same one who had entered the apartment building just as she herself was leaving. This made no sense. Clearly, the young woman must have followed her there and retrieved the bulky envelope from the mailbox, but why? The young woman stepped forward, put down her coffee cup, removed the note from the front of the file and raised it for Verona to see.

'You've been having an affair,' the woman accused, 'with a Russian.'

Verona swallowed hard. Dear God! They must have found out about Aleks. But how? Her heart began racing. She wondered if they were here to arrest her. She felt the urge to blurt out her guilt and get it over with, but a sense of self-preservation immediately kicked in and she decided to plead ignorance and to say as little as possible.

'What?' she spluttered. 'What do you mean?'

'This note,' the blonde said.

Verona immediately recognised the bold, black handwriting, which was the same as that on the envelope. The young woman read the message out loud.

'My Darling. Was this what you wanted? I cannot see you

tonight. Things are heating up here. I should be able to get away on Wednesday. DV.'

'You're having an affair with Natalie Schoen, aren't you?' the blonde accused.

'Me? No. Absolutely not,' Verona protested.

'Verona,' Harris interjected gently. 'These people are from the Security Service in London. They need to know why you delivered a file containing some highly sensitive and highly classified documents to that woman. Do you know her?'

'No,' Verona said. 'I've never met her. I had no idea what was in the envelope. And as for that note, that isn't my handwriting.'

'You signed it '*DV*'. What does that signify?' the blonde asked. 'Darling Verona, perhaps? Is that what she calls you?'

Verona looked again at the note which the blonde now slapped down on the desk in front of her. Her heart was throbbing rapidly. She could hear it pounding in her ear drums. She hoped her interrogators couldn't hear it. She could also feel her cheeks reddening. Panic rose in her chest and suddenly she was finding it hard to breathe. She tried to steady her nerves and to think clearly. Maybe they didn't know about Aleks after all. She suddenly felt her vision narrowing and for one awful moment she thought she might be about to faint. It didn't help that she hadn't eaten anything since breakfast. Taking in a deep breath, she steeled herself and focused on the note. The significance of 'DV' now suddenly occurred to her.

'That '*DV*'. I don't think it's a signature. I've seen it written somewhere before. I think it means '*Deo volente*'. That's Latin for 'God willing', isn't it? But it's not a phrase I would use. I don't normally use Latin phrases,' she said, shifting uncomfortably in her seat but glancing across at Harris, hoping he would remember who in their embassy *was* addicted to spouting Latin.

'What phrase *would* you use when writing to your lover?' the blonde asked.

'Well, I assure you I don't have a lover, but if I did, it wouldn't be a woman. And the phrase I would use would be '*inshallah*'.'

The blonde looked blankly at Verona.

It was Simon Harris who chipped in next: 'One of Verona's previous postings was Pakistan, wasn't it, Verona? And *Inshallah* is Urdu for 'God Willing', isn't it? So, Verona, if you didn't write the note, who did?'

Verona fell silent for a few seconds. She suddenly realised she had been stitched up by Peter Cross. She had been compromised. She had unwittingly become involved in something potentially even more serious than her affair with Aleks. She now found herself in a similar situation to that which the unpleasant Tiffany Munro had experienced, although this situation was shaping up to be a whole lot more serious than Tiffany's. The theft of the Defence section's documents had arisen through carelessness. The removal from the embassy of this file, however, had been a deliberate act. Why, she wondered, would the DHM have asked her to deliver classified documents to the Schoen woman? If Schoen were indeed some kind of US official, someone entitled to have the information on the documents, surely, he could have invited her over to view the file? Or he could have sent her information from the file electronically. Why the subterfuge, she wondered?

'Verona,' Harris asked again, gently, 'who wrote the note, and who asked you to deliver the file?'

'Oh dear. I don't know what to say, Simon. I wouldn't want

to get anyone into trouble,' she began, although she knew full well that was exactly what she was about to do.

CHAPTER TWENTY-THREE

In London the following day, Adrian Curtis had been invited to meet with Corey Hart at the US embassy. He decided to take a pleasant stroll along Riverside Walk from Vauxhall down to Nine Elms. Hart's well-appointed office had a pleasant view north east over the river and, soon, Adrian was sitting drinking coffee with his NSA contact. Hart quickly got down to business.

'So, have you any idea yet what happened to Walt Edelman?'

'Well, you were right,' Adrian said. 'There was foul play. And although the incident happened in a spot not covered by CCTV cameras, we've identified two individuals who'd been following him and who seem to have made off with his laptop case. There's no actual evidence they caused the incident, nothing that would stand up in a court of law, that is, but it's highly probable they targeted him and killed him.'

'So, do you know who they were?'

Adrian removed a manilla folder from his case and slid it across Hart's desk. The American opened it and began perusing the printed CCTV images.

'They were Russian, as you'd suspected. The one with the beard is Igor Ignatiev. The clean-shaven one is Zoltan Cherny. At least, those are the identities they used when they applied for UK visas. We do know for certain, though, that they're GRU thugs.'

'Have they been traced? Have you arrested them yet?' Hart asked, hopefully.

Adrian picked up his coffee cup and averted his gaze into the hot, comforting foam.

'Unfortunately, they had flights booked back to Moscow within hours of the incident.'

He took a sip of his coffee. He didn't like lying to Hart, which was why he phrased it the way he did. Their relationship was a good one, based on mutual trust. However, it was essential that the Security Service kept a hold on the two Russian intelligence officers for the time being. He knew that, once every last bit of useful intelligence had been drained out of them and verified, he could arrange for them to be made accessible to the Americans, and in a location which wasn't on British soil. They could be dealt with later on by whoever Corey Hart chose to task with administering justice to them, whatever form that justice might take.

'That's too bad. I don't suppose Edelman's attaché case was recovered?' Hart asked.

'I'm afraid not. It'll be in Moscow now. Any idea what was on it? Anything compromising?'

'We're beginning to suspect there was. But, it's kinda disappointing how these Russian assassins seem to have no trouble getting into Britain. You guys don't seem able to stop them.'

'Well, we allow in the ones we can identify as GRU and FSB in order to keep an eye on their movements. If we didn't do that, the Kremlin would simply get their people in by other means, using identities we wouldn't be able to spot. Mostly, it's a strategy that works well. It's just unfortunate that, in this instance, owing to our involvement in an inordinate number of pressing operations, our surveillance failed. I'm truly sorry about that.'

'Yeah. Well, Edelman's family are pretty sorry, too. As far as they're concerned, though, it was just an unfortunate accident. There seems nothing to be gained by us telling them otherwise.'

'You know, you chaps aren't much better at preventing them getting into the US either, if you don't mind me saying,' Adrian countered, thinking that he couldn't put it more tactfully than that. 'So, I need to let you know about a Russian sleeper whom we've uncovered during our investigation into Edelman's death.'

'Oh, yeah?' Hart frowned.

'A couple of my people are out in Moscow right now, looking into a security issue involving our embassy there. Seems the embassy's sprung a bit of a leak and my people have got to fix it. The individual on the receiving end of outpourings from that leak is a US citizen who is working for the Russians.'

'Who is he?' Hart's face darkened.

The American's concern was both palpable and understandable, Adrian thought. It wasn't that long ago that a significant network of long-term Russian sleepers had been uncovered in the US. The network had set up fairly foolproof American identities and had also established solid, respectable lives in small town America, whilst awaiting the call from Moscow to infiltrate key organisations. Luckily, as part of the FBI's *Operation Ghost Stories*, the entire network had been arrested before they could actually achieve anything. Adrian knew that the revelation of another sleeper would greatly alarm both Corey Hart and Washington.

'She,' Adrian corrected him. 'Doctor Natalie Schoen.'

He thought Hart looked thunder-struck to be told this. He guessed the name would almost certainly be one which was familiar to the American. She had, after all, appeared in the US news quite a bit of late. He imagined this was why Hart looked stunned.

'The great grandparents of Natalie Schoen were Jews who emigrated to US from Russian-occupied Poland in the eighteen nineties,' Adrian continued 'Natalie Schoen's fourth generation American, born in Brooklyn. She holds a doctorate in political science and economics and she lectures in politics at two US universities.'

As Adrian was speaking, Hart was already tapping on his keyboard, searching the internet for details of Natalie Schoen.

'Yeah, I have her details here,' Hart replied, as he scrolled through several sites. 'She's published a number of papers in US. There's quite a bit about her on the web. She's recently been appointed special attaché to the US diplomatic service. She seems well thought of. Numerous academic achievements. A pretty remarkable woman, it seems.'

'Oh, she's an extraordinary woman,' Adrian agreed. 'To have achieved all that when she passed away just two days after birth. That's pretty good going for a dead woman.'

'What? Are you sure?'

'I'm afraid so. It's the classic story of someone assuming

the identity of a deceased infant. That's not so easy to do nowadays, of course, as infant death records are now linked to their birth records. But back when this woman was a child, back in *The Day of the Jackal*, it was much easier. My people traced her records all the way back, through employment, university, school and back to that infant death. We believe that, whoever she really is, and she's not Natalie Schoen, she's been in the US since she was around five or six years old. She's been perfectly assimilated and has been biding her time, getting into the right place to be of use to Moscow.'

'Are you sure about this?' Hart asked.

'Absolutely. There's a copy of the infant's death certificate there in the file. You can check it out for yourself. We could only find one US birth record for a Natalie Schoen within the months preceding the infant's death. Whoever she really is, she's the perfect sleeper.'

'So, I wonder where she is now,' Hart said as he continued scrolling.

'Moscow,' Adrian further informed him. 'She's a minister-counsellor in your embassy there. As an under-secretary level principal officer, she's an advisor and consultant to your government on foreign affairs. In this instance, she's advising on US relations with Russia. And she's perfectly placed to influence US foreign policy in favour of Russia and its current expansionism. She's also perfectly placed to channel your secrets directly to the Kremlin.'

'Dear God!' Hart exclaimed, and he sank back into his well-upholstered swivel chair.

Adrian didn't exactly enjoy witnessing Hart's discomfort, but he did experience a certain degree of satisfaction in being able to tell him something Washington didn't know, and what he did tell him took some of the sting out of Hart's accusation about the ease with which Russians managed to gain entry to the UK.

'Would Schoen have been aware of Walt Edelman's role in the SCG?' Adrian asked.

'Almost certainly,' Hart nodded. 'And she would know he had access to intelligence coming from the special monitors in Russian-occupied Ukraine. Of course, details of the identities and whereabouts of those monitors was restricted to a very few people. She wouldn't have had direct access to that kinda information.'

'But she would have known that Edelman did?'

'Yeah. She would. The question, though, is whether Edelman was carrying that information with him, and if so, did his killers manage to get hold of it? But, tell me, what put you on to Schoen, or whoever she really is?'

'Well, we heard from a Russian defector – a pretty low-level official – that there was a sleeper in your Moscow embassy. He didn't know who it was of course. That knowledge rested well above his pay grade. We naturally liaised with MI6 who spoke to their man in our embassy in Moscow. That MI6 man had suspected for quite a while that there was information being leaked from our embassy. He has his own assets in some useful places, and it seems a car with UK diplomatic plates was seen regularly parked for brief periods outside one of the city's upmarket apartment blocks. It was reported to Russian officialdom, who took no action, naturally, since they already knew what was going on. But one of the Russian officials in the relevant office receiving such tip-offs is the MI6 man's asset, so he passed that snippet on to him.'

'Did he check it out?' Hart asked.

'Yes. Firstly, the residents in the apartment block were all fairly innocuous locals, with the exception of one, a US diplomat. It wouldn't have looked particularly suspicious to our man for a British diplomat to be visiting a US diplomat, but for two things. Firstly, the car belonged to a PA in the UK mission. She's not someone you'd expect to be socialising with a senior counsellor like Natalie Schoen. Secondly, the information being leaked was believed to have come from the office where the PA works.'

'So, the PA was leaking the info?' Corey asked.

'That's what MI6 thought. In their view, the PA fitted the type – a lonely spinster, unhappy in her post and with several good reasons to be resentful. She seemed ripe for turning. So, MI6 asked us to do a bit of delving into Schoen's background and loyalties. Once we realised Schoen wasn't Schoen, we checked the background of the PA. There was nothing adverse known about her here in the UK, so I sent two of my Counter-espionage people out there. Harry and Jo, in fact.'

'And how'd they make out?'

'They weren't known to the PA so they were able to observe her. They followed her to Schoen's apartment block and saw her depositing an envelope in Schoen's mailbox They retrieved the envelope and found it contained highly classified documents.'

'So, the PA's been arrested?'

'Actually, no. It turns out she was just an unwitting dupe. It was her boss who was the leak. As you can see from Schoen's profile, she's not only intelligent, she's quite attractive. She'd been seducing information out of him for some time. He was the source of the leak, but that leak's been plugged now. The PA was simply running errands for her boss.'

'Were those classified papers connected with the SCG monitors?' Hart asked, greatly concerned now.

'No. They were briefing notes including our ambassador's recommendations for a UK response to your government's pull-back on providing funds and military kit to Ukraine. As I'm sure you'll know, there's been much discussion amongst NATO countries as to who could supply what to Ukraine if America really does renege on the promise to continue supplying money and fighter planes.'

'And Natalie Schoen had a major influence on that decision to pull back,' Hart reasoned. 'I see the hand of the Kremlin all over this.'

'Mind you, we don't know what else Schoen managed to get out of our chap. It's possible he'd already given her all sorts of useful stuff on Ukraine. She might already have wheedled details of the SCG monitors out of our man, rather than having stolen them from Edelman. You see, our man regularly attended SCG meetings. He, too, would've had knowledge of the monitors' identities. Alternatively, our man might have declined to give her that info and she might have ordered the hit on Edelman in order to get the details from him instead. The intention might not have been to kill Edelman, just to get his papers and laptop. On the other hand, if she already had the SCG info from our man, then maybe killing Edelman *was* the intention. Edelman might have been killed because he was arguing the case for rescuing those special monitors.'

'He was?' Hart asked, and Adrian was surprised Hart was unaware of this.

'Yes. Our disgraced man in Moscow was at the November SCG meeting in London where Edelman made a strong plea for assistance for the monitors. It seems Edelman had urged member states to issue them with visas, to get them out of Ukraine and give them some financial assistance. Apparently, he spoke most persuasively, comparing the monitors' situation with that of the Afghans who'd worked for the US and UK and who were left behind when everyone pulled out of Afghanistan.'

'So, presumably, the Kremlin wouldn't have wanted the monitors getting out along with the hard evidence they'd been gathering of Russian atrocities and war crimes. The Kremlin woulda wanted them dead. That makes sense. Was Natalie Schoen at that meeting in November, too?'

'No, but I see her name is on the distribution list of the minutes of that meeting. She's been copied in on everything the US and the SCG have been doing in Ukraine. What is unusual, though, is that, from being such a highly-placed sleeper in US, then wielding influence from within your embassy in Moscow, it seems she's also taken on the role of a high-class 'swallow'. She was sleeping with Peter Cross, our number two in Moscow and I'm wondering who else she's been bedding.'

Adrian saw no point in concealing the identity of the British traitor from Hart, since it would soon be apparent to the Americans exactly which member of the UK's Moscow-based diplomatic staff would be leaving post earlier than expected. The Americans could work that out for themselves. Adrian felt he owed it to Hart to save him the trouble. Adrian's approach was to give away a little, so no-one would think you were holding a lot back. Hart looked deeply concerned. Adrian guessed this disclosure had come as an extreme surprise, though he thought he detected an unexpected emotional response in his American counterpart.

'Are you sure Schoen was sleeping with your man?' Hart asked. 'Only, in my experience, swallows are pretty low-key operatives. I can't see why it'd take someone with such a high profile to seduce information out of the guy.'

'I wondered that, too. Maybe it was as much about her influencing our man, and getting him to influence the SCG's decisions, as it was about getting info out of him. It would have taken someone with a good understanding of the issues to exert the right kind of influence. And Natalie Schoen had an exceptionally deep understanding of the issues.'

'Jeez, I guess I need to alert Washington about this asap and get her re-called,' Hart said.

'I think it's probably too late for that. I imagine a lot of damage has already been done. If she's challenged, she'll simply defect. She'll stay put in Mocow and be awarded the Red Star, or whatever gong they give their heroes these days. Naturally, the Russians wouldn't allow her extradition to the US to face charges. No, if exposed, she'll just walk out through the gates of your embassy and into a new life in Russia.'

'Maybe we could leave her where she is and use her treachery against her. You know, feed her disinformation.'

'You could, although that might be difficult, given how much she already knows about US foreign policy. She's actually been instrumental in creating that foreign policy. She'd probably see through any attempt to feed her disinformation, especially when she sees Cross being sent home suddenly. When that happens, she'll realise the jig is up and she'll go to ground.'

'Yeah, she probably will,' Hart conceded.

'You'd also have to be sure the hand that fed her disinformation was a clean one. You don't know who else might be involved with her. She might also have been seducing some of your fellow diplomats or senior men in the US administration. For all you know, the rot might go higher and wider than Schoen.'

'You're right, Adrian. Jeez, what a mess! I guess Washington might decide to terminate her – not just her employment, but Schoen herself,' Hart said, thoughtfully.

'Well, I'll leave that to you, Old Chap. Happily, it's not a decision I'd have to make.'

'And what about your compromised DHM? What'll you do with him when you get him home?'

'Luckily, that's not my decision either. That's one for the Foreign Office to decide, and for SIS's Moscow station to execute.'

'Yes, I'd better get the ball rolling on this right away,' Hart said, and he stood up.

'Indeed. Well, I'll leave you to get on with that,' Adrian said and he also rose. 'No, don't worry, I'll see myself out.'

Adrian headed out of Hart's office. Standing out in the corridor, he put down his briefcase and slowly put on his overcoat. Through the still open door, he could hear Hart picking up the phone and tapping out numbers. Adrian took his time, buttoning up his coat, tucking in his scarf and adjusting his coat collar. He heard his American contact slamming down the handset in frustration.

'Where the hell *is* she?' Hart said aloud.

Adrian was just about to set off down the corridor when he heard Hart's desk phone ring. He decided to linger for a little while more. His instincts told him he might hear something to his advantage. Still fiddling with his coat and scarf, he glanced both ways up and down the corridor to ensure no-one was watching, as he heard Hart snatch up the receiver.

'Yeah, thank God. I've been trying to get you,' Hart said. 'How are you? ... Where are you? ... Are you safe? I've been worried sick about you .... Did you get my voice message? You've been compromised. You gotta get outa there now. *Right now*. D'you hear me?'

Adrian picked up his briefcase and headed down the corridor towards the elevators. He had expected Hart to immediately get on the phone to Washington, but from what he had overheard, it hadn't sounded like Hart was speaking with a Washington colleague. He wondered who it was that Hart felt had been compromised, and who had caused Hart to be worried sick. *'Hmm, curious,'* he thought, *'just a little curious.'*

Back at Thames House, Adrian saw Harry and Jo arrive in the office. They had their luggage with them as they had come straight from Heathrow. He popped his head out of his office and waved Harry in to speak with him.

'How was Moscow?' he asked.

'Cold,' Harry said. 'But for the DHM, it got quite hot.'

'Did he cough to it?'

'Yes. He had little choice, really. As I said when I called you yesterday, the bastard tried to implicate his PA. That proved to be his undoing. The PA's a respectable, middle-aged career woman. You know the sort, classic Foreign Office spinster, dedicated to her job and deeply loyal to her boss. She didn't want to speak out against him, but when she realised he was a traitor, and that he was trying to drop her in it, well ...'

'Good. I just passed the info about Schoen on to Corey Hart,' Adrian advised.

'How'd he take it?'

'He was gobsmacked, as you might imagine. You know, it's quite satisfying, even just once in a while, to be able to tell the Americans something they didn't know, especially if it stops them carping about how lax our border procedures are. He'd heard of Schoen. I suppose that's because her name has featured regularly in the American press. He says he'd never actually met her, though, and it seems the Americans had no idea who and what she really is.'

'We're in credit with the Yanks, then,' Harry grinned.

'Indeed,' Adrian agreed. 'Tell me something, though. Do you and Kit still see Corey Hart and Rosie Leyton socially?'

'Yes, Boss. Occasionally. Not as often as I'd like. Kit's hours are even more unsociable than mine, these days. Counter-Terrorism Command have a lot of major ops on the go right now. Why do you ask?'

'Oh, I just wondered how they were getting on. I remember Rosie got let down somewhat with her previous fiancé, didn't she?'

'Yes, he was a serial philanderer. But she and Corey seem pretty solid. They have a really nice apartment rented by the US embassy. Rosie's a good contact to have in SIS. You know she was Lorna's best friend? Lorna was so pleased when Rosie and Corey got together. She had hoped she'd be going to their wedding one day, but ... it wasn't to be.'

Adrian now wished he hadn't brought up the subject. He had no wish to remind Harry about his former fiancée, Lorna Bayliss, or about the horrific way she had died. It was difficult, though, with Lorna having been one of Adrian's team. Her name often came up, usually in hushed and respectful tones and in connection with past operations and Russian targets. But Harry seemed to have moved on happily enough with Kit, the woman who was now his wife. Adrian knew that, as a detective inspector in the Metropolitan Police's Counter-Terrorism Command, from time to time, Kit McGlone found herself in situations even more dangerous than Lorna might have been expected to face. Adrian hadn't wanted to rake up difficult memories, but he felt he needed to ask about Corey and Rosie's relationship. He had his reasons for doing so.

CHAPTER TWENTY-FOUR

'Is it true?' Tiffany Munro asked.

Verona realised the Defence PA's question was directed at her. She continued to calmly chew then swallow the morsel of chicken mayonnaise sandwich in her mouth before replying.

'Is what true?'

'That the DHM's been recalled under a cloud,' Tiffany expanded.

Verona glanced around the canteen to ensure there were no senior staff sitting within earshot. Lauren's expression suggested she was surprised to hear this, but Caroline cast her eyes down towards her soup bowl. Naturally, Caroline knew. Verona liked Caroline and guessed that, as PA to the embassy's Secret Intelligence Service Officer, she knew how to keep secrets.

'Peter has been recalled to London, yes,' Verona confirmed. 'And my understanding is that his knowledge of the current situation in Ukraine is of great use to the government, so his presence at the Foreign Office is required urgently. But I don't know what you mean about a cloud.'

'Oh, come on,' Tiffany urged. 'I overheard Robin on the phone this morning. I heard him say Cross has got himself in a spot of bother. That's why he's being short-toured. Maybe it'll take the heat off me for a bit.'

'Well, I'm not sure what the DA meant by that,' Verona hedged. 'The homeward despatch of his heavy baggage will certainly prove to be bothersome. Mine still hasn't arrived, and I'm into my fourth month already. This war in Ukraine is causing us all a lot of bother.'

Verona didn't know why she still felt the need to cover up for Peter Cross, especially after what he had done to her, but the approving smile Caroline flashed in her direction persuaded her she was right not to say anything. Verona knew that, if she gave Tiffany the slightest hint about the reason for the DHM being short-toured, it would be all over the embassy within minutes. She wouldn't give her the satisfaction of confirming the gossip. She also knew it was likely Tiffany would be short-toured soon, too, but she wouldn't upset the girl by letting her know that. If Verona had learned one thing from her years of service, it was that the Foreign Office respected discretion, and appreciated employees who could keep their own counsel. Verona was just thankful that her own indiscretions had not come to light – not yet, at least.

'Is he going to be replaced, though?' Tiffany persisted.

'I really don't know,' Verona said, though her immediate thought was *'I bloody hope so'*.

Caroline clearly thought it politic to change the subject.

'Oh, Simon asked if you'd pop up and see him after lunch, Verona. I think he has some good news for you.'

'Oh, and I have some good news, too,' Lauren added. 'We've just been sent the DVD of the second series of *Doctor*

Foster. It's going to be shown in the club this Wednesday. They've also got curry on the menu. You will come, won't you, Verona?'

'I wouldn't miss it for anything, Lauren,' Verona smiled, pleased to be asked.

Harris, too, had a broad smile for Verona when she called in to see him that afternoon.

'Come in, Verona,' he beamed. 'Can I get you a coffee?'

'No, I'm fine, thank you, Simon,' she said.

'Well, take a seat, please. Look, Verona, I'm truly sorry for what Peter did, and for what we put you through. That must have been horrible for you.'

Verona didn't know what to say. She just shrugged, stoically.

'As you know, he's being recalled to London and he won't be coming back to post. Ruth is over in his apartment now, helping Sarah to pack up all their stuff.'

'I am sorry for Sarah, but I don't suppose she'll miss Moscow. Will Peter be replaced?' Verona asked.

'He will be. I understand his replacement has been approached and has already accepted the posting. She'll be undergoing some immersion language training in Russian over the next couple of weeks.'

'She?' Verona asked.

'Yes, a Miss Rena McAvoy. I believe she's a Scottish lady.'

'Rena McAvoy?' Verona brightened. 'Oh, I know her. She was Head of Chancery in Kuala Lumpur when I was there. She's very nice, actually. Oh, that *is* good news.'

'Well, I'm glad you and she are already acquainted. She's new to this part of the world, so you'll be able to help her settle in. She's a bachelor girl, too.'

'I expect she'll be moving into Peter's flat, then?' Verona asked.

'Yes, I believe so. It's a large, two-bedroomed flat, so it's appropriate for her grade, otherwise I would have been asking accommodation section whether you could move in there.'

'Oh, I understand, Simon. I wouldn't have expected to inherit the DHM's accommodation.'

'Well, there will be another slightly smaller apartment in the complex coming free very soon, too, and I've insisted accommodation section allocate that one to you. It's not as big as the DHM's apartment, but it's much bigger than the transit flat, and it has a view out over the river.'

Verona guessed this must be Tiffany's apartment. It had been on the cards that Tiffany would be going home, too. Everyone knew she would be – everyone but Tiffany herself, who clung on to the hope that she would be given a lesser punishment. Clearly, they still hadn't told Tiffany of her fate. Just like Verona, Tiffany had been dropped in it by her boss. Unlike Verona, however, Tiffany was destined to carry the can. Tiffany had never been very pleasant to Verona, it was true, even though Verona had tried to help her avoid being stitched up by the Defence Attaché. Even so, Verona felt bad that she was to benefit from Tiffany's misfortune.

'It'll be a few days before the current occupant can be moved out, and the place will need some re-decoration thereafter, so it won't be ready for a while yet,' Harris added. 'Are you still keen to move?'

'Oh, yes. I'll be delighted to move into the fold. Thank you so much, Simon.'

'Good. Oh, and I have yet another piece of good news for you. Your heavy baggage should be here on Wednesday. We can store it downstairs in the garage until your new apartment is ready.'

Verona returned to her office much lighter of step and heart. Things couldn't have worked out better. Peter Cross was leaving. She would have her office to herself for the next week or two. Her new boss was someone she knew and someone with whom she would feel comfortable – a woman of around her own age, in fact. And, if that weren't cause enough to rejoice, she would also be moving out of the dismal transit flat into a newly re-decorated apartment within the UK's diplomatic enclave. It would be like a new start.

As she reached her office, she was surprised to encounter Cross coming out. He was carrying his briefcase and a couple of carrier bags. She guessed he had been clearing out his desk. She cast him a sympathetic look and she was about to say how sorry she was about how things had turned out. However, she saw the anger in his face and immediately thought better of it.

'Judas!' he hissed as he strode straight past her.

She was deeply shocked at his attitude, knowing it was a wholly undeserved accusation. It was *he* who had betrayed *her*. His comment in the note to Natalie Schoen, that things were getting 'hot over here', told her this was why he had insisted she deliver the papers in person. He had seriously compromised her and deliberately so. She didn't feel she had deserved to be used in that way, and she certainly didn't deserve his insult. She sat down at her desk to think. She felt bad inside. In all her years of service as a personal assistant, she never been anything less than loyal to whoever was her boss. She had gone above and beyond to accommodate Peter Cross, driving him to his sordid assignations, and at her own expense, and cleaning his office and typing his drafts. And hardly a word of thanks had passed his lips.

Thinking things through, she realised she shouldn't feel bad about what had happened. Peter's fall from grace was not her fault. He was a senior diplomat and responsible for his own actions. And, anyway, things were about to change for the better, and she told herself that not even a savage comment from Peter Cross could take away her optimism. She reminded herself she would feel safer and less isolated once she moved, since her accommodation would be a very short and safe walk from her office. She might now be included in more of the social life of the embassy. She knew the PAs often popped in and out of each other's apartments for coffee and chat but none of them had ever felt inclined to walk down to *Nevsky Prospekt* to visit her. They might visit her now. She wouldn't have to spend the following winter trudging home each evening through the snow and start checking the place for bugs. And, more importantly perhaps, she wouldn't have to see Aleks again. Of course, she wasn't absolutely sure how she felt about that.

CHAPTER
TWENTY-FIVE

THE MONTH OF MARCH BROUGHT SLIGHTLY BETTER WEATHER TO Moscow, and Verona's spirits improved with the prospect of her impending move into the embassy and the imminent arrival of both her baggage and her new boss. She had seen neither hide nor hair of Aleks or his parents since Christmas, which was lucky, since she felt she wouldn't know what to say to them, though it did seem odd that she hadn't bumped into them. Verona could smell spring in the air and she rejoiced that the snow had melted from the streets, albeit that there was still the occasional sleet or hail storm. Her sister had also promised to visit, possibly as soon as late March or early April. That also gave her something to look forward to.

A fortnight later, she walked home from the embassy through a light flurry of sleet. She felt the windblown flakes of wet snow sting her eyes and cheeks, but she didn't mind very much, as she knew this evening's would be her very last walk home along *Nevsky Prospekt*. Her move was due to take place the very next morning and she was excited about it. The air was still chilly, though the evenings were beginning to get a little lighter now. Calling in at the little delicatessen to buy some wine and sausages for her supper, she caught sight of the packets of rat poison which she had stupidly mistaken for breakfast cereal. She recalled her embarrassment at that. As she queued up to pay, she couldn't help thinking about Aleks and wondering where he was and what he was up to.

Now that the awful business with Peter Cross was over and done with, and since her own betrayal of secrets had gone undiscovered, she had spent much time reflecting on what had happened. She bore Aleks no ill will. She was grateful to him for having made her feel good about herself. She acknowledged the fact that he had shown her what it meant to be in love, and how to enjoy the physical expression of that love. It was the first time in her life that she had ever been intimate with a man, and it had been wonderful. In some ways, she regretted the fact that it had taken so long for her eyes to be opened to the sheer joy of lovemaking. Aleks had been a gentle and considerate lover, so much so, that, at times, it had given her cause to wonder if he had, indeed, been one of those 'ravens' Simon Harris had warned about. She had sometimes wondered if he had perfected his art of seduction in some spy school. Had he targeted her in order to seduce secrets from her? She had no idea. She only knew he had made her happy – happier, perhaps, than was good for her.

At the same time, however, it was also the first time in her life she had ever relied upon a man for any kind of emotional support. Whether her days would go well or badly had seemed to depend upon whether or not she could enjoy Aleks' company. She now realised that her love for that young man had eroded her self-reliance to a degree. Hitherto, she had always been content with her own company. She had always trundled along on an even emotional keel. Then, she had met Aleks. She had cherished every moment she had spent in his company, it was true, but she had been miserable when he wasn't there. She wasn't used to that degree of emotional dependence. Moreover, it had come so close to ending badly for her, so in many ways, she persuaded herself she was glad it was over. Yes, emotionally, it truly had been a rollercoaster ride, and one couldn't spend one's life on a rollercoaster. The fairground was always going to pack up and move on eventually.

She let herself into the apartment building. Climbing the stairs, she turned her key in the lock and let herself in. Her small air freight trunk was already packed and locked and it stood by the front door, awaiting collection the following morning. Her large suitcase was partly packed and was sitting open in her bedroom. She would pack her toiletries and night-clothes in the morning, after she had taken her last bath in the transit flat. The new apartment had a shower and she so looked forward to using it.

Throwing off her coat and headscarf and stepping out of her damp boots, she switched on a couple of lamps, hoping to add a bit of cheer to the empty sitting room. For once, she didn't bother with her usual nightly routine of checking the lamps for bugs and lifting the handset to listen for suspicious clicks that never came. There seemed no point in that now, especially as no-one was going to phone her, and she was far too weary. Heading into the kitchen, she checked out the fridge. She had emptied it in anticipation of her move and had packed all the float items in a cardboard box which stood on the kitchen counter top, to be collected the following day by the accommodation staff. The kitchen cupboards, too, were emptied. Although she had planned to cook the sausages for her supper, she realised she wasn't actually very hungry. If she did cook, she would only have to wash and re-pack the pans and plates. She had a packet of potato crisps in the cupboard. This would suffice for her supper. She rarely bothered to cook for one, anyway.

On top of the fridge there were a couple of bottles of red wine which she had bought a couple of weeks ago, intending to celebrate Aleks's return from his mission to rescue that Marina woman from Ukraine. Her thinking back then had been that, if she bought wine, that might influence fate and prompt Aleks's safe and quick return. She didn't know whether he had undertaken any other missions or acts of sabotage since then. She didn't even know whether any of that had been true. She now doubted it had been. None of that seemed to matter now, though. Tomorrow, she would be moving out and moving on with her life.

Grabbing one of the bottles and the packet of crisps, she took a clean glass from the float box. Back in the sitting room, she sat down on the sofa. She wouldn't miss the lumpy sofa, or the lumpy bed. Somehow, though, the bed hadn't felt quite so lumpy or uncomfortable when Aleks had shared it with her. She'd been promised a new mattress in her new flat, however, so she told herself she wouldn't mind so much not having anyone to share her bed.

Unscrewing the cap and pouring out a glass of wine, she took a long draught. She had never been much of a drinker before she had met Aleks. Drinking wine, however, had certainly made her feel a little less buttoned-up and a lot less inhibited. She felt like drinking wine this evening to celebrate the changes which were about to happen. She was celebrating her escape from this miserable little flat. She was also celebrating Peter Cross's departure. After a few sips, she could feel the disappointment at her betrayal by Peter Cross melting away. So what if he had accused her of being a 'Judas'. There were several words for what he had done to her – disloyalty, treachery, betrayal, unkindness.

She tore open the crisp packet and began to eat. That, too, made her feel slightly better. She finished the crisps. Soon, she had polished off more than half the bottle of wine, too. Placing a cushion behind her head she felt herself relaxing. She felt she had behaved stupidly and recklessly where Aleks was concerned. There was no escaping the fact that she, too, had been guilty of betrayal. She had betrayed her country. She had quite possibly betrayed those brave but unfortunate monitor people in Ukraine, as well. She couldn't be sure if their fate was her doing but, in the light of Peter Cross's treachery, she persuaded herself it was not. Luckily, she had got away with what she had done. She had not been found out, and it now seemed unlikely she ever would be. Thankfully, Simon Harris regarded her as a victim, not a traitor. The events of her first few months in Moscow had taken quite a toll on her emotionally, but the wine now began to dull both the memory and the anxiety. Maybe, once she moved into the embassy enclave, she would be able to put it all behind her. Gradually, she slipped into deep and welcome sleep.

The sound of sirens in the street awoke her. Glancing at the clock, she realised she had been asleep sitting upright on the sofa for a couple of hours. It was very dark outside now. The sirens grew louder then stopped. She could hear voices from the street below. Curious, she arose, crossed to the lounge window and opened it to lean out. The light snow was still drifting down, and snowflakes blew in and landed on her eyelashes, making it difficult for her to see what was going on down in the street. Squinting, she could make out two vehicles with flashing lights, and there was quite a bit of activity on *Nevsky Prospekt*. She saw several uniformed men emerging from the vehicles. Their bulky military-style overcoats and sheepskin *Ushanka* hats suggested to her they might be policemen, or some kind of military.

She was shocked to realise the men were entering her own apartment building. For a second, she wondered if they were coming for her. However, she dismissed the thought instantly. Even if Simon Harris and the two Security Service officers had decided to take some sort of disciplinary action against her, they would have done it long before now, and they certainly wouldn't involve Russian law enforcement. She watched the goings-on for a while and, to her surprise, she saw the uniformed men escorting a man and a woman out of the building and taking them towards the cars. She could hear the woman's voice apparently protesting. Suddenly, she recognised the voice. It was Olga Petrenko. Verona pushed the window further open and leaned out to get a better view. For one horrible moment, she feared the man being arrested might be Aleks, but then she recognised the portlier figure of his father, Vitaly. She continued to watch until the vehicles, one of which held the Petrenkos, drove away. Silence again returned to the street.

Closing the window, she went and sat back on the sofa. She feared the Petrenkos' arrest was likely to be connected with Alek's activities in Ukraine. Did this mean that Aleks was genuine? Had she been right to trust him after all? The horrible thought struck her that perhaps he had been arrested already.

Yes, that seemed possible. Maybe he had been interrogated. If the authorities had found out what Aleks had been involved in, that would explain why they had come for his family. Maybe he would have told them about the English woman who had given him classified information. Was it possible she might be betrayed by two men, by her boss and by Aleks? Once again, her heart was troubled. She sat there for some time, wondering whether she should do anything. But it seemed there was little she could do. Not knowing what had happened to Aleks, however, was eating her up.

As she sat and reflected, more of Simon Harris's words from the security briefing came back to her. Once again, she remembered what he had said regarding the risks Russian citizens took when entering into friendships with westerners, and so why would they take such risks? Why would Aleks take such a risk? Following the betrayal of the Ukrainian monitors, she had persuaded herself that he hadn't actually risked anything in befriending her, because he had been working for the Russians and she had been used by him. But if he had now been arrested, did that mean he wasn't working for the Russians? Had he really risked his and his parents' freedom for the love of Verona? And now she had turned her back on him.

However, she could still picture him sitting in the *Konditeskaia Kafé* alongside Anna. It had been the sight of them together which had made her suspicious in the first instance. Yet she had believed him when he had described Anna as just a friend, and not someone with whom he was having a physical relationship. But why *wouldn't* he want such a relationship with Anna? Why wouldn't she want to be his lover? He was an extremely attractive young man, and Anna was a beautiful young woman. How could he possibly prefer Verona?

It had been easy, she told herself, to believe Aleks when he was here. She had been so happy and distracted whenever she was in his company that she had been willing to believe everything he told her. Did the Petrenkos' arrest make it more likely it was Cross who had betrayed the Ukrainians or less likely? She hadn't been told exactly what was in the file Cross had her deliver to the Schoen woman. Maybe he, too, had passed on their details, and not to Aleks's network but to the Schoen woman. Who were the real traitors in all of this? She no longer knew what to think.

She remembered the night of the Christmas concert at the embassy. She had introduced her neighbours to Simon Harris, and he had spoken to them in both Russian and Ukrainian, and they had understood. She had no doubt the Petrenkos were Ukrainian. Then again though, they lived in Moscow and not all Ukrainians were anti-Russian. Many held pro-Russian sympathies. Aleks had said he was conceived in Odessa, but had he been born there or in Russia? He hadn't said. Once again, all sorts of thoughts ran around in dizzying circles in her head.

But she had just seen for herself, from her lounge window, the arrest of the Petrenkos. The snowflakes had stung her eyes and had made it difficult to see, but the Petrenkos hadn't been roughly handled into the police vehicle. They weren't handcuffed or anything and nor were they escorted out at gunpoint. Sure, she had heard Olga's voice raised in what she took to be a protest, but supposing it wasn't genuine? Suppose their 'arrest' was a set up. Could this all be a show for her benefit, to encourage her continued co-operation in betraying her own country? She began to have serious nagging doubts yet again. She was totally and utterly confused. She was also afraid.

She felt she just wanted to crawl into a hole and hide. She needed to sleep and to put behind her everything which had happened here. She told herself that, once she moved into her new flat in the embassy, everything would be different. Everything would be fine. She would be immune, both in the diplomatic sense and in a psychological sense. There was nothing she could do to help the Petrenkos if they truly were in trouble, and tomorrow, she would be leaving *Nevsky Prospekt* for the safety of the embassy enclave. There she would be insulated from whatever it was Aleks and his parents were involved in. She decided she should go to bed now. Things might just seem clearer tomorrow. Perhaps she would just wait and see what might happen.

Despite the lumpy mattress, she had fallen into a deep sleep when a noise again awoke her. She wasn't sure at first that she had heard anything at all, until it came again. There was an odd tapping sound. She sat bolt upright and listened. The tapping came again. It seemed to be coming from the Kitchen. She guessed it was coming from the apartment's back door which led out to the fire escape. She wondered if the police had left officers behind to search the building. But why would they come up the fire escape? Wouldn't they come up the internal stairs? They wouldn't tap on the back door. They would hammer on the front door.

Gingerly, she arose, went to the kitchen and peered into the darkness. To her alarm, she could see a figure silhouetted against the glass of the back door. Whoever it had indeed come up the fire escape. The figure tapped again. She grabbed a sharp knife from the kitchen drawer and switched on the kitchen light. She now recognised the man at the door. It was Aleks. Placing the knife back in the drawer where, for safety's sake, she also kept the back door key, she grabbed the key instead and rushed to unlock the door. Aleks almost fell into her arms.

'Aleks!' she exclaimed. 'What is it? Are you all right?'

She helped him into the living room and guided him to the sofa. He was out of breath, and now she noticed his clothing was dishevelled. He had mud on his shoes and on his jeans.

Panting heavily, he glanced anxiously towards the front door of the flat.

'It's all right. It's locked and bolted,' she reassured him. 'I'll lock the back door, too.'

Locking the kitchen's exterior door again, she returned the key to the kitchen drawer and ran back to his side.

'What happened?' she asked again.

'We blew up a major munitions factory over on the east side of Moscow,' he gasped. 'I thought we'd made it away unobserved, but we were stopped as we drove back across the city. There was a roadblock. They were waiting for us there. We must have been betrayed because they called out my name. I leapt out of the car and I ran.'

Alek winced. He was out of breath, but he was also in pain.

'They knew about me, Verona. I think someone must have revealed our plans to the authorities. I didn't dare go to my parents' apartment. I hope you don't mind me coming here, only I didn't know where else ...', he broke off.

'Oh, Aleks, the police must have been looking for you at your parent's flat. They arrested Olga and Vitaly earlier this evening.'

Aleks sat forward, his head in his hands, distraught.

'I'm so sorry, Aleks. Is there anything I can do?'

'I should go. I don't want to get you into trouble, too.'

'No, stay,' she urged. 'If the police come to my door, I'll show my diplomatic ID and I won't let them in. They won't arrest me. Our ambassador would make a stink if they did. You're probably safest here. It's a flat rented by our embassy. They'd have to get the embassy's permission to come in and search the place.'

He sat back again his head resting against the sofa. He seemed thoroughly exhausted.

'Can I get you anything?' she asked. 'Some water? When did you last eat?'

'Thanks, but I'm not hungry. Just tired. And worried. My parents don't know anything, so the police won't be able to get anything out of them. But the interrogation won't be very pleasant for them.'

'I'm sure they'll let them go when they realise they know nothing,' Verona said, though she wasn't sure at all. 'But look, you're all wet, and cold. Why don't I run you a hot bath?'

Aleks nodded. She went to the bathroom, ran the bath, took a large, clean bath towel from her trunk and laid it out on the radiator for him. He joined her in the bathroom and began to remove his clothing, starting with his sodden, muddy shoes.

'Give me your clothes and I'll run them through the washing machine,' she offered, and she gathered up his garments as he discarded them. It was then she noticed the large blood stain on his shirt. She saw a corresponding wound in his side – a large purple wound surrounded by bruising.

'Oh, Aleks, what happened to you?' she pointed to the wound.

'We were shot at as we ran away. A bullet just grazed me. It's not too bad. It'll be okay when I clean it a bit.'

'I don't have any medical dressings,' she said, 'but I have

some antiseptic cream. I'll fetch it and you can put some on when you've had your bath.'

She left him to soak in the bath and she took his clothes into the kitchen. Removing his personal documents and change from the pockets, she put them into the kitchen drawer before putting his clothing into the washing machine and switching it on. She held his shoes over the sink and ran the tap over them to get most of the mud off. She hadn't got any clothes for him to wear but she took the warm fleecy dressing gown, her Christmas gift from Romola, into the bathroom and hung it up on the back of the door for him to wear. She also left the antiseptic cream out for him. She gazed at his beautiful, naked body as lay back in the bath, his eyes closed, and she hated to think of him being in pain. She glanced again at the wound in his side and it looked far worse than a graze. It still bled into the bath water. She wondered whether the impact might have broken his ribs.

Whilst he bathed, she sat on the sofa, thinking. She would have to get his clothing dried this evening and get him out of the flat first thing tomorrow, before the embassy driver came to collect her and her luggage to take her to her new accommodation. He couldn't stay here because the accommodation staff would be coming back again to check out the flat. Eventually, Aleks emerged from the bathroom, wrapped in her dressing gown. Moving very stiffly, he sat beside her on the sofa.

'Can I get you something?' she asked. 'Some aspirin, or a hot drink?'

'No, I feel better already,' he smiled. 'Just being here with you makes me feel better. I haven't seen you in so long. I missed you very much. Did you go away somewhere?'

'Uh, yes, my embassy sent me ... to London ... at short

notice. But tell me, what happened? Did your friends manage to get away, too?'

'No, they didn't. I saw one of them get shot and he fell down. I think he was dead. I had no choice but to leave him. I couldn't see Anna anywhere.'

'Anna was with you?' Verona asked. 'Do you think she got away?'

'I don't know. I just don't know.'

He flinched, and she could see he was in pain from the wound in his side. She feared he might have other injuries, too.

'I don't suppose you'd have any whisky, would you?' he asked.

'Oh, no, I haven't. Would a glass of wine help?'

'Yes. That might help me sleep. Things might look a bit clearer in the morning.'

She poured him a large glass of wine and he drank it down in just three or four gulps.

'Listen, Aleks. You can't stay here beyond tomorrow. They're moving me out of here in the morning. They've got me an apartment within the embassy and someone will be along to collect me and my baggage at around half past nine. We'll have to get you out of here before then.'

'Okay. I don't want to make any trouble for you, Verona. I need to rest now, but I'll leave before your embassy people get here.'

'But where will you go?'

'I'll work that out in the morning. I have friends I can stay with. I'm just so weak and tired, right now. But I'll be fine after a few hours' sleep.'

She helped him to the bedroom and eased him into the bed. He looked so pale and vulnerable. She realised letting him stay wasn't the best idea, but she could hardly turn him out into the night. It was still sleeting down out there, and he needed to rest if his wound was to heal. She waited until the washing machine had completed its cycle and she removed his clothes and placed them in the tumble dryer. They should be dry by the time she needed him to leave. She placed his shoes in the airing cupboard to dry out. Then she climbed into the bed beside him.

It felt good to feel his body against hers again. She realised how much she had missed him. Her earlier resolve to avoid him and move on had melted away the moment she had set eyes on him again. He was heart-achingly handsome and he was needy. He needed her help and she felt partly responsible for his situation. She didn't know what she would do next or whether she would be able to continue to see him. She just knew they both badly needed to sleep right now. Things might just look clearer in the morning. She listened to his breathing as he fell into a deep sleep, and then, eventually, she allowed herself to drift off too.

CHAPTER TWENTY-SIX

The following morning, Verona awoke at seven. She had slept so deeply that she had forgotten the startling events of the previous night. As she gradually remembered what had happened, she was aware Aleks was still lying alongside her. His presence felt so natural, so comforting, but she realised she must get up and get dressed. With her practical head on now, she realised she had to ensure that Aleks was out of the flat before the embassy driver arrived to take her and her luggage to the embassy. The driver was unlikely to appear before nine. She had been advised the accommodation staff would be returning later that day, too, in order to carry out the archaic process they termed 'marching out'. This meant a complete inventory of the flat's furniture and fittings would be taken, and the state in which she had left the accommodation, would be noted. She would be held liable for any damage or breakages of the float items which might have been incurred during her occupation.

Reluctant though she was to disturb Aleks, she knew she would have to get him up and get him on his way. She could at least make him a coffee before she turfed him out, though she would have to remember to wash the cup and return it to the box of float items. She reached out and grasped his arm to awake him gently. His arm felt cold to the touch. She shook it.

'Aleks,' she said. 'Time to get up now. You must go soon.'

He did not respond and she suddenly became aware that his breathing was very shallow. In fact, it was so shallow it was imperceptible. She sat upright and felt his brow. It, too was cold – very cold. She now saw, in the dim morning light, that his eyes were open, their focus fixed on the ceiling. She leapt up in great alarm, as she realised he wasn't sleeping at all. He was dead! Aleks had passed away in her bed. She pulled away from him in shock. She started to shake uncontrollably and an involuntary whine escaped her lips. The body beside her in the bed was no longer her Aleksander. It was a dead man. But how? How could he have died?

Pulling back the covers, she saw there was a large blood-stain on the sheet corresponding with the wound in his side. She realised that the wound must have been deeper than he thought. He must have bled to death in the night. He had died alongside her. She sprang out of the bed, stepped away and gazed in horror at his poor, dead body. She had never seen a dead body before. She had been overseas when each of her parents had passed, and dealing with their deaths had been left to her sister Romola. This wasn't the same as losing an aged parent, however. This was awful. Her first thought was how on earth would she explain this away?

She slumped down on the bedroom chair, staring at Aleks and wishing him back to life. She couldn't stop shaking. She wondered how long he had been dead and the revulsion she felt at the thought that she had spent the night next to his dead body drained the blood from her face. As her shock and revulsion gradually gave way to grief, the shaking stopped and she began to weep. She wept for the loss of the beautiful young man who lay before her. She wept out of regret for the loss of his young life and the loss of the future he had so joyfully anticipated. She cried for what might have been, and she also cried for herself.

She sat, traumatised and unable to move. The enormity of the situation left her paralysed with grief and fear. Before she knew it, over an hour had passed. Eventually, however, she realised she needed to pull herself together. She had to set aside her grief and work out what to do. At any moment, the embassy driver might come knocking. She needed to get dressed and finish her packing. She also needed to compose herself and to act normally when the driver arrived. And yet everything was far from normal. How could things possibly be normal when there was a dead body in her bed?

She realised she would have to move or dispose of Aleks' body. But how? There was no way she could carry his body down several flights of stairs to his parents' apartment. She hadn't found keys in his pockets when she had washed his clothes, so she didn't think she would be able to access his apartment. In any case, if anyone should see her trying to move a body they would certainly call the police. No, that wouldn't work. She struggled to remain calm and work out what she should do, yet both her body and her mind were numb. Aleks had said the Russians knew of his involvement in sabotage. They had been waiting for him. They had shot at him and they knew where he lived. That's why they had arrested Olga and Vitaly. They would come back to look for him and they might search the whole building.

She reasoned that, if they came whilst she was still here, she could produce her identity card and persuade them they must seek her ambassador's permission before searching her apartment. However, if she did that, and if his body was later discovered in the flat, which of course it would be, she would certainly be implicated. She knew she must leave *before* the authorities came looking for him. She now saw her own night-dress was stained with Aleks' blood. The sight galvanised her.

She rose from her chair and went to get herself washed and dressed. Then she packed the last of her clothes and toiletries in her suitcase. She also bundled up her bloodstained night-dress and the equally bloodstained dressing gown which Aleks had worn and she squashed it into her case. Next, she dragged her small trunk and the suitcase out of the flat and onto the landing so the driver and his assistant who would be coming to collect her luggage would have no reason to enter the flat. Returning to the kitchen, she washed and dried the final few items of crockery and glassware and placed them in the box on the kitchen counter top along with the other float items.

Removing the plastic bin liners from the waste bins in her kitchen and bathroom, she took them out through the back door to the small dustbin out on the fire escape. She stood outside for a few moments, breathing in the cool morning air and trying to clear her head. As she stood looking at the back door, a very basic plan began to form in her head. She spotted the half-brick which lived on the fire escape and which she imagined previous occupants of the flat had used to prop open the back door in summer. Slipping the sleeve of her sweater over her hand to avoid leaving fingerprints, she picked up the brick. She pulled the back door shut, then glancing around to ensure no-one could see, she used the brick to smash the window pane just above the lock. Dropping the brick, she slipped back into the kitchen and closed the door behind her. The key to the back door was still in the lock. Leaving it in place, she used her sleeve to wipe her finger prints from the key and from the door handle.

Satisfying herself that everything in the flat seemed to be in order – apart from the presence of a deceased young man in her bed – she went into the bedroom and gently pulled the covers up over Aleks' shoulders. She surveyed the scene and hoped that whoever found him there would conclude that, following her departure, he had broken in via the back door, had found the apartment empty and had decided to climb into the bed she had so recently vacated.

His clothes! She suddenly remembered his clothes were still in the dryer. Surely, a mortally wounded man wouldn't have taken the time to wash and dry his clothes before falling, exhausted and dying, into bed? She retrieved the clothes from the dryer and laid them on the bedroom rug. As an afterthought, she took his shirt, turned back the bedclothes and pressed the torn side of the shirt into the still damp bloodstain on the sheet, then she threw it back onto the rug and covered Aleks up again.

She next retrieved his wallet and his personal documents from the kitchen drawer and left them on the bedside cabinet, which seemed a more logical place for him to have placed them. Taking his shoes out of the airing cupboard, she placed these on the bedside rug alongside his clothes. When she was satisfied she had done all she could to make it look like Aleks was simply a fugitive from the law who had broken into what would be an empty flat, she stood by the lounge window and waited, nervously, until, after what seemed an eternity, she saw the embassy driver pull up. She took one last look around the flat, shivered, and then, locking the front door behind her, she stood on the landing to wait. The driver and his assistant collected firstly her trunk which they carried between them down to the car. She remained on the landing, just in case they had a spare key and thought to enter the flat, in which case she would assure them there was no need.

The driver's assistant then returned for the suitcase. She followed him downstairs and settled herself with some relief onto the backseat of the embassy vehicle. As they pulled out of the street and headed for the *Smolenskaya* embankment, she did not look back. She had no wish to take a last look at *Nevsky Prospekt* and, indeed, she hoped she would never have to return.

CHAPTER TWENTY-SEVEN

Adrian Curtis accepted the mug of pleasantly strong coffee Corey Hart proffered.

'So, you said there were a coupla things you wanted to discuss with me,' the American smiled. 'Well, fire away.'

'Yes, thanks for seeing me, Corey. I won't stop long as I'm on my way to a lunch engagement anyway, but it's about the Russian sleeper, Natalie Schoen. Did you ever meet her.'

'Me? No. I don't think our paths ever crossed. Why do you ask?'

'I just wondered, but, when last we met, you said you thought Washington might want to ... how did you put it ... terminate her?'

'Yeah. I guess they're still considering what action to take. No doubt they're still reeling at the shock of learning how deeply she'd infiltrated the establishment. I'm real grateful to you for sharing your intelligence on her. It all checked out, just as you said.'

'Well, I've been giving some thought to ways in which she

could be stopped but without implicating Washington in her demise.'

'Uh huh? What would you suggest?'

'Supposing it could be arranged for the Russians to terminate her?'

'That'd be good, but how could that be arranged?'

'You could leave the details to me. I have an idea which would mean there would be no come-back on Washington. What do you say?'

'I say, that'd be great, if you think you can arrange it. I'd say go ahead. And the sooner the better. If we're to ensure Ukraine gets our practical support and weaponry, it needs to happen under the current administration. If the President loses the next election, though, it's almost certain that funding will be cut.'

'Okay. I'll put that plan into action today, then. Now, I completely forgot to ask you last time I was here, how's Rosie?'

'Rosie? Aw, she's just great. And, by the way, if your diary isn't too full, you might care to ring-fence the first Saturday in September, as Rosie and I are getting married that day.'

'You are? Oh, that's fantastic news. Congratulations, Corey. I do love it when people I really like decide to get hitched. That's wonderful. Where will it be?'

'Down in Kent. Her mom and dad live in a village down there. You and Ellie will get an invite in due course. So will Harry and Kit. But before then, there'll be even more excitement. We're expecting a baby in the summer.'

'You're going to be a dad, too? Wow! So, the baby's arrival is in the summer and the wedding in the autumn, how very modern of you. Do send Rosie my best wishes. I hope the pregnancy goes well.'

'Actually, she's not pregnant. We're not producing our own offspring. Just between you and me, Adrian, I can't have kids myself. I'm firing blanks, so to speak. That's the reason my first marriage broke up years back. No, Rosie and I are adopting a baby. That's why the timing is as it is. We've made arrangements with a surrogate mother and she's due to give birth in July.'

'Well, that's wonderful. So, will the baby be a bridesmaid or a pageboy?'

Hart laughed, 'a bridesmaid. The scans suggest it's a girl. Rosie's already planning a little bridesmaid's dress for a two-month-old infant. Actually, you might be able to tell me who I should speak to about UK visas and such.'

'Visas? For whom?'

'The birth mother is in eastern Europe. She's someone I've known professionally for a coupla years and she suddenly found herself pregnant. Her circumstances are a bit difficult right now and she said she would be putting her baby up for adoption. Since Rosie and I had been discussing adopting, this seemed an ideal opportunity. We'd like to bring the young woman over a few weeks before the birth, so that she can have the child here. That way, we can get all the registration issues done here.'

'I see. Yes, I'll put you in touch with people I know at the Home Office. I believe if you arrange the adoption here in the UK, using a UK adoption agency, the baby might be entitled to UK citizenship. And I imagine you'll register her birth with your consular people, too, so she'll qualify for a US passport as well. But the Home Office will be able to give you the best advice on the adoption. Well, that is wonderful news. I can't wait to tell Harry.'

'You said there was another issue you wanted to discuss?'

'Oh, yes, I almost forgot. Ignatiev and Cherny, the two Russians we believe killed Walter Edelman.'

'Yes. Have you managed to trace them?'

'I told you they were booked on a flight to Moscow the same evening Edelman was killed. Well, after I spoke with you, I had further enquiries made and it seems that, although they'd checked in, they didn't actually leave on that flight. They doubled back and they didn't actually return to Russia, at all.'

'Adrian, please tell me they're somewhere we can get at them.'

'They are. They're hiding out in a rented farmhouse in the Republic of Ireland.'

'Do you know exactly where?'

'Yes,' Adrian grinned, as he slid a printout across the desk. 'County Donegal. Here's the address and also the map co-ordinates. My sources tell me they aren't armed, by the way. I don't need to know what you intend to do with them. Suffice it to say we have no interest in them.'

'Thanks, Adrian. I really appreciate this. As you would say, you can leave the details to me.'

Adrian left the US Embassy and flagged down a taxi to take him to London Bridge. Alighting in front of The News Building, headquarters of *The Times* newspaper, he glanced up at the seventeen-story building, which nestled in the shadow of The Shard, before making his way into the impressive glass atrium and announcing his arrival to the reception desk staff.

'Adrian Curtis to see Ronan Rogers. He's expecting me.'

The Times editor was always delighted to see his old friend and golfing partner, not least because their lunches together often brought forth snippets of information, the disclosure of which suited Adrian's purpose and often formed the basis of a 'scoop' for the newspaper.

'You said you wanted a bit of a tête-à-tête before we head off to lunch,' Ronan said as he motioned Adrian to take a seat on the leather sofa in his office, from which he had a superb view out over the Thames. 'I've booked us a table for twelve-thirty, so we've plenty of time. Coffee first?'

'No, thanks. I just had a strong one over at the US Embassy. But I thought you might like to be the first to know about a major political scandal which is about to hit the Washington fan.'

'Indeed, I would,' Rogers sat back in his leather armchair in anticipation of receiving another of his friend's intelligence-fuelled bombshells. 'Fire away, Old Chap. I'm all ears.'

'Okay, well, have you heard of a Doctor Natalie Schoen?'

'The name rings a faint bell,' Rogers said. 'American?'

'That's right. An academic. A Politico. US government advisor on diplomacy, foreign relations and foreign policy.'

'Yes, I know who you mean. What about her?'

'What would you say if I told you she was a plant – a Russian sleeper?'

Ronan's jaw dropped and he sat forward in his chair.

'Bloody hell! Are you sure?'

'Absolutely. And, as we speak, she's based at the US Embassy in Moscow as a senior counsellor. She's actually influencing US policy on Russia and advising the President on the advisability, or otherwise, of US support for Ukraine. She has a direct line to the White House.'

'Bloody hell! Do the Americans know?'

'They do now. I just told them. But she needs to be stopped.'

'Indeed, she does. But if she's based in Moscow, that could be difficult.'

'It could. But supposing it got out that the Americans had known about her for some time. Supposing it was revealed that she'd been turned by the Yanks and was acting as a double agent for them. What do you think might happen?'

'Since she's in Moscow, I think her life expectancy would be seriously reduced. I think ..., ah, I see what you mean. You're telling me this because such a disclosure would stop her dead. Literally. But, Adrian, would the Russians fall for it?'

'They would if the disclosure included a bit of information the Russians didn't know we knew,' Adrian added, mischievously.

'What sort of information?'

'Information such as the death of a US diplomat back in November at Hammersmith Broadway Tube station.'

'That was an accident, though, wasn't it?'

'No, it wasn't. Walter Edelman was murdered by two Russian agents. Two GRU thugs pushed him down the steps at the tube station, then they stole his briefcase containing highly sensitive information.'

'How do you know that's what happened? The police said it was an accident.'

'It would be very helpful if it became known that Natalie Schoen had confirmed Russian involvement in the death of Walter Edelman. If it got out that she had named his killers as Igor Ignatiev and Zoltan Cherny, two Russian state employees, it would be very helpful indeed.'

'Do you think that would upset Edelman's family, though? I mean, if they've been led to believe it was an accident?'

'I don't think so, somehow. I'm told he was a fairly fit man. Not the sort to die from a clumsy misstep and a tumble down a set of steps. That would have been a stupid and needless way to go. Maybe being murdered by a hostile state would seem a more ... heroic death. Maybe the Yanks would feel moved to give him some sort of posthumous award, or at least a hero's funeral. The family might be okay with that.'

'I'll tell the editorial staff to hold tomorrow's front page,' Rogers beamed. 'But, do the Americans know we're going public on this?'

'Not yet. They'll find out tomorrow. Thing is, Old Chap, we don't know who else in the US administration might be involved with Schoen. She's not averse to sleeping with foreign diplomats, apparently.'

'You don't think the Yanks will be upset when we hang out their dirty linen in our yard?'

'Very probably, but how does that saying go? Better to seek forgiveness than to ask for permission. Oh, by the way,' Adrian grinned, 'if you're looking for a catchy headline, you could perhaps refer to the Edelman incident as 'The Black Friday Murder', since it happened on Black Friday.'

''The Black Friday Murder'? Yes, I like that. I like that very much. I'll call downstairs and get them to set this up, then we'll head over to St Thomas Street. I've booked our usual table at the bistro. Lunch is on me, of course. The special today is roast lamb, and there's sticky toffee pudding on the menu – your favourite.'

'With proper custard?' Adrian asked.

'Of course.'

CHAPTER TWENTY-EIGHT

VERONA KNEW IT WAS BOUND TO COME, THE SUMMONS TO SIMON Harris's office. Although the bed in her new apartment was exceptionally comfortable compared to the one in the transit flat, she had hardly slept a wink during her first night there. She had gone over and over in her head the scenario in which she would be asked to explain about the body, and she had rehearsed what she might say in response. She had even got up in the early hours of the morning and practised some hopefully convincing facial expressions of shock in front of the bathroom mirror.

Her experience with, and love of amateur dramatics told her she must avoid being too melodramatic in order to seem genuinely surprised. Her facial expression would need to start off puzzled, then progress through concern to mild shock. She really didn't know how well she would hold up under any form of questioning, and she was far from confident she could pull it off. She recalled how she had reacted when she had been accused of Peter Cross's treachery. Given the fact that she had blushed, stammered and come close to fainting despite knowing she was innocent of those accusations, she now feared she might really crumble when faced with the guilt of her association with Aleks.

Harris was his usual charming and courteous self, however, as he invited her to take a seat in his office.

'How's the new accommodation?' he asked.

'It's wonderful, Simon. I can't thank you enough. You know, I never felt particularly safe in the transit flat,' she said, pointedly.

'Well, I'm sorry you had to put up with it for as long as you did. You didn't have the happiest start in post, did you? And that business with Peter would have sent a lesser mortal heading for home. He had no idea that Schoen woman was under surveillance. And neither did you, of course.'

Verona didn't know how to respond. She hadn't been expecting a compliment, and that really did sound like a compliment. She just shrugged, modestly. She wondered, though, if this were the gentle preamble to a much tougher interrogation. She scanned his face for any hint that he might be about to accuse her of treachery. She searched for that furrow she had seen between his brows when he had asked her to explain her actions in dropping off those classified documents at Schoen's apartment. However, she could not discern any such sign of suspicion. Harris was still smiling at her sympathetically.

'I think your move was quite timely,' Harris continued. 'And I don't want you to be alarmed, Verona, but after you left, it seems an intruder broke into the transit flat.'

'An intruder?' she exclaimed, with an expression of mild concern but saving her practised alarm for the next wave of revelations. 'A burglar, you mean? But there wouldn't have been much there for him to steal.'

'No, not a burglar, perhaps. It seems to have been someone looking for a place to sleep.'

'Oh, dear. He must have been really desperate to have chosen the transit flat. Then again, I suppose it was the only empty flat in the building. Did he ... do any damage?'

'Not a great deal. It looks like he came up the fire escape at the back and he smashed a pane of glass in the back door. The door key was left in the lock so he was able to gain access.'

'Ah, well I'd left it there because that's where it was when I moved in. Oh, I also left the box with the float items in the kitchen. Did he take those?'

'No, he didn't. They were still there when the accommodation staff got there to clean the flat. Actually, the intruder was still there, too.'

'Oh?' was all Verona could think of to say, since she knew worse was to come.

'Yes. Unfortunately, it seems he'd lain down on the bed and had passed away.'

'Oh, the poor man. It's bad enough for homeless people having to sleep out of doors in London. It must be far worse in a Moscow winter. Was he an elderly chap?'

Verona anticipated his next bit of news would be the revelation that the man was known to Verona, that, in fact, he was her downstairs neighbour. Indeed, he was the rather personable young man she had brought to see the embassy's Christmas production of 'Cats', the young man she had introduced to Harris, and the very same individual she had joked was her 'clandestine lover'. She was well prepared to express shock and even a little distress at that piece of news, whilst rushing to add that she hadn't known him all that well, being more of an acquaintance of his mother. It now crossed her mind that, perhaps, she should have removed Aleks' identity documents in order to hinder identification of the corpse, but she realised it would have looked bad if she'd been caught in possession of them.

She expected Simon would also drop the bigger bombshell of Aleks having been shot and that he bled to death in Verona's recently vacated bed, and, naturally, he would ask Verona what, if anything, she knew about that. It now occurred to her that the local police might already have estimated the time of death of her former lover, in which case, she might have a great deal of explaining to do. But, if it had really been the police who had shot Aleks, maybe they wouldn't even bother with a post mortem. To her surprise, however, Simon didn't seem inclined to question her further.

'Well, I don't want to worry you with all this,' he said. 'I don't think our accommodation people had realised quite how insecure that flat really is. Someone could have broken in whilst you were living there, and that would have been most distressing for you. Anyway, don't give it another thought. You'll be much safer now within the embassy complex. And, since we've just been given a date for when the Canadians are moving into their new building in *Kursovoy Lane*, I've suggested to accommodation that they give up the lease on the transit flat. We should soon be able to accommodate all our staff, including the King's Messengers, safely within the embassy.'

Verona continued to scrutinise his face. His eyes, as usual, reflected kindness and sympathy for her situation. She was relieved to see no sign of suspicion there. It now occurred to her that perhaps the police had not revealed to the embassy staff the identity of the deceased man. Indeed, why should they? The accommodation staff would not have recognised him, and they would simply have referred the matter to the local authorities. The police might not have known the flat had been used for longer term occupation than for the King's messengers. They could not have known that the most recent occupant of the flat actually knew the dead man who had lived down on the ground floor of the apartments. She felt a sudden and deep relief at the realisation that Harris wasn't going to question her further. He seemed to accept she had left before the man found in her bed had arrived. She was acutely aware, though, that she had been sitting bolt upright with her ankles tightly crossed and one hand grasped firmly inside the other, to stop them shaking. She tried to control the tremor in her voice.

'Well, many thanks again, Simon. I really do feel much happier now,' she said, truthfully enough, and she rose to leave.

She was convinced that, before she reached the door, he would call her back and point out her connection with the dead man, yet he did not. It now seemed certain, therefore, that the authorities had not revealed to her embassy the identity of the man found dead in their rented transit flat. She walked briskly out of the office and, notwithstanding the fact that she seemed to have been let off the hook, she began to feel sick. As she headed back downstairs to her own office, she realised she was actually going to be sick. She took a detour into the ladies' room, locked herself in a cubicle, fell to her knees and, not for the first time, she threw up.

CHAPTER
TWENTY-NINE

In her cousin Nadia's house on the south side of Kherson, Marina Ivanova was also feeling sick. As she lay in bed, uncomfortable and unable to sleep, the silence was shattered suddenly by the sound of an enormous explosion. Seconds later, there came another equally loud explosion. She wondered if the Russians were firing into the city from the positions they still held across the Dnipro River. She sat bolt upright and, immediately, her nausea increased. Leaping out of bed and rushing along the landing to the bathroom, she leant over the washbasin and dry-retched.

She had hoped the morning sickness would have abated by now. The doctor told her it usually did by the start of the second trimester, but, as he explained, all women experienced pregnancy symptoms differently. She could hardly keep food down these past few weeks, not even her cousin's tasty breakfast pancakes. Even the sweet aroma of them cooking made her heave. She hoped the nausea would soon pass, as she had much to do to prepare for her journey to England. She was a little concerned not to have heard from Nadia's sister Anna for a week or two now, especially since Cousin Anna had promised to make all the travel arrangements for her.

She splashed cold water on her face and, cupping her hand under the cold tap, drank deeply. Water was about the only thing she could keep down, these days. She could no longer conceal the growing bump in her abdomen. In fact, the recent weight loss brought about by the morning sickness only seemed to accentuate her swollen belly. Naturally, it was a matter of the deepest regret to her that she would not be able to keep her baby. The foetus growing inside her was all she had to remind her of Andrey. It would have been good to see the child growing up and to see whether she would resemble her own murdered father as well as her mother. But Marina wasn't the type to settle down to parenthood, especially whilst there was a war still to be won. In any case, she could not afford to raise a child on her own, particularly since she had lost not only the regular wage the SCG had been paying her, but also the contractual maternity benefits.

Returning to her bed, she told herself she had made the best possible arrangements she could have made for her unborn daughter's future. Birth in the UK and adoption by an American diplomat and his British wife was about the best possible outcome for the child. She would enjoy so many advantages her birth mother could never give her. She would have the best education, a good home and two loving parents. Corey Hart had been more to Marina than just her handler, she felt. He had been more than simply the recipient of her intelligence. He had been a true friend. Another decent American, Walter Edelman, had tried to fight her corner when the SCG had turned their backs on her and her fellow monitors, but his entreaties had fallen on deaf ears. She could not understand why. Then Hart had offered Marina a way out of her present predicament. He had offered to sponsor her to go to London to have her baby. He had even offered to adopt her child. Maybe she would be able to stay in London permanently as many Ukrainians had applied to. That way, even if she could not raise her child, at least she could see her sometimes.

She tried to go back to sleep, but the nausea and the intense heartburn kept her awake. She tossed and turned for a while. There seemed to be no further explosions, but, even so, she could not go back to sleep. She had too much on her mind. The outcome of Russia's illegal occupation of Ukraine was uncertain. Marina's future was uncertain. At least that of her child was assured. Soon, she heard her cousin rise and go downstairs. One by one, Nadia's children followed. Marina heard Nadia going about her tasks in the kitchen. The everyday sounds of the kettle boiling and the radio being switched on all sounded so normal. Yet these were not normal times. But at least Marina had a roof over her head now. No more hiding out in cellars and scavenging the ruins for food. If only all aspects of life could be this normal, she thought, and for all Ukrainians. One day, perhaps. One day soon, she prayed.

'Marina,' Nadia's voice called up the stairs. '*Snidanok.*'

Breakfast was ready. Marina shook her head. She knew she would not be able to face Nadia's pancakes, no matter how delicious they were. She might try and drink some coffee, however. She dressed quickly and went downstairs to join her cousin's family at the kitchen table. Nadia's sixteen-year-old son, Slobodan, was engrossed in the newspaper and Nadia was listening to the radio as she cooked. Marina hoped the war would be over before her teenaged nephew was old enough to be called up, but the radio news broadcast that morning held no indications that this might be so. She took her place at the table and held out her cup for the coffee Nadia poured her.

'Did you hear the explosions in the early hours?' Marina asked. 'Any idea where it came from?'

Suddenly, they heard a distant rumble. It sounded like a train approaching, yet there were no railway lines anywhere nearby. The rumbling grew steadily louder and louder. Soon, it became a loud roar. Marina wondered what it could be. It didn't sound like tanks. Slobodan arose and went to the window to look out. The roaring noise was deafening now. Surely, Marina thought, the Russians hadn't re-taken Kherson? If they were coming back there would have been some sort of warning, a siren, maybe, and the locals would have gone into hiding again. Marina glanced at the worried face of her sister. What could this be?

'Oh, God!' Nadia exclaimed as realisation dawned on her. 'They've blown up the Kakhovka dam!'

The great wall of the reservoir, which held back the waters of the mighty Dnipro, was almost a hundred feet high and loomed over the towns and villages south of Kherson. Marina knew it had been bombed twice before, during the Second World War. But surely, nowadays, it was reinforced to withstand attack from outside. Then again, the Russians were in control of the dam, and they had already tried to breach the dam from the inside, by launching missiles at the sluice gates, though the dam had stood firm. It now seemed they had tried again, and had succeeded. Suddenly, alarmed by the ear-splitting noise, Slobodan ran to the front door and flung it open in order to see what was happening.

'No!' Marina shouted, dropping her cup to the floor. 'Don't open the ...!'

It was too late, however. As the billions of gallons of released river waters gushed down the valley and engulfed the house, so it also came flooding into the kitchen. Marina found herself swept from her chair as the water level rose with alarming speed within the property. She went with the flow of the water as it infiltrated the downstairs rooms and she found herself being swept into the hall towards the stairs. She found a foothold on the stairs and turned around to see if Nadia and the children were following, but there was no sign of them. As the cold water continued its relentless rise, Marina found herself being thrust up the stairs and along the landing until she was hurled up against one of the bedroom doors which, unfortunately, was closed.

Marina kicked for all she was worth against the door, hoping to break her way into the bedroom and perhaps exit the house through the window. She kicked and kicked in vain. Then, taking a deep breath, she plunged down beneath the water and felt around until she located the doorknob. She wrenched at the knob with both hands and, mercifully, the door gave way. She found herself being swept into the bedroom by the deluge and thrust violently against the glass of the window. She tried to resurface in order to take in another breath, but the water level had now reached the ceiling and she could find no air space. She fumbled around for the window catch and, grasping the handle, turned it in an effort to open the window, from which she hoped she might escape. This did not work, so she kicked and kicked at the glass, but it would not break.

Marina pushed and pushed at the window for all she was worth, her lungs bursting as she strained to hold her breath. She now realised, however, that the water outside the house was even deeper that that within the house. She reasoned that the pressure of water trying to escape the house must be equal to that of the rising waters outside. She realised the window was never going to open. She had nowhere left to go. She knew she was about to drown and that her unborn child would drown along with her. She didn't know if it was the numbing effect of the water or a helpless resignation on her part, but she felt a strange kind of calmness come over her. She ceased struggling and allowed the water to press her entire body against the window glass. She slowly breathed in and felt the ice-cold water fill her lungs. Her field of vision began to shrink down to pin-points and she felt the baby kicking within her. The kicking grew weaker and weaker until it stopped entirely. Marina's last heart-wrenching thoughts were of Andrey and their child and the life they might have had together.

CHAPTER THIRTY

AS THE MORNING SUN ROSE OVER THE GREEN HILLS OF DONEGAL THE following day, the two Irishmen drove away from O'Carroll's farm and headed down the lonely track towards the main road to Lifford. Igor Ignatiev heard them go. It struck him as curious and he arose from his bed and looked out of the window. They had taken the old Land Rover and there were no other vehicles parked outside the farmhouse. He dressed and descended the wooden staircase. In the kitchen, he made himself a coffee. Hunting around for sugar, he noticed there was an unopened bottle of vodka in the larder cupboard or, as the Irishmen had referred to it, the 'press'. He had found the local accent difficult to follow, and some of the local expressions were new to him, but, if it were intended that he and Cherny should settle in this area, he supposed they would get used to it.

Soon, his compatriot joined him.

'Did they just leave?' Cherny asked.

'Yes. Probably gone to get more food. There's very little in the ... press. Coffee?'

Cherny nodded and, whilst Ignatiev made him a coffee, he

checked out the contents of the kitchen cupboards. Spotting the bottle of Stolichnaya, he lifted it up to examine the label.

'Latvian, not Russian,' he grimaced, but he shrugged as he unscrewed the cap and poured a liberal amount of the spirit into his coffee.

'Strange that they left the vodka but took the scotch,' Ignatiev remarked.

'Irish.'

'What?'

'You don't call it scotch if it's not Scottish. The whiskey they gave us is Irish whiskey – well, it was, since they've taken it away.'

'I liked it,' Ignatiev said. 'I could get used to it. What was it called – Millbush?'

'Bushmills,' Cherny corrected him. 'How long do you think they'll be?'

'They were only gone thirty, maybe forty minutes last time they went shopping. I hope they bring something good back for breakfast. Those sausages were good, also those potato pancake things. They were like *draniki* or *latkes*, but smoother.'

It was almost midday when the two Russians heard a vehicle coming up the track. Cherny went to fill the kettle for tea. The Irishmen seemed to drink a lot of tea, he noticed. Meanwhile, Ignatiev went outside to stretch his legs and get some fresh air. As the vehicle pulled into the farmyard, he saw it wasn't the Irishmen's Land Rover. He didn't recognise the Range Rover, and nor did he recognise the two men who got out of it. He supposed they must be here to replace the minders. It made sense to him that the minders would work in shifts. The Irishmen hadn't mentioned that they would be replaced today, but, yes, it made sense. Ignatiev walked forward to meet the new arrivals. Too late, he noticed them both produce hand guns fitted with silencers. He turned to run back into the farmhouse, but the first shot shattered his shoulder blade and the second penetrated his lung. He fell to the ground. The shooter walked up to him and stooped to deliver the *coup de grâce.*

The shooter's armed accomplice quickly entered the farmhouse. In the kitchen, unaware of his comrade's fate, Cherny had just made himself a second cup of coffee and was pouring vodka into the cup.

'You want a *caffè correto?*' he called out as he heard footsteps entering, and he raised the vodka bottle.

Turning around, he saw it was not his comrade who had entered the kitchen, but a stranger with a gun. As the first 'phfft' sound emerged from the stranger's gun, it smashed the vodka bottle in the Russian's hand. Before Cherny could react, however, a second shot hit him in the throat and a third in his chest. He fell to the floor instantly. Leaving the bodies where they fell, one in a puddle of vodka, the other face down in the dirt of the farmyard, the two assassins calmly walked back to their vehicle, started the engine and drove away.

It was not vodka which was exciting UK Prime Minister Ivan Thompson that same morning at the cabinet office meeting, but champagne. He breezed into the meeting room, via the door which separated the Cabinet Offices from Number Ten, brandishing a half bottle of champagne in his hand. He was followed, as closely as his own shadow, by Brexit Opportunities Minister Jonah Rhys-Maddox. Taking his place at the head of the conference table, Thompson placed the bottle on the table in front of him then sat down, triumphantly.

'Are we having a raffle, Prime Minister?' Sir Henry Mortimer, Cabinet Secretary, asked.

'No. But you're right, Henry, this is a prize, all right. We have Jonah to thank for this.'

Jonah Rhys-Maddox gave a modest half smile as he acknowledged the Prime Minister's praise.

'It's very generous of you, Jonah,' Lillian Fleming, the Work and Pensions Secretary said, 'but there's a dozen of us here. There won't be enough in that bottle for us all to have a snifter.'

'No, no. You misunderstand,' Thompson explained. 'This isn't for us to drink. It's for us to admire. This is Jonah's latest achievement.'

'You've branched out into the wine making business, have you?' Transport Minister Gordon Tripp asked.

'No, not at all,' Rhys-Maddox protested. 'This is a new innovation.'

'Tautology, Old Chap,' Sir Henry advised. 'All innovations are new.'

'Quite,' Rhys-Maddox brushed aside his criticism. 'This symbolises a post-Brexit win. We are going to introduce wine and champagne in pint bottles. The humble pint measure is a fundamental element of our British heritage. This bottle represents a return to our traditional values. We're going to bring back the pint measure.'

There was a stunned silence, until, at last, Tessa Butler, the International Trade Secretary burst out laughing.

'Why on earth would you want to do that?'

'Because there's nothing British about the litre, or the centilitre or the millilitre,' Rhys-Maddox expanded. 'Winston Churchill himself extolled the merits of a pint measure of champagne. He said it was the ideal amount for two people to share at lunch or for one to have at dinner. He always bought his champagne by the pint.'

'How's that possible?' Gurminder Singh, Minister for Farming, Fisheries and Food, asked, 'since the UK doesn't produce champagne. Champagne is only produced in France, and the French have always produced theirs in seventy centilitre bottles.'

The Brexit Opportunities Minister looked flummoxed for a second but soon recovered his composure.

'Well, I don't know, Gurminder, but that's what he espoused, a pint of champagne. Anyway, we can ensure that all the manufacturers of wines and sparkling wines in England sell their products in pint bottles.'

'But who can afford English wines?' Tessa Butler asked. 'Most of us drink wines from the continent, or the New World. Will you be expecting the French and the Australians to start producing one pint capacity glass bottles just for wine intended for the UK? I can't see them agreeing to that.'

'Well, if this excellent English vineyard here can produce wine in pint bottles like this one,' Rhys-Maddox declared, holding aloft the bottle he had brought, 'there's no reason why any wine producer cannot.'

Tessa Butler reached out for the bottle and the Brexit Opportunities Minister handed it over for her to examine. Slipping on her spectacles, she scrutinised the label.

'This isn't a pint, Jonah,' she said. 'It's five hundred mils. That's half a litre.'

'Is it?' Rhys-Maddox gasped as he snatched back the bottle from her and checked the label for himself. 'Well, that's *about* a pint, isn't it?'

'No, it isn't.' Gurminder contradicted him. 'A pint would be five hundred and sixty-eight mils. If you sold this as a pint measure, you'd be giving short measure. You'd be prosecuted under the weights and measures act.'

'Well, this is just a rough guide as to how a pint bottle would look,' an irritated Rhys-Maddox responded. 'It would only be slightly bigger.'

Sir Henry Mortimer was the next one to pour cold water on his Cabinet colleague's wine plans.

'But you can get six standard glasses out of a bottle of French wine. You'd only get three glasses out of a pint bottle. Drinkers would think they'd been given short measure. Or are you planning to also reduce the size of wine glasses? This all has cost implications, I'm sure.'

'I'm not sure pint bottles would fit nicely in my wine rack,' Tessa Butler added. 'They might fall through the slots. Would wine racks have to be re-designed, too? Then there's my Fortnum and Mason wine cooler bag. It fits two regular bottles quite nicely. Smaller bottles would rattle around.'

'Yes, well,' the Prime Minister interrupted testily, 'there's no point worrying about the little details. Those can be ironed out later. But surely, we're all agreed on the principle, aren't we?'

A number of voices broke out in dissent at this and the argument looked set to continue. Eventually, Sir Henry Mortimer raised a hand and the hubbub quickly died down.

'Whilst we're on the subject of wine, Ladies and Gentlemen,' he said, 'I have a question for the PM.'

'Fire away, Henry,' Thompson nodded, pleased to move the meeting on and avoid further criticism.

'Well, I was just wondering when we're going to see an

estimate of the government's wine stocks. We usually get an annual breakdown and we've been promised the latest assessment is coming four times now, but it hasn't been released.'

'Why would you be interested in that, Henry?' Thompson asked.

'Well, it's been five years since we saw the last estimate. That was before the Covid epidemic struck. The last estimate showed the stocks of wines, spirits and champagnes, available for entertaining UK and overseas dignitaries, stood at around two thousand three hundred bottles, valued at over three million pounds. I imagine the figures must still be the same, so I don't see why you haven't released the estimate long before now.'

'What? Well, these things take some working out, I suppose,' Thompson said. 'I imagine someone's got to count the bottles. I don't see why you think the figure would still be the same.'

'Well, because the period in question covers the Covid epidemic and the two lockdowns, during which time partying was forbidden, wasn't it?' Sir Henry clarified. 'So, if government departments were not able to entertain visiting dignitaries, then, surely, the wine stocks should have remained at exactly the pre-Covid level, shouldn't they? So, why not just confirm that?'

The Prime Minister stuffed a hand into his thatch of unruly black hair, as he often did when perplexed or challenged, and he looked decidedly uncomfortable. Sir Henry wasn't the first person to have suggested the staff at Number Ten might have been partying during lockdown, when the rest of the country had been forbidden to do so, and it was likely he would not be the last to make such an accusation. Thompson looked to

Rhys-Maddox for support, but the Brexit Opportunities Minister simply shrugged.

'I'll see if I can chivvy along whoever's responsible for counting the bottles, then,' Thompson said.

'Good,' Sir Henry beamed. 'Now, then, to matters more serious. Anyone seen the front page of *The Times* this morning? Washington seems to have scored quite a coup. Looks like they turned a Russian sleeper into a double agent.'

'Yes, I did see that, Henry,' Jonah Rhys-Maddox snorted in the direction of the Cabinet Secretary. 'Now why couldn't *we* have done that? We couldn't even catch the Russian assassins you claim killed that American diplomat on the London underground.'

CHAPTER THIRTY-ONE

In Moscow's *Nikitskaya Ulitsa*, that morning, Doctor Natalie Schoen left her apartment early, intending to enjoy an early breakfast of pancakes, bacon and maple syrup in the US Embassy's cafeteria before her working day would begin. Collecting her post from her mailbox in the lobby of the apartment building, she placed the letters in her attaché case then took the back stairs down to the basement car park. Unlocking her car, she was about to climb into the driver's seat when two men stepped out of a transit van parked nearby and strode briskly towards her. One of them snatched the car keys from her hand whilst the second bundled a coat over her head and forced her into the back seat of her own car before climbing in beside her. The man clutching the car keys leapt into the driver's seat, started up the engine and took off up the ramp and out of the car park.

From the transit van there emerged a team of FSB intelligence operatives. Dressed in suspiciously clean overalls bearing the logo of Moscow's Tele-communications provider,

'MGTS', and armed with large evidence bags, they headed up the back stairs to Dr Schoen's apartment to begin their intensively thorough forensic search of the premises.

A few blocks away, in the British Embassy enclave on *Smolenskaya Nabrezhnaya* – or 'Luhansk People's Republic Square', as nobody ever called it – Verona stood gazing out of her apartment window, across the Moscow River. The ice had long since disappeared from the river and the weather was growing milder now. This view was so much nicer than that she'd had from the dark and depressing transit flat. In fact, she felt the *Nevsky Prospekt* episode was well and truly behind her now. She took a sip of Earl Grey tea from her pretty blue and white china cup and sighed contentedly.

She had enjoyed arranging her treasured china and glassware in the pristine cupboards in her newly re-decorated kitchen. It was a small thing, organising her kitchen with the same precision with which, on first arrival, she had organised her office desk, but it cheered her and it really made the place feel like home. Doubtless, Tiffany Munro would have thought this a prissy thing to do, but no matter, for Tiffany was long gone. The Defence Attaché's disgraced PA had been recalled to London to spend the next year or three updating staff movement files in the Ministry of Defence's personnel section.

Glancing around at her lounge, now adorned with her books, her stylish prints of Moghul emperors, her gaily printed Indian mirrorwork cushions, and the other knick-knacks and souvenirs she had picked up on her travels over the years, Verona felt she was in control of her life once more. She felt settled now and more self-contained. She no longer regretted having stayed in Moscow. She didn't even regret her relationship with Aleks, especially since she now believed he really had been truthful and genuine. She knew in her heart that he hadn't just made love to her in order to coax secrets from her. She was sure she hadn't been a victim of what Simon Harris had called 'sexpionage'. No, she was now fully convinced Aleks had been exactly what he said he was, an ethnic Ukrainian wanting to preserve his heritage and fight for the freedom of his parents' homeland.

She told herself she believed in Aleks because, well, because she had to. She still couldn't understand what he had seen in her, but she told herself that perhaps, despite her age, Aleks had nevertheless found her just a little bit attractive. He had loved the English language and had loved learning all about the English way of life, so maybe he had found this middle-aged Englishwoman just a little bit exotic.

She found herself wondering what had happened to Olga and Vitaly. She hoped they would have been released eventually and allowed to give their son a decent funeral. They had shown her such kind hospitality and she felt deeply guilty that she had not been to see them and that she hadn't attended Aleks' funeral. It seemed a harsh decision to make, but she couldn't afford to incriminate herself. There really had been an attack on a major munitions base in Moscow. The reports and bulletins crossing the DHM's desk had confirmed that. And she believed Aleks really had been involved in that attack. He must have been. He really had been a brave and patriotic Ukrainian, not any kind of a Russian *gigolo*. She believed in him. She could never allow herself to think otherwise.

She could see how things might appear differently to others, though, and so she was relieved that her relationship with Aleks had not come out. It would remain her secret. She told herself she did not regret what had happened between her and Aleks. She didn't even regret having given Aleks the information he had sought, albeit that some might consider that treachery. She doubted Aleks would have let that information fall into the wrong hands. No, the real treachery, she told herself, was down to Peter Cross. Of course it was.

Her only regret was that she had lost Aleks. He had lost his young life and she had lost the love of her life. That would take some getting over. But she told herself that love and passion were not for her after all. Maybe she had left it too late in life to fall in love. Maybe she was too set in her ways to give herself entirely to the kind of love she ought to have experienced decades ago. She had now known love, indeed she had, but it wouldn't have been the kind of love which would have lasted. She and Aleks wouldn't have had a happily ever after. Eventually, he would have left her for someone his own age.

'Better to have loved and lost ...' she murmured to herself, but her deep introspection was interrupted suddenly by a knock at the door. For a second, she experienced that sudden thrill she had felt whenever Aleks had come knocking at her door – but only for a second, as she knew no such lover would come knocking ever again. Putting down her cup and saucer, she went to answer the door.

'Good morning, Verona,' a cheerful Rena McAvoy greeted her in friendly Edinburgh tones. 'You still up for introducing me to Moscow's best cakes this morning? You haven't forgotten, have you?'

'Of course not, Rena,' Verona smiled back at her new boss. 'Come in and I'll just grab my coat and bag.'

'What's the name of this place you're taking me?'

'It's the *Konditeskaia Kafé*. It's in a lovely old building in that gorgeous *fin de siècle* style, and the cakes are to die for. Coffee's good, too. It's not too far to walk. In fact, the walk there and back should cancel out the calories in the cakes.'

'Splendid. And tell me, Verona, have you used the embassy swimming pool yet? I like to get in an early morning dip each day before work and I seem to be the only one there at six each morning. Maybe you'll join me some mornings? We could do a few lengths and then have breakfast and a bit of a natter in the cafeteria. Oh, and you must tell me all about the play you're putting on. I hear you're directing it as well as taking the female lead?'

'Yes. It's an Agatha Christie murder mystery.'

'How wonderful,' the fifty-five-year-old career diplomat beamed. 'I love amdram.'

'May I ask you something, Rena,' Verona asked.

'Yes.'

'Have they told you whether you'll be taking Peter Cross's place as UK rep on the Security Co-operation Group?'

'Yes, I believe I will be. Why?'

'Well, there's an aspect to that which I'd like to discuss with you. There's a group of former SCG employees who desperately need our help, but we can talk about that later. Now, tell me, have you ever had Kyiv cake?'

As the two women walked together along *Smolenskaya Naberezhnaya*, chatting enthusiastically, Verona told the new DHM of the city's museums she had visited and those she still had to visit. She felt her life might not be quite so exciting now as it had been with Aleks, but it was pretty much back to normal and she was in control of it. That was the important thing. The city's trees had now burst into colourful blossom and the spring sunshine reflected off the millions of ripples and wavelets all along the breezy Moscow River. Verona now reflected that there were many different routes to happiness. And she really was happy – now.

ALSO BY THIS AUTHOR

More books in the series *The Thames House Files*, a series of standalone international espionage novels:

The Hunt for WOTAK

When the Grey Wolf Sings

A Long Road to Revenge

Shearwater Point

The Kohat Connection

True crime:

Odd Man Out: A Motiveless Murder?

The Cheetham Hill Murder: A Convenient Killing?

The Forgotten Forty-Four: Victims & Survivors of America's First Serial Sex Killer*

*Awarded a 'Highly Commended' in the True Crime Awards 2024

'Book of the Year' award

ABOUT THE AUTHOR

Denise Beddows is an award-winning author of true crime and crime/espionage fiction. With a background in research, investigation and intelligence analysis, and having lived, worked and played in various countries across three continents, she speaks six languages. Based in Buckinghamshire, she is a member of the Society of Authors and the Crime Writers Association. She actively supports the Chalfont St Giles & Jordans Literary Festival. The 'Chiltern Kills' Crime Writing Festival, based in Gerrards Cross, was her brainchild. Writing also as DJ Kelly, she has published the following local histories:

The Chalfonts and Gerrards Cross at War
Buckinghamshire Spies and Subversives
The Famous and Infamous of The Chalfonts and District
Chalfont St Peter Old Burials and Curious Deaths

Printed in Great Britain
by Amazon

46261983R00169